STANDI̶̶̶̶̶̶̶̶̶̶ ̶̶̶̶̶̶̶̶̶̶̶̶̶̶̶̶̶̶̶̶̶̶̶̶̶̶̶̶MIRROR,
SYBILLA LET JOSHUA
TIE HER CRAVAT . . .

We look well together, thought Sybilla dreamily as she gazed at their reflections. Dark and
fair, blue eyes and gray. We're exactly the
right height, too. The top of my head comes
just over his shoulder. Suddenly she was
acutely aware of the tautly muscled male body
behind her. She felt a shiver of excitement
when his long slender fingers brushed against
her face as he tied the cravat. She breathed in
his scent, a compound of fresh crisp linen,
fine soap, and something indefinable, uniquely
masculine and alluring. Their eyes met in the
mirror. He drew a quick breath, and his
fingers stilled in their task. Slowly, gropingly,
his hands slipped to her waist and his arms
began to close around her . . .

CHANCE ENCOUNTER

DIANA DELMORE

DIAMOND BOOKS, NEW YORK

CHANCE ENCOUNTER

A Diamond Book / published by arrangement with
the author

PRINTING HISTORY
Diamond edition / September 1991

ISBN: 1-55773-585-9

Diamond Books are published by The Berkley Publishing Group,
200 Madison Avenue, New York, New York 10016.
The name "DIAMOND" and its logo
are trademarks belonging to Charter Communications, Inc.

PRINTED IN THE UNITED STATES OF AMERICA

10 9 8 7 6 5 4 3 2 1

FOR ANN
IN LOVING MEMORY

CHANCE ENCOUNTER

Prologue

THE WARNING blast of the guard's long brass horn, clearing the road ahead, jerked Sybilla Trent out of her cramped slumber. She lifted her head to stare groggily out the window of the mail coach, unable to perceive more than the vaguest outlines of buildings in the first faint glimmerings of a summer dawn.

"Awake at last, be ye, lad?" said the kindly old gentleman who had been Sybilla's seat partner since she boarded the mail coach in York. He chuckled and added, "I envy ye young'uns, able to sleep anywhere, anyplace. Ye didn't open your eyes when we made our last two stops at Ware and Waltham Cross."

"Are we in London?" asked Sybilla, rubbing the sleep out of her eyes.

"That we are, lad, and unless I miss my guess, we're at journey's end. About time, too. We've been almost three days on the road," said the old gentleman as the coach slowed and made the sharp turn into the brightly lit innyard of the Bull and Mouth in St. Martin's-le-Grand.

When the Edinburgh to London Mail rolled to a stop, Sybilla stumbled down the steps, her country-bred eyes widening at the frenetic bustle of activity in the innyard. Passengers were tumbling out of an overnight coach that had pulled in ahead of the Mail, while other travelers were racing down the steps from the first- and second-story galleries of the inn to take their places in an outgoing coach headed for Manchester. Ostlers and stableboys, chambermaids and porters added to the din as they darted about the yard attending to their duties. One of the porters, a youth of about Sybilla's own age, heavily laden with luggage, bowled into her, knocking her back against the mail coach.

"See 'ere, cull, keep yer winkers open, so's ye don't bump inter yer betters," the porter growled sourly, casting a disdainful eye on her sober coat and breeches, dusty boots, inexpertly tied cravat, and unfashionable low-crowned, broad-brimmed hat.

Sybilla stepped out of the youth's way, smothering an inane impulse to giggle. How different the porter's attitude toward her would be if he realized he was addressing not an insignificant country bumpkin of a boy, but a Yorkshire heiress, a baroness in her own right, Lady Trent of Castle Wycombe in the North Riding!

"Come along and have some breakfast, young feller," said Mr. Finch, the elderly yeoman farmer who had befriended her during the journey from York. "The Bull and Mouth has a very fine coffee room, so I'm told."

Sybilla retrieved her modest valise from the guard and followed Mr. Finch inside, where they sat at a long table in the coffee room. Listening with one ear to the old farmer as he happily anticipated the joys of visiting his daughter in Hans Town and seeing his new grandson, Sybilla gazed down at her cold pigeon pie and her plate of ham and bacon and realized that her normally healthy appetite was failing her. Suddenly she was aghast at the enormity of what she'd done. Stealing away from Castle Wycombe in the dead of night disguised as a boy, catching a ride with an early rising farmer to Harrogate and thence a cross-country stage to York, she hadn't paused to reflect on the consequences of her flight. Family and staff at the castle must be frantic with worry about her safety. The note she'd left had said merely that she was going off on a short trip to sort out her thoughts and do a bit of sightseeing. It wasn't the truth, of course. Not the whole truth, anyway. Sybilla's slender body tensed. Perhaps she didn't really know the truth. Perhaps she'd misunderstood that cryptic, low-voiced conversation she'd overheard at the castle the night before she left. . . .

"Be ye not hungry, lad?" Mr. Finch inquired over the tumult of sound in the coffee room of the Bull and Mouth Inn. "Ye haven't touched a bite o' that pigeon pie. Ye look a mite pale, too. Not feeling well?"

"I'm fine, Mr. Finch, truly," Sybilla said hastily. "A little excited, perhaps, about my first visit to the big city."

Mr. Finch nodded understandingly. "That's right. It will all be very new to ye, and I think ye said ye hadn't seen yer godmother these many years. Well, now, I'm off to see that new grandson o' mine. The best o' luck to ye, my son. It were a pleasure having yer company on the journey."

Saying a smiling goodbye to the old gentleman, Sybilla abandoned the effort to eat her breakfast and beckoned for the waiter so she could pay her shot. She left the coffee room, then put down her valise on the floor of the corridor outside in order to free her hands to tuck the change from a five-pound note into her long knitted stocking purse.

" 'Ere, wot did I tell ye? Git out o' a working cove's way," growled a rough voice, and Sybilla looked up to confront the same young porter who had nearly knocked her down earlier. He stood still, glaring at her for blocking his way. Then his eyes dropped in a long fixed stare to the plump stocking purse in Sybilla's hand.

Turning her back on him with a scornful toss of her head, Sybilla picked up her valise, slipped her purse into her coat pocket, and continued down the corridor into the courtyard of the inn. There she paused to watch a heavily laden coach lumber into the yard, marveling at the mountain of parcels and portmanteaus fastened to its roof and at the number of passengers perched precariously beside the luggage. After a few moments she intercepted one of the scurrying ostlers to ask, "Where could I find a hackney cab?"

Obviously unimpressed by an unfashionably dressed country youth, the ostler said impatiently, "Cabstand up the street a ways. Or ye might catch one driving by wi'out a customer."

Emerging from the archway of the courtyard into St. Martin's-le-Grand, Sybilla looked uncertainly up and down the street, empty of both vehicles and pedestrians. It was much lighter now in the last brief interval before dawn. Feeling rather than hearing a presence behind her, she turned her head, catching a glimpse of furtive, shadowy forms before she felt a shattering blow to her head and slumped, barely conscious, to the pavement.

Seconds or even minutes later, she didn't know which, she sat up groggily, placing a groping hand to her aching head. Withdrawing her hand, she stared unbelievingly at her bloodied fingers for a moment, and then scrabbled to her feet, reaching for the support of the outer wall of the courtyard as she felt a sudden wave of dizziness and nausea. Lifting her head, she found herself looking into the face of a solemn-eyed urchin.

"Hello . . . Did you see what happened?" To Sybilla, the thready sound issuing from her throat didn't sound like her voice at all.

The child shook his head. "Ain't seen nuffin'." He added, with the air of being helpful, "Lots o' coves do be waitin' ter bite the cole when the rattlers come in."

"Bite the cole? Rattlers?"

"Bowman prigs wif' their winkers on the passengers' rhino when the stagecoaches rolls in," explained the urchin, as if he were instructing a rather dull pupil.

Sybilla was to learn later that posting inns and coach stops in London abounded with pickpockets preying on unwary travelers, but for the moment she made no effort to unravel the child's cant vocabulary. She had more pressing problems. A quick glance around her revealed that her valise was gone. With a sinking feeling she slipped her hand into her coat pocket. Her stocking purse with all her funds was missing, too. It was her own fault. She should have been more careful about flashing her money in public. In her mind's eye she could see clearly the fixed stare of the inn porter as he watched her put away her change from the five-pound note. She couldn't prove it, but she was sure the porter had alerted acquaintances to the fact that the country bumpkin was carrying a large sum of money.

The urchin was still there, dividing his curious gaze between her and the stagecoach that was rounding the turn at the corner. Swallowing the lump in her throat, Sybilla inquired, "Can you tell me how to get to the West End?"

The child looked at her blankly. His small world was probably bounded by the few streets around his home, Sybilla thought. She tried again. "Which direction is the river?" she asked. After a long pause he pointed an uncertain finger to his right.

At least she had a vague notion that the Thames River bisected the city from east to west, Sybilla reflected as she waved a hand to the urchin and headed for the nearest intersection. Newgate Street, the sign said. And over there to her left she could see rising above the surrounding buildings the luminous dome of a great church. St. Paul's. So she must now turn right, to the west.

She felt light-headed, her head ached, she hadn't eaten since dinnertime the night before, she didn't have a penny to her name, and it took enormous effort to put one foot ahead of the other; but for all that she had to keep walking. She had one advantage over the hordes of the destitute in this vast alien city. If her legs held out and if she could outlast the waves of nausea and faintness pouring over her, she could find sanctuary in her godmother's elegant mansion in the West End.

Chapter 1

IN THE drifting moonlight the Dutch Garden of Holland House was a magical place. A gentle breeze mingled the fragrance of the multihued blossoms in the geometrically arranged flower beds with the redolent scent of the box borders, while from the Jacobean mansion behind the garden came the soft strains of music from the ballroom. Strolling the paths with his fiancée on his arm, Joshua Waring, 7th Viscount Linton and late Major of His Majesty's 4th Dragoons, got carried away by the romantic setting—influenced, too, by several glasses of arrack punch and the better part of a bottle of claret—and swept Lady Verity Heston into a passionate embrace.

A moment later he recoiled from an unladylike buffet to his cheek. He lifted a finger to wipe away a trickle of liquid coming from the vicinity of his right eye. In the moonlight it looked like blood. It *was* blood. "What did you hit me with?" Joshua inquired, bewildered.

Lady Verity inhaled an indignant breath as she twisted the stone of her antique ruby ring to the outside of her finger. "The prongs of the setting must have scratched you. The ring belonged to Mama, you see, and it's a bit large for me. The stone keeps shifting to the inside of my hand." She looked at Joshua reproachfully. "I'm very sorry, I didn't mean to hurt you, but you shouldn't have seized me like some savage Indian on the warpath."

Joshua lifted a surprised eyebrow. "Good God, you're talking as if I'd committed the Rape of the Sabines or some such thing."

Turning her head away, Verity murmured, "Must you be so coarse?"

"Coarse? We're engaged. We're to be married next month. Why shouldn't I kiss you?"

Even in the dim light Joshua could discern the expression of cool distaste that crossed Verity's perfect features. "That wasn't a kiss. It was a—a bear hug." She turned back to him with an air of candor. "Of course, I realize you've been away from polite society for a long time, fighting with dear Lord Wellington in the Peninsula, but surely you haven't forgotten that ladies and gentlemen of our class don't indulge in unseemly public displays of affection."

Joshua glanced around the deserted gardens. He said, his eyes gleaming mischievously, "Nobody observed my bold behavior as far as I'm aware." He reached for her again, and she jerked away.

Now there was an edge to her soft voice, almost as if she were gritting her teeth. "You know what I mean. Unlike the lower orders, people in our class marry because of compatibility of family background and interests, not for mere carnal reasons like . . . like . . ."

"Like the enjoyment of a romp in the hay?" Joshua asked, suddenly nettled.

Her slender back stiffening with outrage, Verity said coldly, "I must ask you to apologize for that vulgar remark."

"I'm sorry," Joshua responded instantly. "It *was* a vulgar remark."

"Thank you. I should like to return to the ballroom, please. I've promised the next dance to Lord Aldermayne."

A little later, lounging against the wall near the entrance to the ballroom, Joshua watched his fiancée as she went down the line with her partner, the tall and darkly handsome Lord Aldermayne. He thought, as he'd thought from the first moment he met her, that Verity Heston was one of the loveliest women he'd ever seen. She had spun-gold hair and violet eyes, small classic features and creamy skin, and a slim figure that moved with incomparable grace. In her gown of wispy white and silver gauze, she was easily the most beautiful woman in the ballroom.

She was also practically a stranger to him, he reflected with a slow bemusement. Last December he'd met and wooed her in a whirlwind courtship of less than a month. They hadn't met again until he'd arrived back in England a week ago, shortly after the glorious battle of Vitoria on the twenty-first of June, 1813.

He put his finger inside his collar, trying to ease the high, stiffly starched shirt points that were digging into his cheek and preventing him from turning his head easily. It occurred to him also that his exquisitely tailored coat from the inspired hands of Weston was impossibly tight. He could move his arms only with difficulty. Damn his expensive new London finery! His thoughts turned nostalgically to the comfortable, loose-fitting old gray frock coat he'd worn in the Peninsula more often than his uniform. Wellington didn't care what his officers wore, provided they were good fighters. For a moment Joshua felt a surge of longing to be back with his dragoons as they joined in chasing the last of Napoleon's armies across the Pyrenees.

"There you are, Linton. I've scarcely had the opportunity to exchange a word with you tonight." The speaker was a trim elegant man in early middle age, whose aloof eyes and tight-lipped smile conveyed little warmth.

Easing his tall rangy form away from the wall, Joshua bowed to his future father-in-law.

The Earl of Dunsford eyed him speculatively. "Nothing amiss, I trust?"

"My lord?"

"I thought Verity looked a trifle—distressed when she returned to the ballroom. I'd hate to think you two had quarreled."

"Indeed, sir, so would I," Joshua replied coolly. He was damned if he was going to give anything away to Dunsford. Reportedly the earl ruled his own household with an iron hand. His faded wife was dead, and his son and heir was a nonentity who did what he was told. It was obvious he doted on his only daughter, but Joshua suspected, from his brief acquaintance with Verity and Lord Dunsford, that she would think twice before she went against her father's wishes. Well, sooner or later the earl would have to face up to the fact that his about-to-be son-in-law was his own man.

"Of course, you and Verity are only beginning to know each other," the earl went on smoothly. "It's a pity the two of you haven't had the opportunity to improve your acquaintance over the past months. Now, if you had taken my suggestion to stay on in London over the winter and spring instead of—"

"Instead of returning to my regiment for the start of the spring campaign?" It was an old bone of contention. Joshua refused to allow his annoyance to show. "I thought I'd made my reasons for that very clear. When we managed to extricate ourselves from the siege of Burgos last November, all of us in the Anglo-Portuguese army suspected that one last big push would drive the French out of the Peninsula for good and all. After four years of hard fighting I wanted the satisfaction of being in on the kill. And I was. The battle of Vitoria ended French rule in Spain, and I came home."

"And you might have been killed yourself, is it not so? With a disastrous effect on the Linton title and estate, not to speak of my daughter's happiness." The earl's lips curved in a wintry smile. "But come, that's all behind us. I spoke to your man of business yesterday and to mine. They've come to agreement about the marriage settlements."

Joshua's thoughts were wandering. A few months ago his demise from a French bullet would have been of little interest except to his grieving father and brother. He was the younger son—by only five minutes, it was true, but still the younger son—of Francis Waring, 6th Viscount Linton, and he had never expected to inherit the title. Had never wanted to do so. He'd joined the cavalry at eighteen and had taken to a military existence with enormous relish. He loved the camaraderie, the informality, the rough and tumble of life in the field in foreign parts. For more than ten years it had never crossed his mind to envy his twin brother Geoffrey's position as the heir to the Linton title and estate.

Then, last December, as Joshua was settling into winter quarters in Portugal, he received the crushing news: Geoffrey had been killed in a hunting accident. Returning to England for his brother's funeral, Joshua had discovered that his father was seriously ill from a recent heart attack.

"Your campaigning days are over, Joshua," his father had informed him ruefully. "The doctors say I could go at any time. You'll be the seventh Viscount before you know it. Best to resign your commission immediately and start looking around for a suitable wife. If you're not married by your thirtieth birthday, you'll be hard put to maintain the estate. I haven't been the best steward of your patrimony, I fear. I put most of my time and money into my hunters and my carriages and my wagers at Newmarket, and I allowed Geoffrey to do the same."

"Married? Before my thirtieth birthday?" Joshua had stared at his father in stupefaction. Then understanding had dawned. "Good God. Uncle Lucius. I'd almost forgotten. In his will he left all the money from his Barbados estates to Geoffrey—"

"Or to you, as next of kin, if Geoffrey died childless," reminded his father.

"Yes, to Geoffrey or to me, provided he—we—married by our thirtieth birthday."

"My brother Lucius had great family feeling," Lord Linton had said dryly. "He wanted you and Geoffrey to marry early, in order to ensure the continuation of our line. The next heir, you may recall, is my second cousin Marmaduke. Lucius always detested him." Casually Lord Linton had added, "Just before he died, Geoffrey told me he'd taken a fancy to Lady Verity Heston. Dunsford's daughter, you know. She'd have been a splendid *parti* for Geoffrey. Fine old family. An ample settlement, no doubt. Smashingly pretty girl, too, so I'm told."

And so, between his dead uncle's will and his dying father's hints, the thought had more than once crossed Joshua's mind that his engagement to Verity had been almost inevitable, especially after his first glimpse of her white and gold beauty. After the danger and grinding hardships of the retreat from Burgos, Verity had fallen on his senses like a vision from heaven, and he'd daydreamed about her ravishing violet eyes and softly beguiling voice all during the months he was serving with the Anglo-Portuguese army during the spring campaign.

Joshua was aroused from his reveries of courtship by Dunsford's voice. "Perhaps you and I and the solicitors can meet soon to make the final arrangements for the settlements," the earl suggested. "Not too much room for delay, I think you'll agree. Here it is the first week of July, and the wedding is set for the twentieth of August." He nodded, with another of his wintry smiles, and moved off to have a word with his hostess as the music ended and couples began walking off the floor.

Observing Verity standing with her partner nearby, Joshua crossed over to them. "Evening, Aldermayne," he said. He smiled at his fiancée. "I hope you've saved the next waltz for me."

"Doubtless it's very different on the Continent, Joshua, but here in London the waltz is still considered *dégagé*," said Verity primly. "I wouldn't dream of dancing it in public."

Joshua reached for her program. "Well, then, what about the next country dance?"

"Sorry, old chap, I'm ahead of you there," crowed Aldermayne. "You should have claimed your dances when you first arrived. Lady Verity's next dance is mine, and the one after that, too."

After studying the dance card, Joshua folded it in two and tore it across, handing the fragments to Aldermayne. "I think not, *old chap*. Lady Verity will be sitting out the next dance with her fiancé. We have important matters to discuss, as you can well imagine."

Verity's arm in her long, elbow-length glove felt rigid beneath his hand, but she made no attempt to hold back when Joshua guided her to a chair at the side of the ballroom and sat down with her. Though her lips were fixed in a pleasant smile, her voice cut like a whip as she murmured, "How could you be so rude? What will Lord Aldermayne think of you—of us?"

"He'll think I want to spend some time with my betrothed. What's wrong with that?" Joshua put his hand over hers as they lay in her lap, holding her tiny embroidered reticule. "Verity, we nearly quarreled out there in the garden. I wanted to put things straight between us."

"Pray remove your hand," she muttered, lowering her head to hide the faint pink flush that suffused her cheeks. "Didn't you hear what I was telling you in the garden? Gentlefolk don't engage in indelicate behavior in public."

"Or any other time?" Joshua snapped before he could bite back the words. To his horror, he heard his voice adding, "Have you given any thought to what will happen after the wedding ceremony? Will you expect me to retire to my bedchamber for a night of celibate slumber?" Verity's expression was one of pure shock. He said immediately, "I apologize again." A rueful smile curved his lips. "Perhaps you're right, I've been away from civilization for too long."

Verity's face was unsmiling. "Perhaps you have."

A cheerful voice broke into the rather brittle silence that fell between them. "I say, Linton!" exclaimed Lord Aldermayne. "I'm not going to let you cheat me out of *this* dance."

Rising, Joshua stood aside politely as Verity walked away with Aldermayne without a backward glance. He felt vaguely resentful and dissatisfied, remembering how eagerly he'd longed to be with his golden-haired enchantress of a fiancée while he was dodging French bullets in Spain. Tonight, at least, the reality was very different from his imaginings. Had he made a mistake in becoming engaged to Verity?

Oh, he'd taken for granted that she wasn't madly in love with him when he proposed to her. Young ladies of Verity's social standing didn't marry solely for love. She was expected to make a suitable match with a man of good family and large fortune, and Joshua, especially since he was the heir to Uncle Lucius's vast piles of money, fit the specifications.

But if she didn't love him, did she even like him? Hadn't she overreacted a short while ago in the garden when he'd tried to kiss her? After such a short acquaintance, such a short courtship, he couldn't expect Verity to feel a passionate attachment to him, perhaps, but now he wondered if he was actually distasteful to her. He'd never had that problem with the pretty Portuguese and Spanish girls he'd met in the Peninsula. . . . Of course, they weren't ladies like Verity. He moved his shoulders restlessly. Was he being unreasonable in wanting some kind of physical response from her? He'd never thought much about marriage before Geoffrey died, but now that he'd committed himself to it, he wasn't looking forward to an antiseptic marriage bed!

"It's Waring, isn't it? I mean Linton, of course."

Blinking, Joshua roused himself from his musings. The sleek, exquisitely dressed apparition standing in front of him was a mirror of fashion, from his artfully arranged brown curls and his wonderfully tied cravat to his wasp-waisted coat and his black breeches that hugged his slender limbs as if he had been sewn into them.

"You don't remember me, Linton? I was two forms behind you at Eton. I'm Cranborn. Augustus Cranborn."

Reaching back into his memory, Joshua recalled with difficulty a weedy undersized youth who'd hero-worshiped him during his last year at Eton, when he was the captain of the cricket team. "Of course I remember you, Cranborn. Pleased to see you again."

"I shouldn't blame you for not recognizing me," said Cranborn with a complacent glance downward at his elegant person. He shuddered slightly. "When I think of what a grubby urchin I was in those days . . . You've resigned your commission, I understand. I was sorry to hear about your father and brother," he added rather perfunctorily.

"Thank you. Er—what are you doing these days?"

"Listening to the Muse, dear boy, listening to the Muse." At Joshua's uncomprehending look, Augustus explained, "I'm a poet. My father wanted me to go into the church or the army or government service, naturally. I'm a younger son without a bean and all that. Well, you know about the travails of being a younger son, don't you, old chap? My feeling, however, is that a man shouldn't betray his talent. If I were to accept some kind of mundane position, I wouldn't have the time to think, to create, to allow the breezes of inspiration to blow across my soul. Don't you agree?"

"Ah. Just so." Joshua eyed Augustus with a baffled stare, rather like a hunting dog encountering some puzzling new variety of prey. "This poetry writing, it keeps you busy? Have you written a great many poems?"

Augustus looked pained. "It's not quantity that matters, dear boy. One must aim at quality. I've composed a sonnet sequence on the theme of divine love as opposed to human love. And an ode to His Royal Highness the Prince Regent on the occasion of his assuming his new duties. I'm told the Regent was quite affected by it. At the moment I'm in the throes of working on a verse drama."

"Splendid. I look forward to seeing your play performed," said Joshua with perfect insincerity. He wasn't a literary man. When it came to serious drama, he much preferred pantomime or light comedy or even a spot of juggling.

"Kind of you to say so, but there won't be any *official* performance for some time, mind. I won't permit public exposure of my work until I've polished it to a gleaming jewel." Augustus put his hand to his head. "Lord, I'm very nearly forgetting my manners. I wanted to wish you happy on your betrothal to Lady Verity Heston."

Joshua bowed. "Thank you."

"Not that there's the slightest need to wish you happiness with a paragon like Lady Verity, I hasten to add. Beauty, grace, charm, accomplishments—she has them all in over-flowing measure." A slightly self-conscious tone crept into Augustus's voice. "She and I have become fast friends this past year, since she came out. She's been kind enough to read my work and to give me some very helpful suggestions. As I'm sure you've observed yourself, Lady Verity has an ethereal nature far above the grimy realities of this imperfect world."

"Er—quite." Measuring Augustus with a glance of pure frustration, Joshua drew a deep breath. "Look, will you do me a tremendous favor? Please present Lady Verity with my compliments and tell her I'm obliged to leave the ball early.

I've suddenly remembered a pressing engagement else-where."

"Certainly, but there's Lady Verity just coming off the floor after the country dance," said Augustus, plainly bewildered. "Wouldn't it be best to speak to her yourself?"

"I'm in a great hurry. She'll understand. I must visit a sick friend. An old acquaintance of the family, at death's door. I rely on you, Cranborn."

Driving away from the Portland-stone gateway of Holland House in his town carriage, through Kensington and past Hyde Park Corner into Piccadilly, Joshua felt his irritable mood gradually lighten. Talking to Augustus Cranborn had been the last straw in a disastrous evening. It wasn't that he was jealous of his former schoolmate. Verity was always surrounded by respectful but platonic admirers, and she was entirely too circumspect to encourage them. Just for this one night, however, he'd had enough of frigid fiancées and budding poets. He was going to a place where he could have a little uncomplicated male companionship. At White's he could eat and drink in peace, exchange a raucous story or two with any army acquaintances who happened to be there, and perhaps find a likely partner for whist.

Some hours later, bleary-eyed from lack of sleep and too much wine, and with the first clear light of dawn filtering in through the windows, Joshua pushed back his chair from the whist table. Checking the pile of counters in front of him and looking over his card, he discovered with profound surprise that he had won almost thirty thousand pounds. It was time to go home.

Leaning back against the squabs of the carriage, he dozed off intermittently during the drive north to his town house in Bedford Square, rousing occasionally to ponder a perplexing question: Why was it that when he was the impecunious Major Waring, playing cards at White's during his infrequent leaves from the army, he always returned to duty with his pockets to let? And why, on the other hand, metamorphosed into Lord Linton without a financial care in the world, had he been able to win a small fortune at the same club so effortlessly?

Joshua opened one eye when the carriage made the wide swing from Bond Street into Oxford Street, then settled back to sleep again, only to be jerked awake a few minutes later when the coachman pulled the horses to a jolting stop. Letting down the side glass, Joshua peered out the window and called up to the coachman, "What's amiss, Jepson?"

"Can't rightly say, m'lord. A lad dashed inter the street in front o' the carriage an' fell, or slipped . . ."

"Oh, the devil!" Opening the door, Joshua leaped to the pavement. His coachman was already bending over the crumpled body lying in the street only inches away from the front hooves of Joshua's team. A curious crowd of pedestrians was converging on the accident scene.

Pushing his way through the onlookers, Joshua knelt down to examine the slender figure lying still as death in the roadway. The victim's face beneath the tumble of short black curls was marble-white, except for the ugly gash on his temple, and his modest clothing was torn and stained. The wound to the temple wasn't fresh; the youth must have been in a fight—or he'd been assaulted—some hours before. Now he didn't seem to be breathing. Slipping his hand inside the boy's coat to check for a heartbeat, Joshua sharply caught his own breath as his fingers found a yielding softness. Moments later a pair of intensely blue eyes opened to stare up at him, and a slurred, bewildered voice said, "What happened? I remember deciding to cross the road, and then . . . Oh! Did I frighten the horses? I'm so sorry." Then the translucent eyelids closed again over the cornflower-blue eyes.

"Well, 'e ain't dead, anyways," commented the coachman uneasily. "I 'opes ye don't blame me fer wot's 'appened to the lad, m'lord."

"No, of course not," said Joshua slowly, his forehead furrowed in thought. "I feel sure the child was injured elsewhere and simply fainted in the street."

"So what's to do now, then? We can't jist leave 'im 'ere in the gutter, I suppose. P'raps I should take 'im to St. Bart's?"

"No," snapped Joshua. A charity ward at St. Bartholomew's Hospital might be the place for an injured youth of low origin. He couldn't send a girl there. Not this girl, who, despite the fact that she was dressed in boys' clothes and had come to his attention under distinctly questionable circumstances, was obviously not a member of the lower classes. That soft, slurred, cultivated voice could only belong to a lady of quality. He picked up the slight figure and carefully deposited her on the seat of the carriage.

"Drive home, Jepson."

Chapter 2

THE FINE linen felt smooth against her cheek, and the feather mattress cradled her in softest down. Sybilla opened her eyes slowly, blinking against the bright morning sunlight streaming in through the windows. She was lying in a strange bed, an imposing piece of furniture with a high domed tester, hung in pale blue silk. A sliver of memory returned, bringing panic with it, and she pushed herself into a sitting position, wincing with pain as her right temple began to throb. Somewhere in the room she heard a door open.

"So you're awake at last," said a dry, forbidding voice.

Sybilla looked up dazedly at the plump, dark-clad middle-aged lady standing by the bed. All but a trace of the woman's graying hair was tucked beneath an elaborate lace cap, making even more prominent the black currant eyes directed at Sybilla in an unfriendly stare.

"Who are you? Where am I?" Sybilla stammered.

The woman moved a delicate gilded chair close to the bed and sat down in it. "I'm Sarah Roper, housekeeper to Viscount Linton. You're in His Lordship's house in Bedford Square. More's to the point, who are you?"

"I—My name is Smith. How did I get here? The last I remember I stepped off the trottoir into the street . . ."

Her eyes widened. "There was a man kneeling beside me . . ."

"That was His Lordship. He brought you home at the crack of dawn this morning, saying you'd collapsed practically beneath the wheels of his carriage, and I was to take charge of you. And a bedraggled specimen you were, too, with those boys' clothes of yours all ripped and dirty."

Glancing down at herself, Sybilla realized for the first time that she was swathed in a voluminous garment she had never seen before. "Oh," she gasped, her cheeks flooding with color, and pulled the coverlets up around her shoulders.

"And so you might blush, my girl," said Sarah Roper severely. "That's my shift you're wearing. Mind, I don't begrudge any help to those in need, and perhaps His Lordship is right and you should be given the benefit of the doubt, but *I* find it hard to understand how a respectable young female could be found lying in the gutter dressed like a man! Well, enough of that. I've brought your clothes back to you, cleaned and mended as best may be, and I'll be back soon with some breakfast for you. As soon as you're presentable, His Lordship wants to speak to you in the library."

Half an hour later Sybilla stood hesitating at the door of the elegant bed chamber with its painted satinwood furniture, damask wall hangings, and delicately molded ceilings. She felt safe—well, comparatively safe—in this room, and she had no idea what she'd be facing when she left it. Once again a feeling of panic began to overwhelm her. How on earth had she gotten herself into such a fix? It had started, she supposed, when she first became aware that the silken chains of family obligation were beginning to interfere with her freedom of action. . . .

It had been a lovely, golden day on the moors, and after a long, satisfying gallop she and her cousin Barnaby had thrown themselves down on the soft turf to rest near a flock of sheep grazing in the shadow of the sharp bony ridges of the Pennines.

"Sybilla? Have you thought about Father's idea for us?"

Barnaby had inquired, his brown eyes in his round, boy-
ishly handsome face reflecting an uncharacteristic nervousness.

Sybilla didn't answer immediately. She'd grown fond of
Barnaby, in the two years since her father's death when her
uncle Hubert had come to live at Castle Wycombe with his
son and to assume the duties of guardian during her
minority. She and her cousin were virtually the same
age—they were now nineteen—and Barnaby's company
and friendship had in some measure filled the void left by
the loss of her father. Raised as an only child on the remote
moorland estate that had been in the possession of the Trent
family for many generations, Sybilla had turned to her
father for companionship during the long illness of her
mother, an immensely wealthy coal heiress from Lancashire. After the death of Lady Trent, Sybilla had become
even closer to her father, spending long hours with him
riding and fishing and learning the skills of estate management. Save for the obligatory time spent in the schoolroom
with her governess, she was never far from Baron Trent's
side.

"Sybilla?" Barnaby sounded plaintive.

She roused herself from her thoughts. "I heard you,
Barnaby, and yes, I *have* considered Uncle Hubert's 'idea.'
But, you see, I don't want to be married now."

"I thought you liked me. I thought you enjoyed being
with me."

Sybilla rolled over on her stomach in the soft grass and,
leaning on her elbows, looked down at Barnaby's hurt
face. "I *do* like you. I love you very much. But—don't
you see, we're almost like brother and sister. We've been
playing together these past two years like children, not
like lovers. And even if that weren't true, I don't think we
should get married until we've both seen something of the
world. Why, I'm nineteen years old, and I've scarcely been
away from Castle Wycombe since I was born, except for
short stays these past few years in Harrogate to take the
waters. You know Papa hated socializing. Before either you
or I settle down in marriage, we ought to travel a bit, meet
new people. Wouldn't you like to go to London, for
example?"

Sitting up, Barnaby clasped his knees and buried his head in his arms. "No," he said in a muffled voice. "All I want is to stay here at Castle Wycombe for the rest of my life with you."

Sybilla stared at her cousin's bent head. She was genuinely fond of Barnaby, but she was also beginning to resent the undercurrent of reproach, silent or otherwise, that had been enveloping her since Uncle Hubert had first suggested that she marry his son.

The idea was sensible enough from a number of angles. She was a young and very wealthy heiress, her uncle had pointed out, sure to be the target of fortune hunters. If she married one of these strangers, not only her fortune but also her title would pass out of the family, since the Barony of Trent was one of the few old peerages that could descend in the female line. What better way to preserve the Trent name and heritage than for her to marry Barnaby? And if the marriage enabled Uncle Hubert to live on in the home where he grew up and to provide for the future of his only son, what was wrong with that? Uncle Hubert might be a little high-handed in his management of her affairs, but he'd never shown her anything but love and kindness. Perhaps she owed a duty to Uncle Hubert and Barnaby. Arranged marriages in the family interest, after all, were more the rule than the exception.

But Sybilla didn't want to be sensible or dutiful. She suddenly felt hemmed in. No doubt she'd marry some day, and possibly she'd choose Barnaby as her husband, but first she wanted to spread her wings. . . .

Sybilla shook off her memories. She had to decide how to deal with the man who was waiting for her downstairs in his library. What kind of a person was he, this man who had plucked her off the street this morning? Would he expect some kind of payment for his chivalrous gesture, if that was what it was? Even in the wilds of Yorkshire she'd heard tales about what could happen to country innocents set adrift in this great impersonal city! Would she have to put up some kind of a struggle when she wanted to leave the house?

Sybilla straightened her shoulders. She was no helpless female, and she wasn't going to allow herself to be stampeded by nameless fears. After closing the bedchamber door firmly behind her, Sybilla headed for the staircase. As she neared the foot of the stairway, a footman appeared in the marble-paved hallway to intercept her.

"Miz Roper says I'm ter show ye ter the library, sir," the footman told her, speaking with a curious mixture of civility and curiosity as he eyed her woeful-looking garments, which all the housekeeper's brushing and cleaning and mending had failed to make presentable. With a start, Sybilla realized that he'd called her "sir." So Mrs. Roper had kept to herself the fact that her master's unexpected visitor was a girl. Sybilla wondered why.

Stopping at a door halfway down the corridor, the footman opened it and stepped aside. Slowly, choking back her nervousness, she entered the room. The man seated behind the polished mahogany desk lifted his head to look at her. "Lord Linton?" she inquired.

"Yes." He rose, coming around the desk to stand in front of her, his hands clasped behind his back as he gave her a long, considering look. Lifting her chin, Sybilla looked back at him. He was a tall man, broad-shouldered and rangy, with a mop of red-gold hair and rather lazy gray eyes set in a handsome, lean-planed face.

"My governess always told me it was rude to stare," said Sybilla tartly.

The gray eyes crinkled with instant amusement. "So it is. I was forgetting my manners. You see, it's something out of the usual way for me to pluck a young lady masquerading as a boy from beneath my horses' hooves! But, please, won't you sit down?" He moved to the chair behind the desk, leaning back comfortably as she settled into an armchair opposite him. "How are you feeling?" he asked. "That looks like a nasty cut on your temple."

"I'm very well. Lord Linton, I'd like to thank you for rescuing me. I understand I fainted in front of your carriage." Curiosity got the better of Sybilla, and she added, "You weren't responsible for my injuries, such as they were. You had no obligation to help me. Why did you bring me to your home?"

Lord Linton lifted an eyebrow in faint surprise. "I didn't think it right to leave a young woman unconscious in the street."

"But you didn't know I was a female, not until Mrs. Roper told you after she . . ." Sybilla's voice died away, and her cheeks flooded with crimson as she looked at Lord Linton's telltale face.

"I didn't know if you were dead or alive," he said defensively. "I had to—to open your shirt to see if your heart was still beating."

"Oh!" Turning an even deeper red, Sybilla leaped up from her chair and ran toward the door. Before she could open it, strong fingers removed her hand from the doorknob.

"Mrs. Roper told me you didn't have a penny in your pockets," said Joshua grimly as he grasped her arm. "It's obvious from your speech and bearing that you're a gentlewoman who's experienced some kind of misfortune. I can't let you leave until I'm satisfied you have a place to go and friends who will take care of you."

Sybilla glared at him. "My affairs, sir, are quite outside your concern. I do, indeed, have a place to go, and I intend to do just that if you'll only release my arm."

"Splendid," replied Joshua, laughter lurking behind his eyes. "Come sit down again and tell me about it."

"And then you'll allow me to leave?" Sybilla said suspiciously.

"But of course. More than that, I'll take you wherever you wish to go." He returned to the chair behind his desk and stood, keeping a cautious eye on her until she gave in to his request and sat down. "Mrs. Roper also tells me your name is—er—Smith. Jane Smith, I daresay?"

"Yes." Why not? she thought. Then, as she intercepted his look of smiling mockery, she decided not to let him have it entirely his own way. "Actually, it's Sybilla Smith," she said coldly.

"Sybilla Smith. A charming name. Now, then, how did a gently reared female like yourself get into such a fix, and who is this friend who you say will extend a helping hand?"

Sybilla felt the pangs of a headache coming on. She'd decided to conceal her real name from the housekeeper, out of an instinctive fear that Uncle Hubert might be able to trace her whereabouts, but why on earth had she picked a patently false name like Smith? Stealing a glance at Lord Linton, she failed to detect any dangerous libertine impulses in his handsome, smiling face, and for a moment she was tempted to confide in him. Immediately she decided against it. If she told him her story, he'd no doubt escort her back to her godmother's house, as he'd promised. But then, she was convinced, he'd feel obliged to notify her family back in Yorkshire that she was safe. And after that, in three days' time, Uncle Hubert would arrive on her godmother's doorstep, and that would be the end of her fling at independence.

"The fact is, I'm a runaway," she informed him with an air of candor.

"Ah. Somehow I'd guessed as much. A runaway from what, pray?"

"From my father."

"A man named Smith?"

"Sir Frederick Smith," Sybilla agreed defiantly.

Joshua broke into a chuckle. "I'm put in my place. If I don't know his real name, I can't contact him to tell him where his daughter is, which I certainly ought to do as a responsible citizen! Very well, we'll play by your rules for the time being. Tell me about your troubles with 'Sir Frederick.'"

"Well . . . Papa owns a large estate near—near Durham, and I'm his only child," Sybilla began, allowing her always vivid imagination full rein. "He's trying to force me to marry a man I detest, an old rake who lives on an adjoining estate, so I decided to run away. I was planning to stay with my godmother, who lives in the West End. Unfortunately, I was robbed of everything I owned soon after I arrived in London. If I could just get to my godmother's house, I'm sure Aunt Lucretia—she's not really my aunt, only my mother's distant cousin—I'm sure Aunt Lucretia will let me stay with her for a little while, and perhaps while I'm gone, Papa will realize how unhappy I am and he'll reconsider this dreadful marriage."

"I see." Lord Linton sounded thoughtful. "You're very sure you're being pushed into an unsuitable match?" he asked after a pause. "It couldn't be that your father has only your best interests at heart? Perhaps you might come to change your mind about your suitor?"

"I'm no flibbertigibbett miss, my lord," flared Sybilla. "How would you like to marry somebody three times your age who's already buried two wives and who has gout and—and unpleasant breath?"

"Now that you put it that way, it sounds very lowering." The firm, rather sensual mouth twitched, and Sybilla realized with a flash of rage that he was getting a great deal of enjoyment out of the conversation. Obviously he didn't believe in her cruel father and her lecherous suitor. At the same time she felt a pang of compunction at the libels she was fastening onto the memory of her father. Richard, Baron Trent, had been the kindest, most loving father in the world. He bore no resemblance at all to the fictional Sir Frederick Smith.

Lord Linton broke into her thoughts by saying unexpectedly, "Very well. I haven't much taste myself for ill-conceived marital matches. I'll take you to your aunt Lucretia. Where does she live?"

"In Henrietta Place." Well, that was an easy victory, thought Sybilla. Too easy, perhaps? She darted an uneasy look at Lord Linton. Did he have something up his sleeve?

If he did, it wasn't immediately apparent. He rang the bell, ordering his curricle to be brought around, and a few minutes later she walked with him down the front steps of Linton House to the waiting carriage. As he helped her into the curricle, she gazed, impressed, around the square. Linton House was one of four stuccoed and pilastered mansions occupying the central position on each side of the square; the other houses were substantial brick structures ornamented with wrought-iron balconies and doorways of Coade stone.

Driving out of the square through the gate held open by Joshua's diminutive tiger, who then leaped nimbly onto his perch behind them, they passed St. Giles Circus and turned west on Oxford Street. Soon they paused before a trim brick house with iron railings.

"Your godmother lives at Number twenty-one, you said? Here we are." Tossing his reins to the tiger, Joshua followed Sybilla, who had jumped out lightly as soon as the curricle stopped, scampering up the short flight of steps to the front door. He stood beside her, unobtrusively observing her as she lifted the brass knocker and rapped briskly on the door.

She does look like a boy, he thought, like a slender stripling of fourteen or fifteen in her ragtag coat and breeches. Probably he wouldn't have guessed, at least at a a casual glance, that she was really a girl, despite those long-lashed intensely blue eyes, soft red mouth and pert features with the fugitive dimple that popped out unexpectedly. Many girls, it was true, affected her hairdo of crisp short curls, but then so did many aspiring male sprigs of fashion.

"Why don't they answer?" Sybilla muttered, raising the knocker again. Moments passed, and no one came to the door. Sybilla shot a troubled glance at Joshua. "Even if Aunt Lucretia's out, visiting or shopping, surely there must be servants in the house. Unless . . ."

"Unless she's moved, perhaps? Have you been in recent communication with her?"

"N-no, not very recent. Aunt Lucretia hasn't visited me since Mama died, six years ago, and she's never liked to write letters. I remember Mama complaining that she had to write five letters to get one answer from Aunt Lucretia, even though they'd been very close since they were small children."

"Well, I don't think there's much profit in waiting on her doorstep any longer—"

"Wait!" exclaimed Sybilla. "I can hear footsteps. Someone is coming."

The door opened, and a pair of beady eyes in a long face crowned by a thatch of untidy hair peered out at them. "Wot do ye want, poundin' at the door like that?" the man growled.

"I've come to see Lady Madden," Sybilla said eagerly. "Is she at home?"

"Nay. Gone off somewheres."

"Oh. Will she be back soon?"

"Can't say. If'n that be all . . ." The man made a move to close the door.

"Please. Can't you tell me anything about where she went, or how long she might be gone? It's very important."

The note of appeal in Sybilla's voice seemed to reach the man. He scratched his head, saying, "I think I 'eard some'ut about 'er goin' ter Ireland ter visit 'er cousin."

"Ireland! Where in Ireland?"

"Don't rightly know. Miz Endicott—that's the 'ousekeeper—*she'd* know, but she ain't 'ere." The man lifted a hand to forestall the next question. "Nor they ain't nobody else 'ere, neither. The butler, 'e went wi' 'er Ladyship ter Ireland, along wi' the footman an' the abigail. Jist me an' Miz Endicott stayed on, ter watch the 'ouse, like."

"The housekeeper stayed behind?" Sybilla said quickly. "But you said she wasn't here."

"No more she ain't. 'Er daughter's increasin', an' Miz Endicott, she went off ter 'elp wi' the layin'-in."

Gritting her teeth, Sybilla inquired, "Do you know when she'll return?"

"Dunno. A few days, a week? Two weeks?" The caretaker shrugged.

"Thank you," Sybilla said quietly. "I won't trouble you any more, then." After the man had closed the door, she looked up at Joshua, saying, "My thanks to you, too, my lord," and turned to walk down the steps.

He caught up with her as she rounded the iron railings and started down the street. "Where do you think you're going?"

"I don't know," she muttered. "It's nothing to you, in any event."

"Allow me to be the best judge of that." He took her arm, and when she tried to pull free, he increased the steely pressure of his fingers and marched her over to the curricle.

Tossing a coin to his tiger, he said, "I don't need you any more today, Tim. Find a hackney and go home."

"Thank ye, m'lord." His face wooden and his eyes curious, the tiger went off, whistling.

Joshua grinned at Sybilla. "Now that he's gone, we can speak frankly. Hop into the curricle, Miss Smith."

Still trying to release her arm, Sybilla said with a catch in her voice, "I know you're trying to be kind, and I thank you, but please don't offer me money or any other kind of help. I couldn't accept charity. I'll manage somehow."

"How, may I ask, do you propose to do without a ha'penny to your name?"

"I'll find work. I could be a tap boy in a tavern, or a street cleaner, or a—a chimney sweep!"

"Oh, Lord." Joshua rolled his eyes. He said firmly, "Sybilla, you ninnyhammer, I'm not going to let you fend for yourself. Either I take you to Bow Street Magistrate's Court, where I'll hire a Runner to ferret out where you live, or you come with me for a drive and let me talk to you about finding some reasonable way to solve your problem. It's your choice."

"A choice between the frying pan and the fire," Sybilla said resentfully.

"But the only choice you have," he pointed out. Looking at her mutinous, confused face, he added persuasively, "Isn't this your first visit to London? Wouldn't you like to join me in an ice at Gunther's Tea Shop? I'm told the black-currant flavor is especially delicious."

Despite herself, Sybilla's eyes brightened. Even in Yorkshire she'd heard of the famous pastry shop in Berkeley Square, and suddenly she could feel her stomach protesting. In her nervousness earlier, she'd eaten practically nothing of the breakfast that Mrs. Roper had sent up. She could at least listen to Lord Linton, she decided. It needn't obligate her to anything. Certainly she'd be better prepared to launch out on her own if she wasn't weak from hunger. "I daresay it wouldn't do any harm to have an ice," she admitted grudgingly.

Berkeley Square on this sunny afternoon in July was congested with fashionable carriages drawn up beneath the luxuriant shade of the plane trees. Ladies sat at ease in their carriages, spooning daintily at their ices, their gentlemen escorts relaxing against the railings, while apron-clad wait- ers dashed madly back and forth across the road from the tea shop in the eastern side of the square, taking and delivering orders.

"Observe how chic we are," Joshua grinned. "The *beau monde* flocks to Gunther's on fine afternoons. That's the famous Lady Jersey over there, by the way, in the carriage drawn by black horses." Raising a spoonful of black-currant ice to his mouth, he noticed that Sybilla's serving dish was empty. Motioning to one of the hurrying waiters, he gave a brief order. Soon the waiter returned with a large apricot tart and a basket of sugarplums. "Growing boys need extra nourishment," he said solemnly, and after a brief, irritated stare, Sybilla bit hungrily into the apricot tart.

"Feeling more the thing?" he inquired a few moments later. "Good. Now we can talk. And before you try to roll me up horse, foot, and gun, I should tell you I don't believe a word of that gammon you pitched to me earlier. First off, your name isn't Smith. Is it really Sybilla? Yes, I believe it is," he said as her eyes widened. "You're Sybilla some- thing, then, but you're not being forced into a distasteful marriage with an ancient loose fish."

"How—?"

"You were doing it rather too brown," Joshua explained, his eyes twinkling. "I could believe this old gentleman had buried two wives, and that he had gout, but bad breath? Coming it on too strong, my girl!" As Sybilla's lips curved in a reluctant smile, he said, "Shall we have the truth now? What's your surname, where do you live, and what's the real reason you ran away from home?"

Shaking her head, Sybilla said slowly, "I can't tell you who I really am, because you'd insist on sending me home, and I've made up my mind I'm not going back."

Joshua raised an eyebrow. "Are we at an impasse, then? At least tell me why you ran away."

Sybilla looked at him doubtfully. "Well, I daresay there's no harm in that. You see I'm by way of being an heiress, and my uncle, who became my guardian when Papa died, wants me to marry his son. I can't blame Uncle Hu—my uncle for wishing to see his son well married, and I'm really rather fond of my cousin, but I just don't wish to be married right now. I'm nineteen years old, and I've scarcely traveled more than a few miles from where I was born. I made up my mind I was going to see a little bit of the world before I settled down." A note of grievance crept into Sybilla's voice. "I'd have carried it off, too, if only I hadn't been robbed, and if Aunt Lucretia hadn't decided to go gallivanting off to Ireland!" She paused, looking thoughtful. "Of course, my aunt might be planning to come home before very long, or, if not, the housekeeper may return to the house shortly, and she'll be able to tell me where in Ireland Aunt Lucretia is, and then I could write her a letter—"

"That's too many *ifs, mights,* and *coulds*," said Joshua calmly. "Look, I sympathize with your reasons for not wanting to go home at present, and if—Lord, now *I'm* doing it!—*if* your godmother were in residence here, I'd gladly hand you over to her. But as the situation stands . . ." Cocking his head, a quizzical smile curving his mouth, he said, "Let's understand each other. One last time: Are you going to tell me your real name and where you live so I can send you back to your guardian?"

"No," Sybilla said baldly. "And I warn you, no Bow Street Runner is going to make me tell, either!"

"I can well believe *that!* Very well, then, how about a compromise? You'll stay with me at Linton House for two weeks, and if during that time your godmother doesn't return and you can't get any word of her from the housekeeper, you'll allow me to put you on a stagecoach bound for wherever it is you come from. Also, during those two weeks, I'll engage to show you the sights of London. At the very least you'll have seen 'a little bit of the world' before you go home. We can leave a message with the caretaker of your godmother's house, telling her or the housekeeper where to find you. Well, what do you think of my idea?"

Sybilla gazed at him, the confusion of her thoughts showing plainly on her face.

"No strings attached, of course," he added hastily. "My

faults are legion, but no one's ever accused me of being loose in the shaft."

"Thank you, but I already knew you didn't have any designs on my virtue," said Sybilla, chuckling at Joshua's comic look of surprise mingled with a trace of chagrin.

"Good God, Sybilla, I'm no nonpareil, but do I look that innocuous?"

Smiling faintly, she replied, "Only if one examines you with a very keen eye! Tell me, why are you being so kind to a complete stranger? Perhaps you're the type of person who can't resist dragging home stray dogs and cats?"

"Well, I'm fond of dogs and cats," he said with a grin. Then, turning serious, he added, "Let's say I'm doing this for my own peace of mind. I wouldn't sleep nights if I knew you were out there in the city alone, blundering into God knows what kind of difficulty or danger. Look, every morning in the stews of Covent Garden the watchmen find a fashionable young buck or two lying in the gutter unconscious, stripped of clothes and money. Can you imagine what might happen to a green girl like you, loose in the London underworld? Indulge me in this. Say you'll accept my invitation."

Sybilla heard the siren call of temptation. She couldn't recall everything that had happened during her dazed early morning wanderings, but she did remember several of the people who'd accosted her: the drunken beggar, the painted drab, the pathetic street sweeper in his rags and dirt. They were all disquieting people whose desperate faces had demonstrated to her how difficult it would be to maintain herself in London without funds or a place of shelter. Supposing she accepted the invitation to stay at Linton House. Supposing Aunt Lucretia didn't return within the two weeks of grace. Supposing Joshua *did* wash his hands of her by putting her on a stagecoach. She could always get off at the next stop, couldn't she, and request reimbursement for the ticket? As for accepting charity, she thought, it was really no such thing. She had pots of money, though unfortunately at the moment she couldn't get her hands on any of it. Ultimately she could pay back her benefactor every shilling he spent on her.

"Thank you very much, Lord Linton," she said graciously. "I'm pleased and honored to accept your invitation." A gleam of excitement made her eyes sparkle. "Do you think we might visit Astley's Amphitheatre? *I'm* very fond of horses."

"Certainly," said Joshua, climbing into the curricle. "As an ex-cavalryman, I'd fancy that myself. Hop in. And do you think you could stop calling me Lord Linton? My friends call me Joshua."

As they drove out of Berkeley Square, Sybilla said with a dash of foreboding, "I think you've overlooked something, Joshua. Your housekeeper won't approve of my staying at your house. She suspects me of being a woman of loose character."

Chapter 3

❧

SYBILLA WAS correct. Mrs. Roper didn't approve.

Summoned to the library when Joshua and Sybilla returned to Linton House, the housekeeper quite forgot the respect due her employer when he informed her that Miss Smith would be his guest for the next two weeks.

"I'll not have that bit of muslin staying in this house, my lord!" she snapped, the ribbons on her lace cap quivering with outrage.

Sybilla swallowed hard.

"Mrs. Roper." Joshua's voice cracked like a whip, and his eyes were icy. "I think you forget yourself. This is *my* house. I'll invite anyone I please to visit me here."

The housekeeper quailed but stood her ground. "I've served the Waring family for many years, and served them well, nobody can say any different. I'd be remiss in my duty if I didn't tell you that you're about to bring disgrace on this house. If you want to mount a mistress, that's one thing, and it's not my place to try to stop you, but you shouldn't soil your family home by bringing her here. I'm happy your sainted mother isn't alive to see such a thing! And what would Lady Verity think if she knew?"

Dazed at the ferocity of Mrs. Roper's attack, Sybilla stared helplessly at Joshua. "Who's Lady Verity?" she inquired blankly. Was there still another female in the house itching to disapprove of her?

"My fiancée," said Joshua. Obviously trying to keep his temper, he said coldly to Mrs. Roper, "Miss Smith is no bit of muslin, nor is she planning to be my mistress. Even if she were, however, I'd expect you to treat her with courtesy. As it happens, she's merely in temporary difficulties."

With a mounting sense of astonishment, Sybilla listened to Joshua as he told Mrs. Roper a harrowing tale about a sensitive young woman being forced by a cruel and uncaring father into the arms of an aging satyr. Joshua's version was decidedly more inventive than her own, Sybilla reflected appreciatively. She wondered if it would have the persuasive effect on Mrs. Roper that he intended.

"You're telling me this man is over seventy years of age and is suspected of doing away with two of his five wives? He *poisoned* them?" The housekeeper gasped, her eyes wide with horror. "And what's this you say about his own *daughter*?" She turned on Sybilla. "What was your parent thinking of, to force you into the arms of such a libertine? Arranging a good marriage for your child is one thing, but this! Isn't he aware of your suitor's evil reputation?"

"I know Papa means well," Sybilla said gravely, "but he's quite elderly himself, and recently he's been ill. He thinks the rumors about Mr.—this man—are exaggerated."

Suppressing a quick grin of amused approval at Sybilla's resourceful reply, Joshua said to Mrs. Roper, "So you see one can hardly blame Miss Smith for attempting to escape such a fate. Surely you wouldn't begrudge her a place of refuge? For two weeks only. I trust by that time her father may have reconsidered his position."

"Well . . ." The housekeeper seemed to have lost the edge from her hostility, but her manner was still decidedly stiff as she declared, "I won't say as you didn't have cause for alarm, miss, but to run away in boys' clothes! To stay in the house of a complete stranger, and a bachelor gentleman to boot! I can't hold with such goings-on, that I must tell you." She squared her shoulders, her plump face assuming a martyred look. "However, you've asked for my help, my lord, and I shan't deny it, whatever my feelings. Now, then, Miss Smith is to stay here as a young man, I presume?"

"Naturally," said Joshua. "How would I explain the presence of a young unmarried female in my house? You were quite right, Mrs. Roper. We can't have a howling scandal. How about the servants? Do they have any suspicions about Sybilla's—er—sex?"

The housekeeper's mouth folded in a repressive line. "They do not. I personally attended to Miss Smith when you brought her here."

"Splendid. That's one worry out of the way. Let me think, Sybilla. Who are you, and why are you here?" Joshua's brow knit in thought. "I have it, you'll be my young friend Bill Smith. Or perhaps Will Smith. Yes, that has a better ring to it. You're the son of a Peninsular comrade who died at Vitoria. Out of the goodness of my heart and my affection for your parent, I'm showing you the sights of London before you go off to—shall we say Harrow?"

"Harrow or Eton, it's all the same to me," Sybilla replied saucily, her smile fading at Mrs. Roper's expression of austere disapproval.

"And what, pray, is 'Will Smith' to wear?" inquired the housekeeper, casting a withering look at Sybilla's garments. "Your Lordship will hardly wish to be seen on the street with someone who resembles a badly dressed shopkeeper's assistant."

Sybilla glanced down at her rumpled coat and breeches and her scuffed shoes and sighed. "Mrs. Roper has a point. These are my cousin's castoffs. They never did fit too well, and now, of course, they're considerably the worse for wear."

"So they are," said Joshua after a moment's examination of her garments. "Well, that's no real problem. I'll take you to my tailor." He paused, looking a little foolish at the housekeeper's sudden glare. "No, I daresay that wouldn't do," he added hastily. "Mrs. Roper, you'll just have to take Sybilla's measurements." He took out his watch. "As soon as I have the measurements in hand, I'll go see Weston. His premises will still be open."

"I fancy Mr. Weston won't work as quickly as the shoemaker's elves in the fairy tale," Mrs. Roper said tartly. "It will be several days at least before the clothes are ready. Meanwhile, the young lady needs something to wear. Come along, miss. We'll take your measurements and then we'll order the carriage to take us to Grafton House. Heaven knows the place isn't fashionable, but no doubt we can find something. I often buy clothes for my nephews there."

In her small sitting room Mrs. Roper opened her sewing basket and proceeded to measure Sybilla in grim silence. Writing down her figures on a scrap of paper, she sniffed, "There, that should suffice for the likes of Mr. Weston. Let's hope the man never finds out he's making clothes for His Lordship's *chère amie*." She cleared her throat. "I'm sorry," she said, not sounding especially repentant. "That's what the world would certainly call you if it were known you were staying here."

Sybilla studied the housekeeper's face. "You want me to go, don't you?"

"It's not for me to say, I'm sure. Only I should hate to see any scandal cloud His Lordship's life just when he's about to be married. Poor lad. He's had a deal of sorrow lately, losing his father and his brother within so short a time of each other."

Silent for a long moment, Sybilla extended her hand for the slip of paper. "I'll see that His Lordship gets the measurements." She walked down the corridor to the front hallway, where the footman was turning away from the door with a letter in his hand.

"Is that for me, Briggs?" called Joshua as he walked down the stairs, dressed in his caped driving coat and carrying his hat and gloves.

"Yes, m'lord."

Slipping the letter into the pocket of his greatcoat, Joshua nodded a dismissal to the footman and turned to Sybilla. He said cheerfully, "Are those your measurements? Then I'm off to my tailor. In no time at all we'll have you on the road to sartorial splendor. What is it?" he asked quickly. "Has Mrs. Roper been unkind to you?"

"No, she hasn't been unkind, but she *has* been truthful.

She thinks I don't belong here, and I agree with her."
Sybilla rushed her words, afraid she might lose the courage
to say them. "Lord Linton—I mean, Joshua—I think I
should leave. This madcap scheme we've concocted simply
won't fadge. Someone is bound to discover I'm not a boy,
and then there'll be the most dreadful scandal. Mrs. Roper
says you're to be married soon. I won't risk being the cause
of any hurt to your fiancée, so I've come up with a plan. I
know I said I wouldn't accept charity, but supposing you
lend me some money? Say twenty pounds. That will be
enough to keep me until I find employment, and I assure
you I'll pay it back some day—" She broke off, gasping as
Joshua seized her by her shoulders and shook her.

"Listen to me, you little idiot," he said between his
clenched teeth. "We made a pact, you and I, and I'm
holding you to it. If I don't find you here when I come back,
I'll go to Bow Street Magistrate's Court and hire enough
Runners to comb the city until I find you. Do you
understand that?"

"Yes. But Joshua—"

"No *buts*. Do I have your word you won't run away
again?"

"Yes," Sybilla blurted, torn between relief that she didn't
have to leave Linton House and guilt because she knew she
ought to do so, and filled with amazement that Joshua
Waring's lazy gray eyes could suddenly turn into silvery
pools of molten anger.

"Good. Have a successful shopping trip with Mrs.
Roper."

After saying goodbye to Sybilla, Joshua paused on the
doorstep to take his letter out of his pocket. It was addressed
in Verity's tiny, perfect handwriting: "Dear Joshua, I'm
sorry we had a misunderstanding last night. Shall we talk
about it? Please come to tea this afternoon. I'll expect you
at four o'clock. Yours, Verity."

As he climbed into his curricle and lifted the reins,
Joshua felt a stirring of unease. Was he in for a ladylike
tongue-lashing? He and Verity had come close to an
outright quarrel last night, and he presumed his cavalier exit

from Lady Holland's ball without taking personal leave of his fiancée hadn't improved the situation. What had possessed him to do such a childish thing? And would Verity bring up again the subject of that stolen kiss in the garden? Unbidden, a sudden vivid memory of dark-eyed Natividad came into his mind. Natividad, with whom he'd had several heated encounters in the frontier town of Guarda. No one could call her kisses chaste or impersonal, but then, she'd had more practice than Verity. A great deal more, he thought, grinning inwardly.

During the journey from Bedford Square to Bond Street, Joshua found his thoughts wandering from his fiancée to Sybilla. He smiled wryly as he realized he was worrying about the discomfort she might be experiencing from Mrs. Roper's open hostility. It was almost as though he'd become Sybilla's instant parent or uncle! He shrugged. It was no use telling himself that he had no real responsibility for this waif, this girl-child who had descended on him. One look into those cornflower-blue eyes, and he'd known he couldn't abandon her to the terrors of the city streets, even if her predicament was her own fault and she was being headstrong and flighty and unreasonable. Which she was, no *ifs* about it, but he'd always liked people with spirit, and Sybilla certainly had enough of that! He had an apprehensive feeling that complications might disrupt his rash promise to give her two weeks of freedom in London, but he wasn't going to worry about that now. Nor was he going to worry about Mrs. Roper. He'd deal with her later if her barbs got too sharp.

At Weston's establishment in Bond Street the master tailor himself took charge of Joshua. "And what were you thinking of, my lord? A new coat, perhaps? A waistcoat? I've some very fine white embroidered marcella laid by. Or—"

"Actually, I don't require any addition to my wardrobe at the moment. I'd like you to make some garments for a young friend of mine."

"Certainly, my lord. If the young gentleman will come in—"

"Well, but he can't come in. He's—he's injured his leg.

Not a break to the bone, the surgeon tells us, but Will must stay off his feet for a few days. Meanwhile, he needs something to wear. His portmanteau with all his belongings was stolen, you understand, at the time he hurt his leg. So I've brought you his measurements. Make him several coats and some pantaloons and waistcoats. I'll go to Harboro and Acock for his shirts and cravats."

Gazing in dismay at the scribbled figures on Mrs. Roper's scrap of paper, Weston exclaimed, "I'm sorry, my lord! I couldn't possibly create a wardrobe for a gentleman without proper fittings, without even seeing him. Your friend must come in."

"Out of the question. Will can't come in. You needn't worry about how well his clothes fit. The lad's only fifteen, after all, and Carlton House to a Charley's shelter he won't care a fig if he isn't turned out in the first style of elegance! Of course, if you'd prefer I go to Stutz—"

But at this dire mention of his arch rival, the tailor capitulated. "We'll do our best, I can't say more than that." His eye took on a sudden gleam as he walked around Joshua, examining the fit of his coat. "You won't reconsider and allow me to nip in the waist a bit and adjust the armholes?"

"Not on your life. You'll not truss me up like one of those old Egyptian mummies. My coats must be roomy enough so I can swing a saber."

"But, my lord . . . I understood you had left the army."

"Well, so I have," said Joshua loftily, "but I want my coats to be loose enough so I could use a saber if I took the notion to do so."

Leaving his tailor to ponder this heresy, Joshua drove first to Cockspur Street to leave an order with his shirtmaker and then to Lord Dunsford's elegant house on the north side of Cavendish Square. Ushered into the drawing room, he found Verity taking tea with Maria Laleham, a faded creature who had been acting as her duenna since her mother's death some years before. The Honorable Augustus Cranborn was there, too, looking, to Joshua's annoyance, very much at home. Smiling brightly, Verity indicated a seat beside her and poured her fiancé a cup of tea.

"I'm rather surprised to see you here, Cranborn," said Joshua as he sipped his tea.

"Really? Why do you say that?"

"Oh, I always thought that poets, like hermits, required a great deal of solitude."

"No, on the contrary, I need to interrelate with other people to compose or even to recite," Augustus assured him earnestly. "For example, I've asked Lady Verity and Mrs. Laleham to a reading of my poetry at Lady Callan's house this evening. You'd be very welcome, too."

"Well, I—"

"Do come, Joshua, it will be such fun," urged Verity. She added playfully, "Maria is going to honor the occasion by wearing her new cameo, a birthday present from Papa. Isn't it pretty?" As if struck by a sudden thought, Verity said to Mrs. Laleham, "I daresay Mr. Cranborn would like to see the collection of intaglio stones that Papa bought in Italy on his Grand Tour. Why don't you take Mr. Cranborn into the library?"

After Augustus and the duenna, both of them appearing slightly bemused, had left the room, Verity said with a touch of embarrassment, "Do you think I was too obvious? I wanted us to be private." She looked into his eyes gravely. "We almost quarreled last night. That mustn't be. I think we misunderstood each other." A flush of color suffused her porcelain cheeks. "I've no objection to an occasional—an occasional display of affection. A fine state of affairs it would be if a betrothed couple had no feeling for each other!" Closing her eyes, she lifted her face to him in mute invitation. He hesitated a moment, then leaned forward to kiss her gently on the mouth.

She drew back from him, her eyes fluttering open. "There, what did I tell you?" she teased. "I don't dislike kissing at all, provided I'm not being crushed to death in a bear's embrace! Aren't you happy we talked things out like civilized people?"

"Oh, indeed," he replied, forcing a smile. The kiss had been oddly chaste and impersonal, rather like kissing one's schoolgirl niece, or a Vestal Virgin on her way to the sacrifice. Nothing at all like kissing Natividad, but he supposed it represented progress of a sort. By their wedding night Verity might even summon up the passion to put her arms around his neck!

Beaming, apparently feeling their difficulties had been satisfactorily resolved, Verity turned to other matters. "I really think you'd enjoy Mr. Cranborn's reading. Why don't you come here to an early dinner and go on with us to Lady Callan's house?"

Joshua had a sudden vision of Sybilla wilting under the eagle surveillance of Mrs. Roper. "Thank you for the invitation, but I think I should spend the evening at home. A young guest arrived today, the son of an old comrade who was killed at Vitoria."

"Poor young man. He's taking his father's death very hard, I don't doubt. You must bring him to see me. I wonder if he'd enjoy hearing Mr. Cranborn read his poems?"

"Will's a schoolboy, only fifteen," said Joshua hastily. "A trifle young to enter the ton, I fear. I fancy his tastes run more to the Tower Zoo or Madame Tussaud's Wax Works."

"Oh, a schoolboy," said Verity, knitting her brows. "You know, it's very kind of you to take an interest in this lad, but surely you needn't spend every waking minute with him." Leaning toward him, she put her hand on his arm, saying coaxingly, "I really would like you to escort me tonight."

Joshua held his breath. She really was the most beautiful creature . . . "I daresay Will can take care of himself this evening."

The soft knock on the door roused Sybilla from a deep slumber. After returning from shopping with Mrs. Roper at Grafton House, she'd collapsed onto the soft feather mattress for a long nap.

"Yes?" she called out sleepily.

"Mrs. Roper says ter tell ye dinner's in 'alf an hour," came the voice from the other side of the door.

Yawning, Sybilla sat up, swinging her legs over the side of the bed and glancing with a twinge of surprise at the unfamiliar male drawers and muslin shirt she was wearing.

Her cousin Barnaby's soiled and torn hand-me-downs, which had occasioned so many disapproving glances when she'd appeared in them this afternoon at respectable Grafton House, lay in a heap on the floor, where she'd discarded them before her nap. Her eyes moved on to the chair where she'd placed the other garments Mrs. Roper had purchased for her today.

A little later, after she'd donned the new coat and pantaloons and waistcoat and was fighting a losing battle in her fumbling efforts to tie her modest cravat, she found herself staring in shock at the strange youth reflected in the cheval glass. The long nap had refreshed her, and she was thinking more clearly than at any time since the thugs had cracked her skull and stolen her belongings at dawn this morning. Suddenly she was overwhelmed by acute misgivings about the scheme she and Joshua had put in motion.

Her original plan to leave Yorkshire and see something of the great outside world before settling down to domesticity with Barnaby had been a workable one. Running away dressed in boys' clothes might strike most people as unconventional and reprehensible, but few could object to a visit with her godmother. Once she was established in the shelter of Aunt Lucretia's home, Uncle Hubert would have found it difficult to dislodge her. Her godmother might even have proposed to launch her into polite society.

The plan could still work, if Aunt Lucretia came home within the next two weeks, or if Sybilla could manage to prolong her London stay, but it took too much advantage of Joshua's good-natured generosity. Mrs. Roper was quite right. The ton wouldn't blink an eye if Joshua set up a fancy-piece in a snug house in Marylebone, but it would look askance if he established a ladybird in his own house under the very eye of his fiancée. Sybilla took another long look in the mirror. Yes, she could pass as a boy to the casual eye, but her disguise might wear very thin under the watchful gaze of a houseful of Joshua's servants. So, it seemed, she had two alternatives: She could opt to continue her masquerade, or she could turn tail and flee back to Yorkshire before she'd so much as put a foot into Westminster Abbey or the Pantheon.

Clamping her lips tightly together, Sybilla attacked her cravat ferociously. Her mind was made up. She'd be careful, she'd do her best to avoid detection, and she'd make the most of her two weeks of grace. Meanwhile, she was ravenously hungry. The black-currant ice, apricot tart, and sugarplums she'd consumed at Gunther's were now only a faded memory.

In the cavernous dining room of Linton House, however, she almost lost her appetite as she sat at one end of the gleaming mahogany table and stared down its long solitary expanse. She would be dining alone in conspicuous solitude.

"Lord Linton won't be joining me?" she asked the footman.

"No, sir. His Lordship is out this evening."

Fortunately, the arrival of a bowl of delicious soup revived Sybilla's appetite, followed as it was by an excellent dinner. After eating heartily, she trailed out of the dining room, looking around the vacant hallway and wondering if she was expected to spend the rest of the evening in her bedchamber like an obedient child. If so, she could at least find something to read, she decided, and started down the hallway to the library. Halfway there, she changed her mind and headed purposefully for the rear portion of the house.

Shortly afterward, stepping into the kitchen, Mrs. Roper paused in surprise at the sight of Lord Linton's new charge in deep conversation with Cook. Looking up, Sybilla said jauntily, "Hello there, Mrs. Roper. I'm picking Cook's brains. Her jugged hare was magnificent, but it tasted a bit different from what we have at home. Her secret, it turns out, is port. Our cook uses Madeira. And the cream darioles, delicious! I must have the recipe to take home with me."

"And so ye shall, sir," said Cook with an indulgent smile. "We all know that young gentlemen 'ave 'ollow legs fer sweets. 'Is Lordship, now, when 'e was a lad, 'e never could get enough o' my darioles."

Mrs. Roper said, "Mr. Smith, since His Lordship is out this evening, would you care to have coffee with me in my sitting room?" Her voice was pleasant and respectful, but Sybilla caught the hint of iron in it. A few moments later, pouring the coffee, the housekeeper exclaimed, "What possessed you to talk to Cook, miss? Do you want to give yourself away? Gentlemen aren't supposed to be interested in kitchen matters."

"I'm sorry," Sybilla said, sighing. "I was feeling a bit lonely, I guess, and it *was* an excellent dinner." She gazed around the pleasant sitting room, noting its meticulous tidiness. "You have an extremely well-run establishment here. It's a pleasure to stay in a house like this. The Waring family must find you indispensable."

Despite herself, Mrs. Roper bridled with pleasure, and afterward she could never quite explain how it was that she and Sybilla plunged into such a long and satisfying conversation. By the time the housekeeper finally said good night, she might have been talking to a long-lost daughter of the house.

At midnight, when Joshua walked into the library, he stopped short when he saw Sybilla sitting before the fireplace. "Hello, there, not in bed yet?" he said, his tone sounding faintly guilty. "I hope you weren't too much at loose ends by yourself this evening."

"Oh, no, I've managed to entertain myself quite well. Did you have an enjoyable engagement?"

"Oh, yes. Well, to be perfectly truthful, not exactly. I had to listen to a confounded poet!" Joshua glanced at Sybilla's serviceable new garments. "You look much more the thing tonight. Did—I gather you and Mrs. Roper must have kept the peace."

"Mrs. Roper and I are becoming bosom friends," Sybilla assured him.

"I say, really?" Crossing to the sideboard, Joshua poured two glasses of Madeira and returned with them to the chair opposite Sybilla, handing her one of the glasses. "Tell me about this miracle."

"It's simple enough. Mrs. Roper likes to talk about the Waring family, and I'm a good listener." Sybilla grinned. "I heard all about how beautiful your mother was, and what good friends you were with your brother, even though you were so different, and how you sneaked off on your father's prize hunter and failed to jump a fence and broke your leg. Oh, yes, and how you saved your commanding officer from certain capture by the French and carried him off the field with a bullet wound in his chest!" For some reason she couldn't explain, even to herself, Sybilla omitted telling Joshua about Mrs. Roper's lavish praise of Lady Verity Heston's golden beauty.

Joshua grimaced. "By Jove, I hope Mrs. Roper didn't reveal all our family skeletons." He looked over at the small table beside Sybilla's chair. "What are you doing, playing draughts all by yourself?"

"For lack of an opponent. Will you have a game?"

"Why not?" Joshua replied good-naturedly, drawing up his chair. "My brother, Geoffrey, and I used to terrorize our friends with our prowess! Have you played much?" he asked, extending balled fists concealing a counter of a contrasting color in either hand.

"A little, with Papa." Sybilla tapped his right fist, which opened to reveal a white counter. "Wonderful. I prefer to play with the white counters."

After forty-five minutes of concentrated play, Joshua looked down at the board and said in stunned astonishment, "I can't make a move."

Her eyes glinting with laughter, Sybilla leaned back in her chair. "You can't expect to win every game, Joshua. Perhaps I was a bit lucky."

"Lucky! You're as shrewd as you can hold together. Sharp's the word and quick's the motion with you, my girl. Play a little with your father, indeed! You probably sent him into a decline with your devastating game."

Setting up the board again, Sybilla said invitingly, "Shall we see if the last game was a fluke?"

The candles were guttering when Joshua pushed back his chair with a yawn. "Well, a draw is better than nothing. I don't feel quite so incompetent now." He rose, reaching down to ruffle Sybilla's black curls. "It's late, infant. Best you hie yourself to your bed."

"Infant!" The deep blue eyes sparked. "I told you I'm nineteen years old!"

"I beg your pardon. A vast age, indeed." The corners of his mouth turning up in an amused smile, Joshua reflected with a tinge of surprise that it had been a long time since he'd spent such a pleasurable evening. It certainly made up for having to listen to the Honorable Augustus Cranborn's poetry.

Chapter 4

PUTTING DOWN the *Morning Chronicle* with a frown, Joshua reached for his cup. The coffee was cold with a skim of milk on the surface, but he sipped the unappetizing brew without noticing its taste while he pondered the latest war news. So, Marshal Soult had arrived at Bayonne to take command of Napoleon's battered Army of Spain. That meant hard fighting for Wellington's veterans. Soult was a far worthier opponent than Marshal Jourdan or King Joseph had ever been. And before Wellington could advance across the Pyrenees into France, he'd have to reduce San Sebastian and the other border fortresses that were still in French hands. Joshua's eyes glinted with longing. Lord, he'd give a monkey to be with his regiment in front of San Sebastian!

"Well, my lord, what do you think?"

At the sound of Mrs. Roper's voice Joshua looked up at the doorway of the dining room. The housekeeper pushed Sybilla ahead of her into the room. "Mr. Weston finally delivered the clothes you ordered for Miss Sybilla," said Mrs. Roper. "I think they're a fair fit, considering that Mr. Weston never laid eyes on the child to take her measurements. As well he shouldn't have," she added, her severe tone leaving no doubt that she still disapproved of Sybilla's masquerade.

"Turn around," ordered Joshua, and Sybilla, smiling

rather self-consciously, revolved slowly in front of him while he examined her with a critical eye. She was wearing a single-breasted tailcoat of pale blue superfine, a striped marcella waistcoat, tight fitting lemon-colored pantaloons and well-polished Hessians. Despite her slender grace, few people who saw her would fail to accept her as the stripling she was pretending to be, Joshua thought. During this past week of squiring her about London, he'd actually found himself, on more than one occasion, thinking of Sybilla as a boy.

"By Jove, you've turned into a Bond Street Lounger, no less," he grinned. "You'll do me credit at last. I was beginning to fear that my friends would cut my acquaintance if they saw me with a scruffy-looking schoolboy."

Tossing him a saucy smile, Sybilla went to the sideboard, where she lifted the covers to peer at the contents of all the dishes before heaping one plate with boiled beef and grilled kidneys and eggs and another with a tall mound of buttered toast. The size of Sybilla's appetite never ceased to surprise Joshua, especially when he compared her eating habits with those of his fiancée. The dainty and ethereal Lady Verity appeared to subsist more on thin air than on real food.

"While you're consuming that enormous breakfast, I'll be in the library reading the *Times*," Joshua told Sybilla. "Come fetch me when you're ready to go sightseeing."

A little later, feeling comfortably full, Sybilla stood in front of the mirror in the foyer, adjusting the glossy black top hat that had also just arrived from the master hand of Lock in St. James's Street. She did look rather elegant, she reflected, though these certainly weren't the clothes she'd have imagined herself wearing on her first visit to London! Wistfully she recalled the lovely gowns of jaconet muslin and sarcenet and lutestring and crepe that she'd glimpsed during these past few days in fashionable shop windows.

Well, no matter. On her *next* visit she'd contrive to look like the Top of the Trees, but for now she should count her blessings. She had a luxurious, secure place to stay, and she was seeing the city she'd dreamed about all her life. True, she had only one week remaining of the two Joshua had promised her. For that week, however, she could banish from her mind the dark cloud of apprehension that had sent her fleeing from Yorkshire.

"Here, now, young Will, stop preening yourself," said Joshua, striding along the hall from the library. As he came up to her, he gave her a playful poke, saying, "Can't have you getting swell-headed in your new togs, you know. Ready to go? Come along, then."

As she walked down the steps with Joshua to the waiting curricle, Sybilla stole a sideways glance at him, thinking, not for the first time, how odd it was that so tall and powerful a man should have such a lounging grace, such a lazy, good-natured smile. Day after day for almost a week now he'd escorted her around London, giving no indication of impatience or boredom. He'd behaved, as a matter of fact, rather like an affectionate and indulgent uncle. Sometimes, Sybilla thought, he seemed to be enjoying their jaunts as much as she was.

"Well, what shall we do today?" asked Joshua, putting his team in motion after his tiger had opened the gates of the square and jumped onto his perch behind. "It seems to me we've seen most of the great mansions and splendid churches and public buildings. In fact," he added thoughtfully, "I'd as lief I didn't see another church for a while. They all look pretty much alike, don't you think?"

"What a heretic," joked Sybilla. "You mustn't display your lack of culture like that."

"Look who's talking about being uncultured," Joshua retorted. "At the Tower, what you enjoyed most was laying your head on the block where Anne Boleyn was executed, and trying out the thumb-screwing machine in the torture chamber. And at Westminster Abbey the only thing you looked at twice was the corpse of Mary, Queen of Scots because you thought it so odd that vandals had absconded with most of her fingers!"

"Well, at Somerset House *you* said there were too many pictures of ruined Italian castles and abbeys and what you'd like to see was a painting of a nice, comfortable country house!"

Sybilla and Joshua looked at each other and simultaneously broke into peals of laughter. Wiping his eyes,

Joshua said after a moment, "So that's decided, then, we'll be uncouth together. Where shall we go?"

"We could go shopping." Sybilla's eyes lit up with an anticipatory gleam. "Mrs. Roper was telling me that Ludgate Hill is *lined* with elegant mercers' shops."

"The proprietors of which would no doubt take kindly to having their wares turned over by a young sprig of fashion like yourself. You'd look so charming with a length of *crêpe lisse* draped over the shoulder of Weston's new coat."

"Oh. Yes, I daresay the mercers don't see many fifteen-year-old boys in their shops." Sybilla sighed. "Well, could we go to the Smithfield Market, then?"

"The cattle and sheep market?" Joshua rolled his eyes. "Why in heaven's name would a female want to go there?"

"My father once owned a prize flock of sheep," Sybilla replied. "We still raise a few of them on our estate. I could tell my uncle and our steward all about the market when I return home." She repressed a smile, thinking about the great flock of fat Swaledales roaming her Yorkshire acres. A few sheep, indeed!

"Be it on your own head, then," said Joshua. "No accounting for tastes, I daresay."

As they drove along Oxford Street, the sheer variety of the congested London traffic captivated Sybilla's attention, as it never failed to do. Carriages and carts and wagons of every description. Vendors shouting their myriad wares over the noisy clatter of wheels on the cobbles. Match sellers and apple ladies and knife grinders and broom sellers and gingerbread men and dairy maids with their pails suspended on yokes over their shoulders. Even the most fashionable residential squares, she'd noted, were often filled with a rabble of street vendors, beggars, crippled soldiers, pimps and their clients and shady-looking characters who she suspected were after the purses of the unwary.

They spent very little time in the squalid, noisome lanes and alleys of Smithfield Market. When Sybilla turned suddenly pale and stumbled, Joshua put a large arm around her shoulders and half-led, half-carried her away from the enclosure that housed the sheep.

"There, what did I tell you?" he exclaimed. "I knew it

would be too much for you, the stench and the filth and the crowding. It's a wonder both of us escaped being knocked over by someone carrying a quarter of beef or a newly skinned sheep."

Still looking decidedly pale, Sybilla leaned back against his supporting arm while she fought off a feeling of nausea. At length she said in a trembling voice, "How can they mistreat the animals like that? Crammed so closely together they can't move . . . unfed, unwatered. When I think of that happening to my beautiful Swaledales . . ."

She was so preoccupied with the plight of the animals that she didn't notice the curious look that Joshua directed at her. After a moment she moved away from him, saying, "Smithfield wasn't a very good suggestion. What would you be doing today, if you weren't showing a country bumpkin around the city?"

"Oh—any number of things. I might box a round or two at Gentleman Jackson's Saloon. Or cup a wafer at Manton's. Take a fencing lesson from Angelo. See a cockfight at the Cock-pit. Drive to Newmarket for the Midsummer Meeting. Why do you ask?"

"Why don't you take me to one of those places?" Sybilla countered. "I've no wish to deprive you of your usual amusements."

"Take a female to—to Gentleman Jackson's Saloon?" Joshua spluttered. His lips firmed. "No."

Knowing his mind must be filled with alarming visions of half-naked men flexing their biceps in front of her maidenly eyes, Sybilla whooped with laughter. "Very well, I give you Gentleman Jackson's," she said. "Surely, however, there'd be no harm in taking your schoolboy friend to a place like Manton's Shooting Gallery?"

"Don't you try to bamboozle me," Joshua began. Then he paused, a faintly wistful expression crossing his face. "Well . . . What harm could it do, after all? Mind you be careful to keep your voice low, if we encounter any of my friends."

"And don't you forget to call me Will!"

Arriving back at the waiting curricle, they drove away from the market, out of Charterhouse Street into Holborn and then into Davies Street. There, at the premises of the famous gunmaker, Joe Manton, Joshua lingered in the shop to inspect a handsome pair of silver-mounted dueling pistols. Weighing them in his hand, he tested the pull. "Nicely balanced," he told the proprietor.

"Indeed, my lord. Hair trigger, of course."

"I'll have them. Send them around to the house, Joe."

"With pleasure, my lord. Those pistols I made for you last year—before the battle of Salamanca, I believe it was—were they satisfactory?"

"Saved my life more than once," Joshua assured Manton, who beamed with gratification.

"Planning to fight a duel, are you?" Sybilla murmured, walking with Joshua out of the shop to the shooting gallery behind it. Looking surreptitiously around her, she was relieved to observe that none of the other customers was giving her a second glance. In this male bastion, at least, her appearance was passing muster.

"Damn your impudence, my gi—my lad," said Joshua cheerfully. "I like guns, not killing people." As they entered the gallery, he said in a low voice, "Over there—the man in the light blue coat, shooting at the wafer. That's Lord Byron."

Sybilla looked with considerable interest at the romantically handsome, black-haired man. In the flesh he seemed far from being the Satanic despoiler of female virtue she'd heard so much about. Watching the poet engage in target practice, she muttered, "He's not a very good shot, is he?"

Choking on a sudden chortle of laughter, Joshua said, "No more he is. Let me show you how an *expert* shoots." Several minutes later he lowered his pistol with a complacent air. "Nineteen out of twenty. I fancy Lord Byron won't beat *that!*"

"Could I try my hand?"

Joshua gazed at Sybilla with an expression of alarm. "Have you ever pulled the trigger on a pistol?"

"Oh, yes. Papa taught me to shoot."

Speaking under his breath, Joshua grumbled, "I've a notion I'm going to regret this. Have at it, then. Try to avoid hitting any helpless spectators."

When Sybilla lowered her arm after taking her shots, Joshua eyed her with a baffled frown. "Eighteen out of twenty. That was a fluke, Syb—Will. Had to be. Lay you a yellow boy you can't do it again."

"You're on." Sybilla shot him a teasing look. "Although, if I lose, you'll have to loan me the blunt to pay you."

As a baffled Joshua watched, Sybilla split the wafer nineteen times. She eyed him with a challenging smile. "Still think it was a fluke? Shall I try a third time? Perhaps you'd care to raise the stake. Shall we say five pounds?"

Half an hour later, as they sauntered out of the gallery, Joshua asked, "How much do I owe you after all that?"

"Let's see. I make it eleven pounds. I shot four rounds. The stake for the last two rounds was five pounds. I can certainly use the money!"

"Will you please tell me how it was that your father taught you how to shoot like that? It's not generally considered a ladylike accomplishment."

"Oh, I think Papa took me on out of pure frustration. He didn't have any sons, you know. I was an only child. My mother died when I was thirteen. I think Papa was lonely. He liked company in his amusements, so he taught me how to use a pistol. He taught me to ride and to drive, too." Once again Sybilla was oblivious to Joshua's sudden sharp glance.

Back in the curricle, as Joshua flicked the reins to start his team, Sybilla looked longingly at the horses. "I don't suppose you'd allow me to take the ribbons."

"I will not. If I were to tell you what I paid for this team . . . There's a vast difference, I assure you, between driving a dogcart or a gig on a country lane and handling the ribbons behind a perfectly matched pair of Thoroughbreds like mine."

"I've driven Papa's phaeton on the streets of Harrowgate. I'm quite sure I wouldn't damage your team, but, of course, if you don't trust me—"

Joshua glared at her. "Oh, very well. You're a crack shot. Show me you're a first-rate fiddler, too!"

From the perch behind Joshua came a gasp. "Guv, ye

wouldn't let a schoolboy, not dry be'ind 'is ears yet, drive them prize cattle o' yourn," wailed the tiger.

Ignoring the interjection, Joshua handed the reins to Sybilla, stepped down from the curricle to allow her to move into the driving seat, and got in on the other side. Leaning back against the seat, he crossed his arms on his chest and watched her performance with a frankly apprehensive eye.

Showing not the slightest lack of confidence, Sybilla put the horses in motion, sending them down Davies Street in a brisk trot. Soon Joshua relaxed. It was obvious she had fine, light hands and knew exactly how and when to use the whip. When she ventured a sideways glance at him, he grinned, saying, "At home to a peg, my dear Will, at home to a peg."

She grinned back. Approaching Berkeley Square, she asked, "Where to, Joshua?"

"Hyde Park Corner. It's Monday, a selling day at Tattersall's. I've a mind to buy a saddle horse or two. Drive to Grosvenor Place, behind St. George's Hospital."

A little later, following the crowd, Sybilla and Joshua emerged on foot from a narrow lane into a large circular enclosure surrounded by a gravel path bounding a grass plot. Around a tree in the center of this plot handlers were exhibiting a large number of horses.

"Waring, by Gad! Oh, excuse me, I mean Lord Linton! I might have known you were too tough and wicked for the Froggies to kill!"

His face glowing with pleasure, Joshua turned around. "Merry, by all that's holy—" he began. Then he paused, looking stricken. The man who had spoken to him was short and slight, with a mop of carroty hair and bright blue eyes. He was balancing himself on one leg with the aid of crutches. The other leg was gone almost to the hip.

"Merry, old lad," Joshua faltered, eyeing the crutches. "When I heard you'd been wounded, I hoped . . ."

"So did I, so did I." The newcomer grimaced. "Surgeons couldn't save the leg, unfortunately." He glanced at Sybilla. "Care to introduce me to—no, it can't be your nevvy. Your brother wasn't married."

"This is Will Smith. His father served with me. Killed at Vitoria. I'm giving him a little holiday before he goes back to school. Will, I'd like to present you to Captain the Honorable Francis Merriweather of His Majesty's Fourteenth Light Dragoons. Commonly known as Merry."

"How do you do, sir," said Sybilla shyly, extending her hand. Captain Merriweather was the first of Joshua's friends she'd met. The Tower and St. Paul's and Somerset House were not among the usual haunts of a fashionable man about town!

The captain frowned. "Smith. Smith. Can't recall anyone by that name in your regiment, Waring—sorry, Linton."

"Will's father was Ambruster Smith. A late transfer from the First Dragoons, King's German Legion," Joshua invented quickly. Glancing at the empty, folded-back leg of the captain's pantaloons, he said with a trace of hope in his voice, "What brings you to Tattersall's, Merry? Can you—?"

"No, confound it, I can't ride anymore," said Merry without self-pity. "I can still drive to an inch, though. I'm here to have a look at Gabe Masterson's matched grays. There they are, over there to the left."

Horse-mad like her father before her, Sybilla had never before seen so many elegant bits of blood gathered in one place. Her eyes wide with interest, she followed Joshua and Merry about the enclosure as they examined the horses which would be sold later in the adjoining courtyard.

"What do you think of this bay, Merry?" asked Joshua.

Moving slowly and awkwardly on his crutches, the captain edged backward for a better view. He glanced up in surprise when Sybilla said unexpectedly, "Not up to your weight, Joshua."

Merry took another look. "Damned if the lad isn't right. You must go almost thirteen stone, Linton." To Sybilla, he said, "Know something about horseflesh, do you, young Will?"

Coloring, Sybilla said, "Not very much, sir."

"Syb—" Joshua hastily corrected himself. "Will might surprise you, Merry. His father seems to have taken his education in hand." He raised an amused eyebrow at

Sybilla. "Is there anything else wrong with this horse, other than he's too light for me?"

Turning an even deeper red, Sybilla blurted, "He's too leggy. Papa always said a tall, leggy horse lacked stamina."

Merry laughed. "Well, lad, do you see any horse here that might suit Linton?"

Her eyes shining, Sybilla pointed to a black stallion that was pawing the ground nervously and attempting to jerk away from his attendant. "That one. Look at the deep body. Plenty of heart room. The long, sloping shoulders, for endurance. The well-defined muzzle, the large generous eyes."

"Yes, and the brute looks as if he has a temper," said Joshua. "Probably do his best to throw me. Well, let's have a look at him."

The groom walked the horse back and forth in front of them. After a moment Joshua observed to Sybilla, "Moves well, do you think?"

"Splendidly. Oh, I'd love to ride him!"

Joshua grinned at Merry. "That settles it. The oracle has spoken. I'll take the black horse and the brown one with the star on its forehead."

After buying the horses at the auction in the adjoining courtyard and arranging for their delivery, Joshua invited Merry to a late luncheon at Boodle's. Partaking heartily of a beefsteak pudding and a glass of claret, Sybilla sat back quietly, listening to the conversation between the two ex-cavalrymen.

She was seeing a side of Joshua that was new to her as he spoke to the comrade who had shared so many of the experiences that had shaped his young manhood. Indeed, she was becoming aware that her life in Yorkshire had been more isolated than she'd realized. Her acquaintance with male society had been limited to that of her father and Uncle Hubert and Barnaby. The half-bantering, half-serious exchange between Joshua and Merry was a revelation to her.

She didn't understand a good deal of the conversation, which was entirely about battles that had been fought in the Peninsula and battles about to be fought in the Pyrenees and in France. What she did understand, however, was the depth of the longing felt by both men to be a part of the coming campaign. Merry could no longer fight because he couldn't sit a horse. Joshua could no longer fight because his lineage demanded that he marry and provide an heir for the estate. And yet Merry managed to maintain a lighthearted gaiety, and Joshua had taken on his new life with an easy good humor.

Gradually the talk moved on from changes of base and naval escorts and battering trains and overextended fronts to lighter subjects. Chuckling, Merry described a letter he'd received from a fellow officer in the 14th Light Dragoons.

"As you'll well remember, Linton, the French retreat after Vitoria turned into a rout. During the pursuit, Harry Wyndham and a detachment of the Fourteenth caught up with King Joseph's carriage and almost captured *him*. He got away, worse luck, but the carriage was filled with treasures, from among which Wyndham absconded with the king's magnificent silver *pot de chambre*. Harry sent it home to the regimental mess. They plan to use the chamber pot at important functions for drinking champagne toasts. By the way, did you know that Jack Preston was invalided out after Burgos? He wrote me he's coming to town this week. Come have dinner with us."

"Better yet, both of you come have dinner with me at Linton House," said Joshua. "This Friday suit you?"

"Perfectly." Merry grinned at Sybilla. "Now that Major Waring is a lord in his own right with a Bedford Square mansion, Jack Preston and I wouldn't dream of buying his dinner for him."

After the lengthy luncheon Merry refused Joshua's invitation to accompany him and "Will" to a performance at Astley's Amphitheatre, on the grounds of a prior engagement. Sybilla and Joshua, however, spent a thoroughly satisfying evening in the theater on Westminster Bridge Road in Lambeth. Sitting in a box near the great central arena beneath the glow of the magnificent central chandelier, they watched clowns and conjurors and acrobats and a musical melodrama, and best of all, a superb display of horsemanship during a simulated fox hunt.

Returning to Bedford Square in the waning spring twi-

light, they both discovered they were ravenously hungry.
Joshua rang the bell for a footman, and soon they were
enjoying a cold supper in the library.

"Oh, Joshua, thank you for the best day of my life,"
Sybilla was saying in reminiscent delight when Mrs. Roper
entered the library.

"This message came for you several hours ago, my
lord," said the housekeeper.

Even before he opened the note and read it, Joshua's
expression had turned apprehensive. "My God!" he exclaimed. "I completely forgot I was supposed to escort
Verity to the opera tonight!"

Chapter 5

◈

THE NEXT morning Sybilla was playing a game of Patience in the library when Mrs. Roper poked her head into the room. "Still here, miss? I thought His Lordship was taking you to Runnymede today."

"He went to see Lady Verity Heston."

"Ah." There was a wealth of meaning in the syllable. Mrs. Roper said no more, however, though the currant-black eyes were snapping with curiosity.

"Joshua felt he should apologize to Lady Verity for not escorting her to the opera last night."

Mrs. Roper had become so accustomed to hearing Sybilla use her employer's Christian name that she no longer took exception to it. Apparently taking Sybilla's remark as an invitation to talk, the housekeeper shut the door and sat down opposite her. "Indeed, and I think His Lordship *should* apologize," she said severely.

"Well, certainly, but he didn't break the engagement with Lady Verity deliberately, you know. He was just forgetful. He was enjoying himself so much. At Tattersall's—"

"Miss, you never went there!" Mrs. Roper looked horrified. "Ladies don't go to places like Tattersall's!"

"No, but young men do," Sybilla retorted. Mrs. Roper opened her mouth and closed it again, her lips pressed together in a disapproving line. Sybilla continued. "At

Tattersall's we met a great friend of Joshua, a Captain Merriweather. They hadn't seen each other for ages. Joshua had a wonderful time, looking at horses with the captain. Later, at Boodle's, they talked about the war. I think Joshua misses the war."

At the mention of Boodle's, Mrs. Roper blenched, but she went on to a more important subject. "Was this Captain Merriweather short, with flaming-red hair? Ah. I might have known. Francis Merriweather has been a bad influence on His Lordship since they were boys. Would you believe it, he once persuaded His Lordship to put toads into the head-master's bed? *Toads*!"

Sybilla burst out laughing. If she knew Joshua, he hadn't needed much persuasion to torment the headmaster. To placate Mrs. Roper, she said, "Captain Merriweather isn't to blame for Joshua's broken engagement. I'm afraid it's mostly my fault. If I hadn't gone on and on about how much I'd like to see a performance at Astley's, I daresay Joshua wouldn't have forgotten to escort Lady Verity to the opera."

Mrs. Roper's sniff of scorn expressed her opinion of Astley's. "We must hope Her Ladyship wasn't too offended," she said with a worried frown. "I should hate to see anything go wrong. It's such a great match for His Lordship. Lady Verity was considered the belle of her season, you know. She has a very proper fortune, too. They say His Lordship was fair bowled over by her beauty the first time he saw her. He was going down the line in a country dance when he spotted her entering the ballroom. He stopped and stood stock-still staring at her. Threw every person in the line out of step. He offered for her two days later."

"Did Lady Verity accept?" asked Sybilla, fascinated with this glimpse into Joshua's love life.

"Well, no, not for at least a week. It would have been unseemly to accept His Lordship's first offer. Lady Verity's family is very correct, very formal, you understand."

Sybilla found herself wondering how Mrs. Roper knew so many intimate details about Joshua's courtship. Then she answered her own question, remembering how difficult it had always been to keep gossip from spreading from one

household to another even in the remote reaches of Yorkshire. Mrs. Roper undoubtedly had cronies among the upper
servants in most of the great establishments in London.

"I'm sure Lady Verity would never cry off her engagement over such a trivial incident," said Mrs. Roper, as if
trying to reassure herself.

"Well, of course not. And if by chance Lady Verity *were*
that shallow a person, Joshua is well off without her!"

Mrs. Roper looked at Sybilla reproachfully. "It's not
quite that simple. I'm not thinking solely of His Lordship's
happiness. I'm thinking of the very future of his house. If
Her Ladyship were to throw him over—which won't happen, naturally—he'd be hard put to find another wife before
his birthday in September." She explained about Great-
uncle Lucius Waring's will, which stipulated that Joshua
would forfeit his uncle's vast fortune if he failed to marry by
his thirtieth birthday.

Sybilla gasped. "But why would Mr. Waring make a will
like that? Thirty isn't such a great age."

"He was afraid that if His Lordship died early without
issue, the title would go to the next of kin, Marmaduke
Waring."

"So?"

"Well, you see," Mrs. Roper said, lowering her voice,
"Mr. Marmaduke is a little queer in his attic. He talks to
ghosts, and sometimes"—the voice sank even lower—
"sometimes he thinks he's Julius Caesar."

Sybilla chuckled. "I see Mr. Waring's point. It would be
very disconcerting if a peer walked into the House of Lords
dressed in a suit of Roman armor!"

He wasn't looking forward to this visit, Joshua thought
glumly as he made the turn into Oxford Street and headed
west. Verity would be less than human if she didn't resent
his behavior. Perhaps she wouldn't assume he'd deliberately
bypassed her company in favor of attending a vulgar
performance with a schoolboy. The truth would probably
strike her as even worse, however. It would undoubtedly be
the first time in her pampered, popular life that one of her
swains had simply *forgotten* to keep an engagement with

her! And the devil of it was, he couldn't summon up any real sorrow for missing the opera. He'd hugely enjoyed himself with Sybilla last night at Astley's Amphitheatre.

Sybilla. His frown deepened. His opinion of her was changing. What kind of a girl was she, really? How much of what she'd told him was true? She'd certainly lied to him in the beginning. It hadn't taken him long, though, to puncture that absurd tale of the father who'd tried to force her into marriage with an elderly roué. But as long as she'd fit the original impression he'd formed of her, he'd been able to credit the story of the uncle-guardian who was trying to persuade her to marry his son. Now he wasn't so sure.

At first he'd thought of her as merely a captivating sprite, a trifle empty-headed, perhaps, certainly a little spoiled. He'd constructed an imaginary biography for her, filling in the gaps in Sybilla's very sketchy account of herself. He'd guessed she came from the minor gentry. The heiress to a modest estate in the North, she'd been indulged by a doting father. After his death she'd overreacted to the firmer hand of her uncle. She'd run away in a childish tantrum when he made the entirely reasonable proposal that she marry her cousin to keep the property in the family.

Well, now what did he think? Joshua asked himself. For one thing, he knew that until quite recently she'd been the constant companion of a loving father who'd taught her to be a competent shot and a crack driver, and who'd instilled in her a strong compassion for animals. The image of an empty-headed female had quite faded from his mind. And that modest estate he'd envisioned. Its image, too, was fading. From Sybilla's knowledgeable use of the name Swaledales, he wouldn't be averse to thinking in terms of broad acres and large flocks of sheep.

Was everything Sybilla had told him a lie? Even if she was lying, did he really care? In these past few days she'd turned into a delightful companion. In any case, she wouldn't be on his hands for very much longer.

"Bean't we going ter Cavendish Square, Guv?"

Joshua roused himself from his thoughts at the sound of his tiger's voice. He'd overshot the turn for Cavendish Square and was rapidly approaching New Bond Street. "It's all right, Tim. I have an errand here. Look for Number—Oh, there it is."

Joshua stopped in front of Richard Robinson's confectionery shop and went inside. He picked out a large assortment of exotic sweetmeats, including comfits, pistachio nuts, prunellos, and limes. Leaving the shop, he observed a flower seller down the street. When he started up his team again, an enormous bouquet of French roses, with pink blossoms the size of saucers, reposed on the seat beside him.

In Cavendish Square he handed the roses and the box of sweetmeats to a footman and waited nervously in the drawing room for his fiancée to appear. Once or twice he put a finger between his neck and his cravat, which he'd apparently tied much too tightly that morning.

"Joshua! What a lovely way to start the day! A bouquet of roses *and* a box of sweetmeats, too."

Joshua rose as Verity entered the room with the graceful gliding step that gave the impression she was floating rather than actually placing her feet on the floor. Every ringlet of her spun-gold hair was in place, and her gown of sheer muslin sprigged with pastel flowers became her delicate beauty perfectly. As she lifted her face to him, Joshua observed thankfully that her smile was sweet and unclouded. He bent to kiss her lightly on the lips.

Taking a seat on a sofa, Verity patted the cushion beside her. "Come, sit down and tell me to what I owe the honor of a visit from you so early in the morning."

Joshua suppressed a pang of annoyance. Verity was being arch, and he disliked archness in a woman. She must know quite well why he'd come. "I wanted to apologize as quickly as possible for my behavior last night. I'm very sorry I caused you to miss the performance. I know you were looking forward to hearing Madame Toselli sing."

"Oh, I was certain you must have had some very good reason for not keeping our engagement," Verity assured him. "And fortunately, I didn't miss the performance after all. Immediately after I sent my note to your house—wondering, you know, if you'd had an accident, or some such thing—Mr. Cranborn called, merely to leave off a poem he wanted me to read. He kindly offered to escort me to the opera."

One could make a good case that poets were a blight on civilization, Joshua thought sourly. Did Augustus Cranborn spend all his free time trailing after Verity? Actually, Joshua supposed, he ought to be grateful to Augustus. By escorting Verity, he'd probably taken the edge off her resentment toward her fiancé.

Verity said playfully, "And so, what catastrophe, pray, kept you from my box at the Haymarket last evening?"

Joshua cleared his throat. "Well . . ."

Laughing, Verity said, "Let me guess. Did you meet an old friend who inveigled you into attending a pugilistic bout at—where was it my brother was used to talk about, much to Papa's displeasure?—oh, yes, at Daffy's Club? Or was it a cockfight?"

Clearing his throat, Joshua said, "Actually, I took young Will Smith to Astley's Amphitheatre. I'm very sorry. I clean forgot about the opera."

Joshua glimpsed a faint shadow of displeasure crossing Verity's face. Or had he imagined it? He must have done, he decided. Placing her hand on his arm, she said, "I haven't told you how much I admire you for spending so much time with that child. Poor lad, left half an orphan. I do hope he and his mother appreciate your efforts. How much longer will the boy be staying with you? A week? Oh, I really must meet him before he goes. Bring him to tea this afternoon. I'll ask Cook to make some of the delicacies little boys like."

"Ah—you needn't put yourself out," Joshua began.

"Nonsense. No trouble at all. I'm eager to share your interest in this boy, as in all things. Well, perhaps not in pugilism! I think the child will enjoy coming here. Mr. Cranborn has promised to read a portion of his new verse play."

Oh, God, not the poet again, Joshua groaned inwardly. He made a feeble effort to avoid his fate. "I hardly think a schoolboy—"

"It will be an educational experience for Will," Verity said firmly. "I'll expect you at four."

After taking leave of his fiancée, Joshua drove back to Bedford Square in a mixed frame of mind. He was back in Verity's good graces, but the price might be too high. It was one thing for Sybilla to pass as a boy in a crowd of strangers, or even with Francis Merriweather. Merry had never been especially observant. Verity *was* observant, however. Keenly so. Would Sybilla be able to deceive her?

His spirits improved somewhat when he reached his stables. His head groom informed him that Tattersall's had delivered the horses he'd bought yesterday at auction. As he was watching a groom walk the black stallion around the courtyard, Sybilla came hurrying out to join him. "You sent for me, Joshua? Oh—" She stood transfixed, staring at the horse. "He's even more beautiful than I remembered," she said with a sigh.

"Saddle him," Joshua ordered the groom. To Sybilla, he said, "You wanted to ride him. Take him for a turn around the square."

Half an hour later, as he was entering the library, Joshua heard Sybilla's voice calling to him. He swung around to look at her as she came down the corridor. "Well?" he said, gazing at her glowing face. "I needn't ask if you have second thoughts about the stallion."

"No. He's perfect. What are you going to call him?"

"Oh, I think you should choose his name. He's your horse."

Sybilla gaped at him. "If you're trying to roast me—"

"No, I mean it. I bought him for you."

"Oh, Joshua, you—you *darling*!"

Joshua caught his breath as Sybilla threw her arms around his neck and kissed him. This was no boy's body pressed closely to his. Nor could those warm soft lips conceivably belong to a boy. Before he realized what he was doing, he'd wrapped his arms around her and his lips were returning her kiss, eagerly, hungrily, like a man lost in the desert who'd finally stumbled on a life-giving well.

And then, before sanity quite left him, he wrenched his mouth and his arms away from her and stepped back. His heart was hammering against his chest, and he was breathing erratically. Sybilla looked dazed. Glancing up and down the corridor, Joshua breathed a sigh of relief that none of the servants—at least there was none in sight—had observed him passionately kissing his young male guest. Forcing a grin, he exclaimed, "By Jove, I thought you'd appreciate receiving the horse, but not quite *that* much!"

At the sound of his voice Sybilla's cornflower-blue eyes lost their unfocused look. In a moment she'd recovered her self-possession. "If you weren't bamming me about the horse—"

"I wasn't," he interrupted. "He's yours."

"Well, in that case, I thank you from the bottom of my heart, but I can't accept him."

"My eye and Betty Martin, why ever not?"

Sybilla looked away, swallowing hard. "It's far too valuable a gift, for one thing. My governess was used to say that an unmarried lady should accept nothing from a man more costly than a posy."

"Sybilla! Don't you be missish! You can't suspect me of scheming to ravish you!"

The familiar impish spark returned to Sybilla's eyes. She chuckled, saying, "No, no, I absolved you of that long ago, remember? But consider: I'll be returning to—to Durham in a week's time. I couldn't take Midnight with me—" Cutting herself short, she looked a picture of guilt.

"Aha, you've given yourself away," Joshua whooped. "You've already named the animal, so you can't force me to take him back. Tell you what. Ride Midnight during the next week, and then, after you return home, your uncle can send for him."

That afternoon, riding with Joshua to Cavendish Square, Sybilla was so preoccupied that she failed to notice an organ grinder with a particularly appealing monkey on the corner of the Tottenham Court Road until Joshua called her attention to it.

"You're looking a trifle blue-deviled," he said with concern. "Not worried about seeing Verity, are you?"

"Oh, no, not concerned at all. I'm sure Lady Verity will be most gracious." Sybilla spoke with as much assurance as she could muster, but the butterflies were flitting madly about in her stomach. Of course she was worried about this visit to Cavendish Square, more for Joshua's sake than for her own. After all his kindness, it would be sheer tragedy for him if Lady Verity saw through her masquerade. What possible excuse could Joshua give his fiancée to explain the situation? He'd not only spent days escorting a strange young woman dressed in boys' clothes around the city, but he'd also invited her to stay in his own house. Lady Verity might be a paragon, but Sybilla suspected that her first impulse would be to cry off from her engagement.

Adding to Sybilla's guilt feelings was the memory of the kiss she'd shared with Joshua. What had possessed her to fling herself at him like that? He'd be perfectly justified in thinking her a fast, vulgar sort of female. What was worse, she'd enjoyed the kiss, and he must have known it. But, a small voice whispered inside her, hadn't Joshua seemed to enjoy the kiss, too? Sybilla felt her cheeks growing hot and turned her head away to hide her blush.

By the time the footman ushered her and Joshua into the drawing room of Dunsford House, Sybilla had overcome some of her nervousness. Lady Verity's graceful cordiality did the rest, as she made a special effort to put her young guest at ease. "I'm so glad you've come, Master Smith," she said with a sweet smile. "Or may I call you Will, as Joshua does? I'm eager to make all of Joshua's friends my friends, too, from the very old to the very young and everyone in between!"

A single glance had convinced Sybilla, feeling a pang of envy, that Joshua's fiancée was the most impossibly beautiful creature she had ever seen. No wonder he'd fallen an instant victim to that spun-gold hair and those luminous violet eyes. Returning Verity's greeting, Sybilla made a deliberately awkward bow and even managed to produce a squeaky break in her voice. Out of the corner of her eye, she caught the quickly suppressed quiver of amusement that crossed Joshua's face.

Munching at several of the delicacies Verity had provided to tempt a schoolboy appetite, Sybilla studied the other occupants of the room. Mrs. Laleham, Verity's companion, was a faded lady who rarely opened her mouth except to bleat agreement with everything that was said.

Augustus Cranborn was of more interest. Sybilla surmised that he was, or aspired to be, a Dandy of the Dandies. The pinched-in wasp waist of his coat and the inordinately high points of his collar must be hideously uncomfortable, she thought. Augustus might be very fashionable, a very tulip of the ton, but for herself she much preferred the way Joshua's clothes fitted his graceful, rangy frame.

Conservatively dressed and severe of face, the Earl of Dunsford was as unlike the smiling, agreeable Augustus as night from day. From Joshua's slight flicker of surprise, Sybilla had gathered that he hadn't expected Verity's father to take tea with them.

The earl drew up a chair beside Sybilla. "So, young man, your father served with Linton," he began. His smile was difficult, as if he seldom had the occasion to use it and it had become rusty. "Smith. Not an uncommon name, eh? Which branch of the Smiths do you represent, my boy? Would you be related to my old friend Sir Joseph Smith of Boynton? Or perhaps to Lord Robert Smith, who went to school with my son?"

As Dunsford droned through a list of eligible Smiths, Sybilla panicked. Why, why hadn't she and Joshua foreseen that she might be asked questions about her family? Even a few minutes' thought would have enabled them to invent a credible background for her. But now her mind was blank.

"We come from Yorkshire," she blurted. Best stick to an area she knew something about. She pulled out of the corner of her mind the name of a tiny town through which she'd passed on her journey to London. "Midvale," she said. It wasn't a place with which the urbane earl was likely to be familiar.

Unfortunately, he was. His eyes kindled. "Ah. Jasper Smith. I know him well. He has a fine, well-managed estate up there. Your father? No, your father would be a younger man. I presume Jasper is your grandfather?"

The harried Sybilla shot a glance at Joshua. He looked calm, but his hand had tightened on the arm of his chair. He certainly wasn't being of much use to her in this predicament. "Oh, no, Mr. Jasper Smith isn't my grandfather," she said, inventing desperately. "My family is proud to claim the connection, but we're only distantly related. Yes, I believe Mr. Smith's estate is quite magnificent, but we've no expectations in it, worse luck. My father's a younger son of a younger son."

The earl's gaze sharpened. For some reason Sybilla felt chilled. Then, seeming to lose interest in her, he turned his head to speak to Joshua.

"Now, Mr. Cranborn, we've waited long enough," said Verity, flashing the poet a charming smile. "Won't you give us the pleasure of hearing a few lines of your epic?"

Beaming, Augustus said to his hostess, "Allow me to express my gratitude for the privilege of unveiling my new work in such intimate and friendly surroundings." He rose, one hand tucked into his waistcoat, the other behind his back. "I should explain, first of all, that my play is based on the legend of Atalanta and Hippomenes and the race for the golden apples of Venus."

Augustus then proceeded to compare the various versions of the legend in stultifying detail. He also mentioned all the scholarly sources he'd consulted and the reasons why he had and hadn't agreed with them. Sybilla fought the urge to fall asleep. A surreptitious look at Joshua revealed that he was glassy-eyed with boredom. Finally, clearing his throat, Augustus began reciting from the prologue of his verse play:

"Fair Venus, powerful goddess of love,
Faint with desire, I beg thee to help me,
Allow me to win the prize of my heart,
Without fair Atalanta I care not to live."

Several more lines followed, perhaps as many as twenty. Then Augustus stepped back, bowing. He turned his expectant gaze from one to another in his small audience.

The glazed look vanished from Joshua's face. He blurted, "Good God, Cranborn, is that all there is? I understood you to say you'd been composing away at this thing for weeks."

Verity exclaimed, "Joshua!"

Eyeing her gently reproachful face, Joshua swallowed, saying, "Beg pardon, Cranborn. Er—I daresay poetry writing is a slow business."

"One struggles with every word, every line," acknowledged Augustus with wounded dignity. "As an artist, I feel bound by the dictates of quality, not quantity."

"Exactly so," Joshua agreed hastily. "I'm sure your play will be all the crack."

The earl rose. "Mr. Cranborn, I thank you for a delightful reading. Linton, could I have a private word with you?"

As Joshua left the room with her father, Verity exclaimed with an arch smile, "Settlements! I vow, Papa talks and thinks of nothing else! I never realized getting married was quite so complicated!"

"But that's as it should be, surely," said Augustus. "With individuals in our station of life, marriage is a very serious matter. We simply don't go about it in the havey-cavey way of the lower orders."

When Joshua returned alone to the drawing room a few minutes later, he looked so wooden-faced that Sybilla suspected immediately he was in a towering rage.

Verity apparently noticed nothing amiss, however. "My dear Joshua, before you and Will arrived, Mr. Cranborn proposed the most famous scheme! He suggested we all go to Hampton Court tomorrow morning. It will make a delightful excursion, and also it will be an educational experience for Will to see the masterpieces of art at the palace."

"Indeed," murmured Augustus. He lifted his eyes in ecstasy. "The Della Robbia busts in the Western Court. The murals by Verrio in the Queen's Drawing Room."

"Very kind of you, Cranborn, but I must beg off," said Joshua curtly. "I promised to take Will to Runnymede today, and I was unable to do so. We'll go tomorrow."

Verity's great violet eyes seemed drowned in disappointment. Sybilla said quickly to Joshua, "I'd like very much to see Hampton Court, sir. Perhaps we could go to Runnymede another time?"

Shrugging, he said, the edge still in his voice, "Very well, if that's what you wish to do." After making the arrangements with Augustus for the excursion, Joshua took a rather abrupt leave of his fiancée.

In the curricle as they were driving away from Cavendish Square, Sybilla said in a low voice, "Is something wrong?"

"No, I'm in prime twig. Looking forward to our evening at Saddler's Wells, matter of fact."

Joshua's carefree air didn't deceive Sybilla. In the past short week she'd learned to recognize his moods. His eyes were normally lively and good-humored. Now they had darkened to the ominous gray of a thundercloud. He'd quarreled with his future father-in-law, that was obvious. It was just as obvious he had no intention of talking about it.

Joshua stalked into the library, shut the door, and poured himself a large glass of claret. After tossing down the wine, he took decanter and glass and sat down in an armchair, where he poured himself another glass.

His thoughts were mutinous as he sprawled back in his chair, sipping his wine. Confound the Earl of Dunsford. If the man were younger, or if he weren't Verity's father, he'd be nursing a very sore jaw at the present. Joshua's eyes smoldered at the memory of his encounter with his future father-in-law. . . .

"My dear Linton, I know you'll accept this bit of advice in the spirit in which it's offered," the earl had begun.

Naturally, Joshua's hackles had risen immediately. "Sir?"

"Yes, well, Verity is too sweet-tempered to make any objection, but have you thought you might be embarrassing her by jaunting about town in the company of that—that urchin, Will Smith? Last evening, I understand, you actually failed to keep an engagement with my daughter because you'd taken the boy to some vulgar place of amusement."

Trying to preserve his temper, Joshua said levelly, "Coming it a bit too strong, aren't you, sir? Perhaps you've forgotten that Will Smith is the son of an old comrade in my regiment? And that many people in good standing with the ton see fit to patronize Astley's Amphitheatre?"

Lord Dunsford's eyes snapped angrily. "No, I haven't

forgotten this Will Smith is the son of an officer in your regiment. I'd venture to say, however, that admission standards for His Majesty's cavalry regiments have deteriorated since my day."

"Meaning what, sir?"

"Meaning that Will Smith's father is a disgrace to his family and his regiment, and in my day he would never have been allowed to purchase a commission. Oh, yes," the earl added, seeing Joshua's eyes widen in bewilderment. "The boy told me he was distantly related to my close friend Jasper Smith of Midvale. The only member of that family who went into the army that I know of was Richardson Smith, a black sheep who forged his uncle's name to a promissory note and eloped with a Viennese actress."

Joshua had been torn between irritation and the desire to laugh. He didn't doubt for a second that there was a real Richardson Smith who'd gone into the army. The Earl of Dunsford, a snob to the core, was rarely wrong in the matter of pedigrees and lineage. Of course, Richardson Smith had never joined the 4th Dragoons. There were no Smiths at all in the 4th Dragoons. But, Joshua's hands were tied. He couldn't deny that Richardson Smith had been a member of the regiment *or* that he was "Will's" father without laying bare Sybilla's unfortunate lies.

"Now, perhaps, you'll understand why I take it amiss that you should neglect my daughter, your fiancée, in favor of a young nobody," said the Earl of Dunsford.

Joshua had made an instinctive movement toward the earl, and as quickly curbed himself. He'd managed to say with a chilly politeness, "My fellow officers and I considered Will's father a fine gentleman who died for his country. I'm happy to perform any small services I can for the son. As to my fiancée, if she feels I'm neglecting her, she has only to say so, and I'll immediately mend my ways. Good day, sir."

Joshua reached for the decanter of claret. Unfortunately, the wine hadn't yet cut the edge of his anger. Why couldn't his future bride have been an orphan, he wondered morosely. Verity's behavior had been everything he could have asked for today. She'd been charming and sweet, generously overlooking their broken engagement to attend the opera. She'd gone out of her way to be gracious to "Will Smith." But her father . . . !

No, he decided, he didn't regret at all having given Dunsford a setdown, though he doubted it would keep the earl in his place. Lombard Street to a China orange, Dunsford would still be attempting to interfere in his life when he was a graybeard! It was a glum prospect for his future married life. Joshua poured himself another glass of wine.

Chapter 6

A FOOTMAN emerged from the door of Number 14, Cavendish Square, and deposited a large hamper on the seat of the landau that was waiting in front of the house. Joshua handed Lady Verity into the carriage and, after her, the elderly companion, Mrs. Laleham. Augustus Cranborn climbed into the landau, sitting beside the picnic hamper on the seat facing the ladies. It was a beautiful July morning under a cloudless, brilliantly blue sky.

Putting up her parasol, Verity smiled at Joshua and at Sybilla, standing next to him beside the carriage. "What a lovely day. I'm quite looking forward to our excursion. Mr. Cranborn thinks it might be better, Joshua, if you and Will lead the way in your curricle."

"Yes, I'm familiar with the route. Come along, Will."

Seated in the curricle, Sybilla eyed Joshua covertly as he picked up the reins. He was more his usual self this morning. Last night at Saddler's Wells he hadn't warmed even to the high jinks of the great clown, Grimaldi. Once again she wondered what the Earl of Dunsford had said yesterday to Joshua to dim his sunny high spirits.

Starting up his team, Joshua began to thread his way slowly through a small group of loiterers who were obstructing traffic in the square. As often as she'd seen them, it still astonished Sybilla to observe the hordes of itinerant vendors and beggars who frequented even the most exclusive residential areas of Mayfair.

Suddenly she clutched at Joshua's arm. "Look to your right. That man is beating that one-legged beggar over the head with one of the beggar's own crutches!"

Joshua had seen the incident and was already reining in his horses. Tossing the ribbons to his tiger, he jumped down from the curricle, with Sybilla close behind him. Before they could reach the two men who were fighting, the crippled beggar had fallen to the pavement. His opponent continued to strike at him with the crutch. Grabbing the attacker's arm, Joshua swung him around and delivered a sharp, hard blow to the man's chin. The man crumbled, unconscious, to the ground, and Joshua turned his attention to the beggar, who had pulled himself into a sitting position. Blood streamed from a cut on his temple.

"Are you badly hurt, man?" Joshua inquired.

Mopping ineffectually at the blood that was obscuring his eyesight, the man muttered, "Nay, 'tis but a scratch. If ye could jist 'and me my crutches . . ."

"First let me help you up."

With Joshua's steadying hands under his armpits, the beggar struggled to his feet, only to collapse with a groan. "My good leg," he gasped. "It's broke, I think."

Kneeling, Joshua slowly ran his fingers along the man's leg. He looked up to say, "I'm afraid you're right. So far as I can tell, there's a break just above the ankle."

At that moment the beggar's eyes met Joshua's in a flicker of recognition. Beneath the grime and the blood the man's face flamed with embarrassment.

At that same moment Joshua's gaze became riveted on the man's worn coat, a single-breasted red jacket with blue turnbacks and eight bars of tarnished silver lace across the front. Joshua drew a startled breath. "That's the uniform of the Fourth Dragoons!"

The man looked away, his face growing a deeper red. "Yes, sir. Major Waring, ain't it? I was in Cap'n Worthing's squadron."

Joshua hesitated. Then, as if the words were being forced out of him, he exclaimed, "God in heaven, why is an ex-trooper of the Fourth Dragoons begging on a street corner? Did you have trouble getting your pension?"

The ex-trooper's embarrassment dissolved into an angry scorn. "Not a bit o' it, Major. I gits sixpence a day, reg'lar as rain. Oh, I'm full o' juice, sir. The begging? I does that fer funning, like, ter fill in my days. There's not many, y'see, that'll hire a cripple."

Joshua flushed in his turn, and Sybilla, standing beside him, gasped, saying, "Sixpence a day? That's—that's three and a half shillings a *week*. Nobody could keep body and soul together on three and a half shillings a week, let alone— Trooper, do you have a family?"

"Wife an' son. The boy, 'e's two year old."

Sybilla turned on Joshua. "This is an absolute disgrace. How does the army expect this man to support his family on sixpence a day when he's crippled and can't work?"

"I had no idea," Joshua muttered. "I'm ashamed of my own country." He cleared his throat, addressing the ex-dragoon. "What's your name?"

"Wyatt, sir. Lem Wyatt." The man hung his head, as if he were ashamed of his outburst.

"Where did you lose the leg?"

"Salamanca, sir."

"Well, Trooper Wyatt, I'm going to get you home, find you a doctor, and after that I'll see what else can be done for you. Where do you live? St. Giles? I'll have you there in a trice." He beckoned to a burly man standing beside his knife-grinding machine, open-mouthed with curiosity at the actions of the gentry. "Here, you. There's a pound note for you if you'll help me get this man into my curricle."

"Major, there's no need fer ye—"

Joshua silenced the trooper's protests. He said impatiently, "Don't make a goosecap of yourself. With only one leg, and that one useless, how do you expect to leave Cavendish Square?"

As Joshua and the knife grinder were lifting the ex-dragoon into the curricle, Augustus Cranborn stepped down from the landau, in which he and the ladies had remained while Joshua was going to the defense of the trooper. Taking Sybilla aside, Augustus said in a low voice, "What's to do here? Who's that creature, and what's he doing in Linton's carriage?"

"That's Lem Wyatt. He once served with the Fourth Dragoons. He can't walk, so Joshua is taking him to his home."

A look of acute displeasure flashed across Augustus's face. He wheeled to accost Joshua, who was slipping the knife grinder the promised tip. "Now, see here, Linton, if this isn't the outside of enough," began Augustus angrily. "First you engage in a brawl in full view of your fiancée and Mrs. Laleham, then you propose to ride off with this"— he gulped at the sudden spark of anger in Joshua's eyes— "with this person when you have an engagement to accompany Lady Verity to Hampton Court. I'd be remiss if I didn't inform you that every feeling must be offended by your behavior."

Joshua glared at Augustus. "Good God, Cranborn, sometimes I think you have no more sense than a zero. Do you expect me to leave this man helpless in the street? A man who lost a leg fighting with my regiment in the Peninsula?"

Augustus looked uncomfortable. "Perhaps you could send someone for a hackney cab. . . ."

Throwing up his hands, Joshua swung away from Augustus and headed for the landau. Sybilla followed him. As she came up to the carriage, Verity was saying in a concerned voice, "You're quite sure you aren't hurt, Joshua? It was kind of you to go to the rescue of that wretched man, but you might have been badly injured."

"No, I told you, the ruffian didn't lay a finger on me," Joshua replied impatiently. He explained briefly about the dragoon's predicament. "The man's quite helpless. I'm very sorry to disrupt your plans, but I feel I must drive him to his home."

"Of course you must," said Verity, all warm sympathy. "That's so like you, to show such loyalty to the men who served under you. We can go to Hampton Court another day."

Joshua flashed her a pleased smile. "It's so like *you*, my dear, to be so understanding. Thank you. We needn't cancel the excursion, however. Wyatt lives only a short distance from here, in St. Giles. It won't take me long to drive him there. You could wait here for me, or better still, you might go on ahead of me with Mrs. Laleham and Mr. Cranborn and Sy—Will." Joshua glanced quickly at Verity. She apparently hadn't noticed his partial slip. "I'll catch you up en route."

"We'd be delighted to have your company, Will," said Verity. "There's plenty of room in the landau."

"No," said Sybilla stubbornly. "I think I should come with you, Joshua. You'll need help in getting Trooper Wyatt out of your carriage."

"No, you aren't coming with me. A curricle was never meant to carry three passengers."

"It's a good thing, then, that I'm thin!"

"What's more, St. Giles isn't a respectable neighborhood."

Sybilla lifted her chin. "All the more reason why I should come along. You may need rescuing!"

"Oh, the deuce—"

Sybilla shot him an imploring glance.

Joshua shrugged in defeat. "Oh, very well, then. You might be useful after all."

During the drive down Holles Street from Cavendish Square and thence west along Oxford Street, Joshua tried several times to induce the trooper to talk about himself. Wyatt answered only in monosyllables. At times it almost seemed that he was slipping into unconsciousness. Sybilla wondered if his leg was giving him increasing pain, or if the blow he'd received on his head was more serious than they had realized. The real reason for his taciturnity became apparent only when Joshua turned the curricle into St. Giles High Street and said, "Where to, Wyatt?"

The trooper seemed to have difficulty rousing himself. "Oh—lemme see, now. Left on Buckeridge Street, an' then the second left again. That'll be Larkspur Lane."

It was hard to imagine a place less appropriately named, thought Sybilla a few minutes later, when they stopped at the entrance to Larkspur Lane. If flowers had ever grown anywhere in Larkspur Lane, they had long since gone. The lane was more of an alley, narrow and dark and evil-smelling, lined with makeshift hovels, strewn with garbage. At the corner the proprietor of a rough stall was selling gin to several slatternly women and slovenly dressed men, who turned to stare curiously at the occupants of the carriage.

"The lane's too narrow for the curricle, Wyatt," said Joshua. "Do you live far from here?"

The trooper said hurriedly, "Jist leave me 'ere. This is the entrance to the 'Holy Land.' One o' the worst rookeries in Lunnon. Ye and the lad wouldn't be safe in there. It be full o' coves on the dub lay, very clever with their fambles. If ye'd be so inclined as ter slip me a meg, or even two, why, I wouldn't say no, but don't ye think o' goin' in there."

"Stow your whids and plant 'em," said Joshua rudely. The dragoon looked startled at the knowledgeable use of cant. "If the 'Holy Land' is all that dangerous, how do you propose to drag yourself to your crib on two hands and one knee without having someone relieve you of the blunt I'm about to give you?"

The trooper stared down at his hands. At last he said in a weary, shamed voice, "Ain't got no crib."

"You don't live here? Then why—?"

"I didn't want ye ter know I was in sich low water. Not even a place ter sleep. Y'see, I *had* a room in there, oncet. Then I couldn't pay the rent, an' they tossed me out, an' my wife, she left with the boy. . . . Well, ye could 'ardly blame 'er, now, could ye? An' since then I've jist been haunting Larkspur Lane, ye might say, hopin' Emmy'd come back, or I'd 'ear somefing o'where she'd gone—"

"Joshua!"

At Sybilla's warning cry, Joshua whirled on the man who had furtively crept up beside the curricle. With an expertly aimed lash of his whip, Joshua sent the man sprawling. Taking a small pistol out of his pocket, Joshua leveled it at the prostrate man, saying, "You'll not get your fambles on my rhino, not this time. Get up. Stand against that wall over there."

Keeping the gun fixed unwaveringly on the would-be pickpocket, Joshua flicked a glance at the proprietor of the gin shop. "You. Do you know—what's your wife's name, Wyatt? Emmy?" Joshua turned back to the gin seller. "Do you know an Emmy Wyatt? You do? Here you are, then." Joshua tossed the man several coins. "There's a yellow boy or two where that came from. If you ever hear anything of the whereabouts of Emmy Wyatt, bring your information to Linton House in Bedford Square."

The proprietor's eyes gleamed with a sudden avarice. "Linton House. Bedford Square. I'll remember, Guv."

"Good." Joshua touched his reins to his horses, and as soon as the curricle had moved on a few yards from the entrance to Larkspur Lane, he tucked the pistol back in his pocket.

"What a dreadful place. I'm very glad to leave it," said Sybilla with a shudder. "Joshua, did you see that woman feeding gin to her child?"

"I daresay it's more the rule than the exception, eh, Wyatt?"

"Yes, sir. I'm afraid so, sir." The trooper's mind, however, was plainly not on the subject of Blue Ruin and its effect on children. After a moment he said hesitantly, "Where be we goin', if ye don't mind my askin'?"

"To find a doctor, which is what we should have done in the first place. Remember our regimental surgeon, Frank Reynolds? Invalided out after Salamanca? He's started up his own practice in Soho in—let me think, now; yes, I have it—in Dean Street. We'll go to him."

Half an hour later, as she sat with Joshua in the waiting room of Dr. Reynolds's surgery, Sybilla asked, "What happens after the surgeon sets Trooper Wyatt's leg? He'll still be quite helpless. You could find him a room, I suppose, and hire someone to care for his needs until he can use his crutches again. You couldn't be sure, though, that you'd found an honest caretaker. And after all that, when he's well enough to walk, he'll be no better off than he was before he broke his leg this morning. He'll still be an unemployed cripple."

Joshua smiled at her troubled face. "One thing I'll say about you, your head is set straight on your shoulders. You don't let yourself be blinded by sentimentality. You're quite right, of course. I can't throw Wyatt a few crumbs of charity and then forget about him."

"No, *you* couldn't do that!" exclaimed Sybilla impulsively.

Joshua looked surprised, then self-consciously pleased, and, finally, embarrassed. Collecting himself, he said, "Clearly, what Wyatt needs is a safe place to convalesce, which he won't find in the 'Holy Land.' After that he needs employment, which he won't find in any other part of London, either."

"So we'll have to take him out of the city, on both counts. Joshua, you've thought of something!"

"Well, I think I have. I inherited a small property from my godfather. It's thirteen or fourteen miles from London, just to the north of Epsom. My godfather used it as a stud farm. I haven't even seen the place for some years, but I know it's in good hands. My tenant on the home farm, Tom Simmons, is acting as my bailiff, and he still raises a few horses. I'll ask Tom to find Wyatt something to occupy him. The surgeons amputated Wyatt's shattered leg below the knee, so I'm sure he can still ride, not like my poor friend Merry. Actually, fitted with a wooden leg, Wyatt could probably make himself quite useful around a farm."

"It sounds like a perfect place for Trooper Wyatt. Thirteen or fourteen miles, though. How will he get there?"

"Why, I'll drive him there, naturally. He couldn't possibly travel alone by stagecoach."

"But—you haven't forgotten our excursion to Hampton Court with Lady Verity? You told her you'd catch her up later this morning."

"And so we will. Hampton Court and Epsom are roughly the same distance from Hyde Park Corner, and in the same general direction. Verity was planning to serve a picnic luncheon before visiting the palace. We'll miss the picnic, but we'll certainly be able to join them in good time to see the palace."

"I'm sure Lady Verity will forgive us for being a little late when you tell her about Trooper Wyatt's desperate straits," said Sybilla, relieved that Joshua was in no danger of breaking another engagement with his fiancée.

The ex-dragoon's injury proved to be less serious than they had feared. The surgeon quickly set and splinted the bone, and soon they were back in the curricle again, driving over the high, balustraded arch of Westminster Bridge with its hooped lampposts and through the streets lined with mean hovels and factories in St. George's Fields.

Though he was obviously more comfortable physically now that his leg was set, Wyatt appeared to find it difficult at first to comprehend where he was going and what he would be doing. When he finally did understand what Joshua was telling him, he accepted his changed circumstances quite docilely. Sybilla had to turn her head away to hide a smile. Without either of the two men apparently realizing it, Joshua had fallen easily into the familiar role of command, and Wyatt had meekly followed his officer's orders.

"If you can locate your family, Wyatt, they can join you at the farm," Joshua said. "I've no doubt my bailiff can find you a cottage."

"I can't never thank ye enough, Major. I don't rightly know why ye're bein' so kind."

Joshua looked embarrassed. "Honor of the regiment and all that. You'd do the same for me."

" 'Twould be wunerful fer the boy, living in the country," said the ex-trooper wistfully. "My wife, now, I dunno. Emmy's a real Cockney. Born within the sound of Bow bells, she was."

"If Epsom is half as lovely as this area, your wife will love living in the country," Sybilla assured him. They were driving through a pretty district of hills and woods and tiny streams in the vicinity of Tooting. Soon they crossed the River Wandle at Merton and entered the great rolling chalk downs of southern Surrey. North of Epsom Joshua turned off into a narrow lane leading to a substantial house backed by well-kept outbuildings and a walled stable area.

As the curricle came to a stop in the cobbled courtyard in front of the house, a plump, middle-aged lady, neatly dressed with a snowy cap and apron, appeared in the doorway. "Master Joshua," she gasped. "I mean Yer Lordship. Is it really you?"

"It really is, Mrs. Simmons. Lord, it's donkeys' years since I've been here! This is my young friend, Will Smith, and Lem Wyatt, who served in my regiment."

When Joshua had explained Wyatt's situation, Mrs. Simmons said warmly, "Indeed, Lem Wyatt, any man who's fought ter save us from that monster Bonaparte is most welcome ter stay here in my spare bedchamber, and very good care we'll take o' ye, never fear. And I don't doubt my husband will find work fer ye when ye're on yer feet again."

With the help of a farmhand Joshua settled Wyatt into Mrs. Simmons's spare bedchamber. When he came down to the parlor, Joshua told the farmer's wife, "Wyatt's a little frightened and unsure of himself. He's never stayed in a house like this before."

"Be sure I'll do my best to make him feel ter home, Master Joshua. Now, then, if ye'll wait fer jist a moment, I'll have tea ready fer ye and the young man. Freshly baked scones, not more than half an hour out o' the oven. Ye was used ter fancy my scones in the old days. While ye're drinking yer tea, ye can tell me about yer exciting experiences in—where's that place?—in the Peninsula."

"Thank you, but I'm afraid we can't stay. We have an engagement to meet friends at Hampton Court."

Noticing the cloud of disappointment descending on Mrs. Simmons's brow, Sybilla said to Joshua, "A few minutes wouldn't matter, surely? While Mrs. Simmons is preparing the tea, you could show me the farm."

"Well . . ." Joshua consulted his watch. "I daresay it will be all right. Verity and Mrs. Laleham and Cranborn will be looking for a picnic spot about this time."

As Sybilla toured the stables and the kitchen garden and a small apple orchard with Joshua, she reveled in the pleasure of country sights and sounds and smells. Suddenly she realized she was homesick for the wild moors and lonely dales and spiny hills of Yorkshire. When would she see them again? she wondered.

Behind the orchard a rushing little stream splashed its way between borders of willow trees and bushes. "Many's the trout I caught here when I was visiting my godfather," Joshua said as they stood on the banks of the brook. He chuckled. "Look. Over there. I'm dashed if I don't think that's the Old Gaffer, the same wily fellow that eluded my fly time and time again when I was a boy."

Sybilla laughed. "Papa was used to get very frustrated about an ancient grandfather trout who lurked in a stream near the castle. Papa tried year after year to catch him and never succeeded." Jumping from stone to stone, she balanced herself on a flat rock in the middle of the stream and bent down to peer into the foaming riffles for the elusive old trout. Her back turned to Joshua, she didn't observe the keen glance he directed to her at the mention of the word *castle*. "There he is!" she exclaimed. As she reached out her hand to point, the rock slipped, and she fell into the water.

"I hope you can swim," Joshua called, choking with laughter. "It's quite deep. All of two feet."

Sybilla opened her eyes, staring up at Joshua in bewilderment as he knelt beside her. The fronds of a willow tree swayed above her head, and she seemed to be lying on grass. She felt very damp and chilled. The sleeves and the front of Joshua's coat looked damp, too. "Where am I?" she mumbled between chattering teeth. "Oh. I fell in the stream, didn't I?"

"You almost drowned," Joshua growled.

"Don't be silly. The water's only a few feet deep. How could I drown?"

"You hit your head on a stone as you fell. At first I didn't realize what had happened. When I finally leaped in after you, you were unconscious and you'd swallowed gallons of water. A lot of water, anyway." He gently touched her bruised temple with his forefinger. "Does that hurt much?"

"A bit." She managed a smile. "This is the second time you've rescued me after I'd injured my head. Have you ever thought what would have happened if you hadn't picked me up off the street that morning and brought me to your house? At best, I'd have ended up a charity patient at some hospital."

Joshua caught his breath. He reached out his hand to smooth the wet black curls away from her forehead. "God, Sybilla," he muttered, "when I think of you waking up, dazed and frightened and penniless, to find yourself in the hands of strangers in an anonymous hospital ward . . ." Slowly, as if he couldn't help himself, he lowered his head, brushing her lips in a warm, clinging kiss that held in it nothing of passion, only an aching tenderness.

Even as her lips responded, Sybilla felt a warning quiver. She moved her head slightly to the side, breaking the kiss. Joshua looked down at her, his face registering a curious mixture of confusion and regret. "Perhaps you should rue the day I brought you to Linton House," he said with a shaky smile. "I'm not taking very good care of you, am I? First I almost let you drown, then I leave you lying drenched on the ground to catch your death of cold." Getting to his feet, he stooped to gather her into his arms."

"Joshua, you needn't carry me. I can perfectly well walk."

"And I can perfectly well carry you. You bashed your head on a rock, remember?"

Mrs. Simmons's eyes widened with concern as Joshua entered her neat kitchen with his sodden burden. "Ye must get into something dry right away, Master Smith, afore ye come down with the ague. Take him into the parlor, do, Master Joshua, and help him shed them wet clothes. I'll bring him an old shirt and breeches that belonged to my son. He can wear those whilst I dry his own clothes afore the fire."

In the parlor Joshua set Sybilla down and closed the door. He raised an amused eyebrow, saying, "Mrs. Simmons gave me my marching orders to help you undress. I presume you want me to turn my back and close my eyes?"

Sybilla glared at him. She had a sudden memory of their

first meeting, when he'd slipped his hand inside her shirt to . . . "I can manage quite well, thank you."

Minutes later she felt little the worse for her immersion in the icy little stream except for a slight soreness at her temple. Dressed in the shabby, much-too-large castoffs of Mrs. Simmons's son, wrapped in a blanket, she sat before a cheerful fire, gorging on scones and biscuits and cup after cup of scalding tea.

Seated opposite her, Joshua eyed the depredations she was making on the tray of delicacies Mrs. Simmons had provided. He grinned, saying, "I've often wondered if you have a worm in your stomach that consumes all the food you put into your mouth. By rights, you ought to be as round as a plum pudding."

Sybilla made a face at him and continued eating. Replete at last, she brushed a bit of butter from her lip with her napkin and set down her cup. "Nothing tastes better than country food and country cooking," she said with a contented sigh. "You know, I've enjoyed seeing London so much, and I'll feel very sad about leaving when it's time to go, but I wouldn't want to live there permanently. I'd die a little bit if I knew I'd never live in the country again. I like your farm. It reminds me of home."

Joshua nodded. "I get my fill of London very quickly. It wouldn't grieve me if I never visited the city. I've often thought I'd like to live in the country year-round. Take this farm, for instance. My man of business tells me that two large adjoining parcels of property are up for sale. If I were to buy these parcels, I'd have enough land for a good-sized stud farm. I could spend several months a year here."

Sybilla's face lighted up. "That would be wonderful. You'd have to enlarge the stables, of course, and you'd want to build a much grander house . . ."

An hour later they were still deep in provisional plans for an enlarged stud farm when Mrs. Simmons entered the parlor with Sybilla's clothes, now only faintly damp. "There, that didn't take so long." She glanced at the clock on the mantel. "Ye might be a bit late fer yer engagement, though, Master Joshua."

Sybilla and Joshua looked at the clock and exchanged stricken glances. It was midafternoon, far too late to drive to Hampton Court to join Lady Verity in her tour of the palace.

Chapter 7

HELPING SYBILLA into the coat, Mrs. Roper stepped back to take a critical look at the garment. "I told you so," she said with satisfaction. "I was sure, once it had been cleaned, we'd find the coat hadn't shrunk at all."

Sybilla looked down at the dark blue coat and pantaloons. After her dunking in the stream at the Epsom farm several days ago, she'd never thought the clothes would be presentable again. "Thank you for refurbishing the coat and pantaloons. I'll be dressed in the first style of elegance for the dinner party tonight, won't I? I was afraid I'd be obliged to wear the same old things I've been wearing every day—the light blue coat and lemon-colored pantaloons— and put poor Joshua to the blush in front of his friends."

"First style of elegance, is it?" sniffed Mrs. Roper. "A black coat and breeches, *that's* what Mr. Brummell wears in the evenings. But that's neither here nor there. There wasn't time for Mr. Weston to make you up a pair of breeches and another coat. In any case, as well you know, it's my opinion His Lordship is making a mistake in allowing you to join his guests for dinner."

The housekeeper had, in fact, been extremely vocal in her objections to Sybilla's appearance at Joshua's entertainment for his military friends.

"Don't be in such a taking, Mrs. Roper. I know you think

it's unwise for me to appear in too close quarters with Joshua's friends and acquaintances. But consider: I've already met most of the guests: Merry—I mean Captain Merriweather—and Lady Verity and Lord Dunsford. Not one of them had the slightest suspicion I'm not Will Smith. I really don't think you need worry about the dinner party."

Mrs. Roper continued to grumble. "Even so, it wouldn't be at all the thing. You're supposed to be a fifteen-year-old boy. Striplings, I assure you, do *not* attend ton dinner parties." She heaved a martyrlike sigh. "Well, that's as may be. I make no bones about telling you that my heart will be in my mouth until the dinner is over."

After the housekeeper had left the bedchamber, Sybilla took off the dark blue coat and pantaloons and hung them in the wardrobe, ready for the evening's festivities. As she changed into the light blue coat and lemon-colored pantaloons, she acknowledged to herself that she shared some of Mrs. Roper's apprehensions. There was a real risk in mingling too freely with Joshua's friends. True, Merry and Lady Verity and Lord Dunsford had already accepted her as Will Smith, but on closer acquaintance her imposture might begin to fray around the edges.

She'd mentioned her doubts to Joshua. "Nonsense," he'd replied impatiently. "I'd feel like a real monster if I knew you were cooped up in your bedchamber for a whole evening while I was enjoying myself with my friends downstairs. You haven't been caught out in your masquerade yet. Don't borrow trouble."

Well, perhaps their luck would hold for a while. It needn't be for long, Sybilla mused as she picked up her hat and went out the door to join Joshua for their morning excursion. Although he'd said nothing to her to remind her of it, she was well aware that she'd been at Linton House for a full two weeks. Soon Joshua would suggest it was time for her to leave, and then the danger of exposure would be over. She'd be on her own in London, losing herself in some anonymous, unfashionable corner of the city where she'd run little risk of meeting any of his friends.

Starting down the stairs, she realized suddenly that her scheme to evade being sent away from London now seemed bleakly unattractive. In a day, or two, or three, when Joshua put her on the stagecoach for her journey "home" to Durham, it would be easy enough to slip off at the first stop as she'd planned. She'd be in no danger of starving for the immediate future, since she still had the sovereigns she'd won from Joshua in their shooting match at Manton's Gallery. During the past two weeks, however, she'd seen a good deal of London, including some of its more seamy aspects. She was no longer so certain that she'd be able to hold her own in this vast, inhospitable, and dangerous place. Nor was it merely the danger and the loneliness that made her future prospects so unappealing. Reluctantly she admitted to herself that she would sorely miss Joshua's large, comforting, good-natured presence. During these few brief days he'd become so much a part of her life that it was hard to imagine a time when she hadn't known him.

When she came down the stairs, he was waiting for her in the hall. "By Jove, you're looking Friday-faced this morning," he said disapprovingly. "Can it be you're not eager to go see the Irish Giant in the Haymarket? I did tell you, didn't I, that the fellow's reputed to be nine feet tall? Of course, if you'd rather do something else—"

Resolutely Sybilla pushed her uncertainties to the back of her mind. Mustering a smile, she said, "No, indeed, I'm very eager to see the Giant. And I'm looking forward to the cricket match at Lord's. Thanks to you, there soon won't be a nook or a cranny in all of London that I haven't seen! Oh, I forgot to ask you at breakfast—how was your evening last night? Didn't you escort Lady Verity to the Countess of Morton's rout party?"

Joshua's lips tightened. "Heaven preserve me from any such affair in the future," he burst out. "Rout! *Squeeze* is more the word for it. Over a thousand people, I'd guess, invited to a house that might comfortably hold four hundred. No dancing, no cards, no music, no *food*. It was almost impossible to move from room to room, and little reason to do so, I must tell you, except to shout and wave to some of Verity's friends. So after we'd done that for a while, we went home. Or tried to. The staircase was so crowded that at least four ladies fainted in the crush. Why anyone in his right mind would want to attend such an affair passes understanding!"

Poor Joshua, thought Sybilla, choking back an urge to laugh. Verity had graciously forgiven him once again for breaking their engagement on the day he and Sybilla had rescued the ex-trooper Wyatt and carried him down to Epsom. But Joshua had apparently felt the need to make amends. For several days now, from late afternoon to the early hours of the morning, he'd dutifully accompanied Verity to functions that normally he would have done his best to avoid. A poetry reading by a friend of Augustus. A private concert by a young lady reputed to be a dabster at playing the harp. A ball so crowded that not once had he succeeded in dancing with his fiancée.

"I'm sorry you didn't enjoy yourself at the rout party," Sybilla murmured.

Joshua brightened. "Well, tonight will be different, I assure you. Good talk. Good food, if I know Mrs. Roper. Good wine . . ." He clapped his hand to his forehead. "Lord, if I didn't forget to tell the butler to make sure we had plenty of champagne—yes, what is it?" he said to the footman hovering at his elbow.

"Yer pardon, my lord, I'm sure. There's a—a person at the door of the kitchens. Says 'e must see Yer Lordship."

Joshua lifted an eyebrow. "My friends and acquaintances usually ask for me at my front door. Any other caller may state his business either to the butler or to the housekeeper."

Plainly discomfited, the footman stammered, "Yes, my lord, but ye see, this person says ye *told* 'im ter come 'ere. Very important, 'e says. Matter o' life and death. I thought I should jist tell ye . . ."

Sybilla said in a low voice, "Joshua, could it be that man from the gin shop with news of Lem Wyatt's family?"

"Oh, the devil. Yes, I daresay it could be." Joshua spoke to the footman. "Show the fellow into the library."

The gin shop proprietor, dressed in shabby, soiled clothing, looked distinctly uncomfortable as he shuffled into the library, followed by a watchful footman. The man stared furtively about him under drawn brows. Sybilla suspected he'd never before come into such close contact with either the homes or the persons of the gentry.

Seated behind his desk, Joshua shot a keen look at the man. "Your name?"

"Archer, sir—m'lord. Frank Archer."

"You have information for me?"

"Yuss, sir. M'lord. I knows wheer that crippled soljer's woman be livin'." Archer paused, waiting expectantly.

"Well? Oh." Joshua tossed the man a sovereign. "That's for now. What do you have to tell me?"

"Emmy Wyatt's livin' in Dirty Alley."

"Good God! Where's that?"

"Near Spring Gardens an' the King's Mews. Not far from the big church, St. Martin-in-the-Field."

Rising, Joshua nodded a dismissal to the gin shop proprietor. "Leave your direction with the footman. If your information is correct, I'll see you get a bit more for your trouble."

After the man had left, Joshua picked up his hat and driving gloves. "Let's be off, Sybilla. We'll find Wyatt's wife, give her some money for her fare to Epsom, and then we'll go visit the Irish Giant."

As they came off the Strand into Charing Cross, Joshua began asking directions to Dirty Alley with little success. Finally a man pointed them toward an area of ramshackle houses and narrow streets between Charing Cross and the end of the Mall.

Joshua drove into the area by what appeared to be a principal street, stopping every few feet to ask for directions from one of the slovenly, listless-appearing men and boys who loitered there. After only a minute or two he began swearing under his breath. "I shouldn't have brought you here. When Archer mentioned Spring Gardens and St. Martin-in-the-Field, I thought he was talking about a poor but possibly respectable neighborhood. This is a rookery, even worse than the one in St. Giles, where we took Wyatt that day. I think we'd better go."

It *was* worse than St. Giles, Sybilla thought, looking around her with round eyes. Pools of evil-smelling liquid filled the potholes in the unpaved street, from which twisting, trash-strewn alleys branched off to small courtyards. These alleys were far too narrow to admit a curricle and pair. The houses lining the street were mere dilapidated hovels, in the doorways of which weary, defeated-looking women stood, holding crying babies. Sybilla could see at least two gin shops as she peered down the street, and both of them seemed well-patronized.

"Let's not give up yet," she begged. "This may be the only opportunity we'll have to find Emmy Wyatt."

Joshua hesitated. His eye fell on a ragged urchin who was standing against the wall of a house, staring at them curiously. He fished a coin out of his pocket and held it up. "Can you tell us how to find Dirty Alley?" The boy nodded, keeping his eyes fixed on the coin until Joshua tossed it to him. Then he pointed to the next twisting lane to their right.

Joshua reached into his pocket for several more coins, shaking his hand so that the coins made a jingling sound. "Do you have some friends who'd like a little of the ready?" As a grin split his face from ear to ear, the boy put his fingers to his mouth to produce a shrill whistle. As if by magic, several more urchins appeared. Joshua looked at them sternly. "Now, lads, if you help Tim here"—he motioned to his tiger, standing tensely on his perch behind the driving seat—"to guard my curricle and pair while I'm gone, you'll each receive a crown when I return from my errand. Understood?"

The beatific smiles on the urchins' faces answered for them. Dismounting, Joshua handed the reins to the tiger, who stood protectively at the horses' heads, whip poised and ready. As Joshua left the curricle and walked toward the alley, he muttered to Sybilla, trotting by his side, "I think the carriage and horses will be safe enough. Those lads would go through fire and torture for a few shillings."

Avoiding fetid puddles and odorous bits of garbage as best they could, Joshua and Sybilla walked along the alley, emerging into a small courtyard surrounded by narrow two- and three-story houses so dilapidated that they seemed in imminent danger of falling down. Joshua stooped to speak to a ragged, toothless crone sitting on the steps of one of the houses. "Does an Emmy Wyatt live here?"

The woman gazed at him vacantly for several moments. Then she pointed to a house two doors away. "First floor, on the right." Looking up at Joshua, she cackled suddenly. "Emmy's comin' up in the world. Not one but two fine young gentry coves ter visit 'er!"

As they turned away from the crone, Sybilla said in a low voice, "Good God, you don't suppose the old lady meant that Emmy Wyatt's become a—a fancy-piece?"

Joshua gave Sybilla a level look. "If she did, she may not have had a choice. When she left Lem Wyatt, she probably had no money at all."

"And she had a child to feed. Poor thing." Sybilla clutched at Joshua's arm. "If it's true—and it may not be, you know—we won't tell Lem. It's not Emmy's fault."

Sybilla soon discovered to her chagrin that her sympathy had been misplaced. She and Joshua climbed a flight of malodorous stairs and knocked on one of the grimy doors. No one came to answer their repeated knocks for several minutes. Finally the door opened. A blowsy redheaded woman, clothed in a soiled wrapper, stood in front of them. Strong fumes of Blue Ruin wafted from her person. She said belligerently, "Well? Wot's a pair o' swells like ye doin' in a place like this?"

Joshua touched his hand to his hat. "Are you Emmy Wyatt?"

The woman's eyes narrowed. "So why d'ye want ter know?"

Quickly Joshua explained about the ex-dragoon's broken leg and his move to the Epsom farm. "Lem is anxious for you and the boy to join him."

"Is 'e now? Always wanted ter muck about on a farm, 'e did. Well, 'e kin do as 'e likes. *I* ain't goin' ter no farm." A loud wail sounded from a corner of the room, where a child of about two years of age sat on a pallet on the floor. The woman sniggered. "The boy, now. Lem's welcome ter 'im. Little Joe, 'e might like ter live on a farm."

"Mrs. Wyatt!" exclaimed a shocked Sybilla. "You're willing to give up your own child?"

"Ain't no good ter me." The woman made a sudden dash to the corner of the room. Bundling the child up in a tattered blanket, she returned to the door and thrust the boy into Sybilla's arms. "There, my lad," she sneered, "take 'im ter Lem, an' good riddance!"

Sybilla gazed blankly at the child, who stopped crying and looked up at her out of solemn eyes. Behind her a rough voice growled, "Wot's this, now?" She turned to face a burly, unshaven man, dressed in soiled, shabby clothes, who stood in the noisome corridor glaring at her and Joshua.

A look of fear crossed Emmy Wyatt's face. "These coves are goin' ter take little Joe ter Lem, in the country. Georgie, ye allus said ye didn't want Joe around. Got in the way o' business, ye said, 'is cryin' annoyed the customers."

Country-bred Sybilla realized she was looking at a pimp.

The man's eyes raked Joshua and Sybilla from head to foot, from their exquisitely fashioned beaver hats to their brightly polished boots. At last he said, "If ye 'was ter 'and over a bit o' rhino, ye could 'ave 'im, wi' my blessings. Say five quid? That's fair enough, ain't it?"

Reaching out a long arm to shove "Georgie" aside, Joshua said curtly, "Be damned to you. We'll take the child to his father, but you'll not get a penny from us. Get behind me, Will," he warned, as the pimp raised his fists and moved toward them.

"They say some o' ye gentry coves be 'andy wi' yer fives," jeered the man. "We'll see now, won't we?"

A small pistol appeared in Joshua's hand. "I could land you a wisty-castor if I had a mind to it, but I'm not willing to soil my hands or waste my time in a mill with you," he said calmly. He waved the man away from the door. "Will, start down the stairs."

Holding the child tightly, Sybilla went down the stairs and across the courtyard, venturing an occasional quick glance behind her to note that Joshua was almost literally walking backward, to cover their rear.

"Cor!" breathed one of the urchins guarding the curricle when he caught sight of the pistol. "Didn't 'ear no shot, Guv. Be ye goin' ter kill somebody?"

"Not immediately. Not unless somebody really annoys me." Pistol at the ready as he faced the alley from which he and Sybilla had just emerged, Joshua called over his shoulder to the tiger, ordering him to help Sybilla and the child into the curricle. Then, pulling out a handful of coins, he gave them to the nearest of his youthful temporary employees, saying, "That's better than a crown apiece. Divide it up among you." Jumping into the curricle, he flicked the reins, sending his horses trotting swiftly down the narrow street.

"Well, now I know why you won't allow your tailor to make your coats too close-fitting," observed Sybilla after they had turned one corner and then another and were moving safely out of the squalid rookery. "You don't want the public to know you're carrying a pistol."

Joshua turned his head to grin at her. "One never knows when it might be useful. These London streets are more dangerous than the wilds of Portugal! This is the first time I've had to act as rear guard, though." He glanced at the child sitting rigidly in Sybilla's lap. "Do you think you can manage him until we get to Epsom?"

Sybilla took her first close look at the child. He was dirty and quite thin, but he bore no signs of actual abuse. He appeared somewhat frightened and bewildered, as well he might, she thought. He'd been handed over to total strangers, and he was probably experiencing the first carriage ride of his short life. She smoothed her hand gently over his unkempt hair. "Don't be afraid, Joe. Nothing bad is going to happen to you. Are you hungry?" When he nodded, she said, "We're going to see a lady who bakes wonderful scones. We'll be there soon."

As they drove into the Surrey countryside, Sybilla continued to talk to Joe, telling him about his father, soothing his fears when they encountered such large awesome objects as cows and horses. Once or twice she was conscious that Joshua was staring at her with an expression she was unable to decipher. There was surprise in it, and approval, and some other emotion she couldn't identify.

When they arrived in Epsom, Mrs. Simmons, the farmer's wife, greeted them enthusiastically, though she seemed somewhat nonplussed to find they had brought a baby with them.

Sybilla felt amply compensated for any danger or difficulty she and Joshua had encountered when she observed Lem Wyatt's overwhelming joy in seeing his son. Unable to move unaided from his comfortable chair in his sunny bedchamber, Wyatt cradled the boy in his arms, alternately crooning endearments and crying, until Mrs. Simmons removed the child to feed and wash him.

"Ain't no words ter thank ye, Major, an' Master Will, too, o' course," said Wyatt when he was alone with Joshua and Sybilla.

"Glad to do it." Joshua hesitated. "Sorry we couldn't bring your wife, too."

A slow flush spread over the trooper's face, and he dropped his eyes. "I knowd 'bout 'ow Emmy was livin', Major. I jist couldn't bring myself ter tell ye. . . ."

The mystique of the 4th Dragoons again, Sybilla thought, as Joshua, looking intensely embarrassed, clapped a hand on Wyatt's shoulder. "It's all right. Mrs. Simmons and her husband treating you decently?"

Wyatt beamed. "Like a king."

In the farm kitchen a little later, Joshua apologized to Mrs. Simmons. "I know you never anticipated being saddled with a crippled ex-soldier *and* a child. You'll hire a nursemaid to care for Joe, of course, until Lem is on his feet."

"Not to worry, Master Joshua. Except—what's the boy to wear? Those rags he's wearing should be burned."

Thus Joshua and Sybilla spent the rest of the afternoon in the mercers' shops of Epsom, engaged in the very unlikely task of selecting lengths of kersey and nankeen and corduroy and Indian cotton to clothe little Joe. At one point Joshua sent Sybilla into a paroxysm of laughter when he said darkly, "At this rate I'll end by spending more time on little Joe's wardrobe than I do on my own. And what's more"—he pulled out his watch—"after we've delivered these parcels to Mrs. Simmons, we'll be hard put to arrive in London in time for dinner."

* * *

With an exasperated sigh Sybilla threw down the square of heavily starched muslin to join several other failures on the floor. In two weeks she hadn't even come close to mastering the art of tying a gentleman's cravat. Tonight her lack of skill was especially irksome. Returning from the Epsom farm, she and Joshua had reached Bedford Square so late that they had only twenty minutes in which to change their clothes before his dinner guests began arriving.

She picked up another square of muslin, folded it cornerwise and wrapped it around her neck. Carefully easing her chin downward to create the proper creases in the cravat, she attempted to tie the front ends in a tasteful bow, only to come her usual cropper. Smothering an unladylike urge to curse, she tore off the offending material and seized another square of muslin. Folding it cornerwise, she started to put it around her neck. Then, struck by a sudden thought, she left her bedchamber and walked down the corridor to Joshua's rooms. His voice called, "Come," in answer to her knock.

Poking her head cautiously around the door, Sybilla said, "It's me, Joshua. Are you dressed? I came to ask your valet to help me with my confounded cravat."

"Yes, I'm dressed. Come on in." As Sybilla entered the room, Joshua put down his hairbrush and rose from the dressing table. "I sent my valet downstairs with a message. I'll help you tie your cravat." He chuckled. "I don't guarantee the result, you know. Just remember I've never given Brummell any reason to consider me a rival for his title as the best-dressed man in London! Come over here to the cheval glass. Put the thing on and crease it. That's it. Now stand with your back to me. . . ."

Staring into the mirror, Joshua reached around Sybilla for the two loose ends of the cravat and began tying them into a knot. "I'm giving you a Trone d'Amour," he murmured, his eyes intent on his mirrored handiwork. "I'm told the Dandies favor it. You'll be all the crack when I get through with you!"

We look well together, thought Sybilla dreamily as she gazed at their reflections. Dark and fair, blue eyes and gray.

We're exactly the right height, too. The top of my head comes just over his shoulder. Suddenly she was acutely aware of the tautly muscled male body behind her. She felt a shiver of excitement when his long slender fingers brushed against her face as he tied the cravat. She breathed in his scent, a compound of fresh crisp linen, fine soap, and something indefinable, uniquely masculine and alluring. Their eyes met in the mirror. He drew a quick breath, and his fingers stilled in their task. Slowly, gropingly, his hands slipped to her waist and his arms began to close around her.

"I see you're an expert in tying cravats," said Sybilla shakily. "I look complete to a shade!"

The sound of her voice seemed to break a spell. His eyes cleared, and he moved away from her. "Next time I'll treat you to a Horse Collar," he said, grinning. Turning to the dressing table, he picked up his hairbrush. "Your hair's not right for a man about town. Here, I'll arrange it 'à la Brummell.'" A moment later he murmured bemusedly as he brushed some curls in place over her temples, "Your hair's like black silk. It clings to my fingers . . ."

A discreet cough sounded at the door that Sybilla had left open. "Beg pardon, m'lord," said the footman. "I don't guess ye 'eard my knock. The butler says ter tell ye that yer guests are arriving."

Joshua pulled the brush from Sybilla's hair so quickly he might have been handling burning coals. A faint red suffused his skin, bronzed from campaigning. "Thank you," he said to the footman. "We're coming."

As he and Sybilla rounded the bend of the staircase, the butler was ushering Captain Merriweather into the foyer. Following the crippled ex-officer into the house was a groom carrying a large square package.

"Hallo, Merry, what have you got there?" Joshua called. "A gift for me? My birthday isn't until September."

Merriweather airily waved the crutch on his good side and almost fell over. "Oh, the devil," he complained. "Don't think I'll ever learn to use these things. Damned inconvenient, don't y'know, to lose a leg." His bright blue eyes began to dance beneath the mop of carroty-red curls. He pointed at the box. "What have I got here, Linton, my

son? Don't be so curious. You'll know in good time."
Briefly he directed his groom to hand the package to a
footman.

Turning to Sybilla, the captain said, "Hallo, young Will.
Been selecting any more horses for Linton? I hope you
charge him a commission. I think you know more about
horses than he does. How did you enjoy your evening at
Astley's Amphitheatre? I'm dashed sorry I didn't go with
you and Linton. Went to the dullest ball instead. Now, I ask
you, what possible use would I be at a ball?"

Merriweather was still chattering in his cheerful, incon-
sequential way when they entered the drawing room, where
Lady Verity was already seated with her companion, Mrs.
Laleham, and Augustus Cranborn.

"There you are, Joshua," said Verity, ethereally beautiful
in her sheer white muslin sprinkled with silver embroidery.

Was there the faintest barb in her voice, Sybilla wondered? Joshua should, of course, have been downstairs to
receive his fiancée.

Verity looked at Sybilla. "Will. You're dining with us?
How—how pleasant." No doubt about it, her sweet smile
didn't quite extend to her eyes. "Let me guess," she said
archly. "You two were off on one of your little excursions
and quite forgot the time."

"Something like that." Joshua raised an eyebrow at
Augustus, who seemed mildly uncomfortable. He was
elegantly dressed in a black coat, black breeches, and silk
stockings, although, as usual, he looked as if the tailor had
squeezed him into garments that were too small for him.

"I must explain to you, Joshua," said Verity quickly.
"Papa came down with the most dreadful toothache this
afternoon. He didn't feel he could inflict his pain on your
guests. So when Mr. Cranborn came by—"

"Bringing you another of his poems, no doubt."

"Why, yes. When he came by, I asked him to escort me
and Mrs. Laleham. To keep your table even, you see."

Sybilla felt a small pang of guilt. Three more guests were
expected: Joshua's officer friend, Lieutenant Preston, and
his wife and daughter, who would make the dinner seating
even at four men and four women. By including "Will

Smith" in the dinner party, Joshua had thrown his table off.

Captain Merriweather poked an elbow into his host's ribs. "Where are your manners, Linton? When are you going to introduce me to this lovely lady who's about to make you the most fortunate creature in the world?"

The introductions made, the captain dropped into a chair beside Verity and proceeded to captivate her into euphoric good humor with his extravagant compliments and his rib-tickling tales of the lighter side of service in the Peninsula. At one point Verity said to Joshua, "I can't think why you've never told me any of these amusing stories."

"It might be because I'm not as accomplished a liar as Merriweather," Joshua retorted.

While Merry clutched his sides, laughing so hard that he was gasping for breath, Verity looked blankly from Joshua to his friend. Sybilla raised a mental eyebrow. Could it be that Verity didn't have a sense of humor? If so, she might find married life with Joshua trying. His lively sense of the ridiculous was one of his more engaging traits.

With the arrival of Lieutenant Preston, a plain-looking, good-tempered man with a pleasant wife and a charming daughter, the party was complete and soon adjourned to the dining room. Verity dimpled with pleasure when Joshua said, "My dear, would you sit opposite me? I have no hostess."

"Might as well, Lady Verity," said Merry with a grin. "Good practice for you. Soon you'll be occupying that chair permanently."

Verity beamed. As the second course succeeded the first, however, her smile became less radiant. The conversation inclined more and more to military matters. As the phrases flew back and forth, faster and faster, the civilians at the table grew mute. ". . . should have enlarged the breach at Badajoz before we attacked . . . Marmont's fatal mistake on his left wing . . . Wellington should have waited for a siege train at Burgos . . . Beresford didn't realize he'd already won the battle . . ."

When it was time for the ladies to leave the men to their port, it seemed to Sybilla that Verity rose from the table with unusual alacrity. Forgetting momentarily her masquerade, Sybilla made an instinctive move to join the other women and then sank back in her seat. Joshua came to her rescue. "Run along, Will," he said, a quirkish smile curling the corners of his mouth. "You're too young to drink port. Besides, Jack and Merry and I have serious business to accomplish. We're going to refight the war for Mr. Cranborn's benefit and point out to him where we'd have out-generaled Wellington."

Feeling relieved, Sybilla went off to the drawing room. "I've been ejected," she informed the ladies as a footman entered the room with a coffee tray.

"And quite rightly, too," Verity said. "Joshua has good sense."

Mrs. Preston smiled at Sybilla. "You *are* a little young to drink port with the gentlemen, but I think you might have enjoyed their conversation. Along about this time, I expect, they're deep in the siege of Ciudad Rodrigo."

Accepting a cup of coffee from the footman, Verity peered over the rim of her cup at Mrs. Preston. "Surely not," she said. There was a definite edge to her voice. "I would have thought that Joshua and your husband and Captain Merriweather had exhausted the subject of the war at the dinner table. Indeed, they talked of nothing else."

Susan Preston laughed. "Oh, I fancy Papa could talk about military matters until dawn without tiring of the conversation."

Her mother nodded. "Jack couldn't wait to get here tonight. Since he retired, he has no one to talk to about tactics or strategy. No, I'm sure my husband and Lord Linton and Captain Merriweather haven't exhausted the subject of the war, Lady Verity. I daresay we'll sit here twiddling our thumbs for some time before the gentlemen rejoin us."

Mrs. Preston was correct. The minutes wore away to the half hour, and Joshua and his guests didn't appear in the drawing room. Glancing repeatedly at the tiny jeweled watch pinned to her bodice, Verity lapsed into a stiff silence. Mrs. Preston and her daughter and Sybilla did their best to keep the conversation going. Verity's companion, Mrs. Laleham, ventured a timid remark or two. At one point the ladies heard a loud, prolonged burst of laughter coming from the dining room down the corridor. Verity flinched.

Shortly afterward, Augustus Cranborn entered the drawing room. His face was flushed, and he was brushing at his breeches with the napkin he'd taken away with him from the table. Verity's eyes went to the vacant doorway behind him. "I've come alone, Lady Verity," he said with a cold dignity. "I couldn't in conscience remain in the company of Lord Linton and his friends."

"Why, what do you mean, Mr. Cranborn?"

Augustus exploded. "I mean that I couldn't lend my countenance to behavior that goes far beyond the bounds of decorum. You'll find this almost impossible to credit, but I assure you it's true, every word of it. As soon as you ladies left the dining room, Captain Merriweather brought out a"—Augustus grew even redder—"a large silver chamber pot, which, he informed us, once belonged to King Joseph Bonaparte. The captain's regiment captured it during the French retreat from Vitoria. Not satisfied with bringing this object into a gentlemen's dining room, the captain then proceeded to order the servants to fill it with champagne."

Sybilla began to laugh. "So *that's* what was in Merry's mysterious parcel. We wondered what caused that shout of laughter a bit ago. You've been drinking toasts from the chamber pot."

Speaking between his clenched teeth, Augustus said, "If that were all, Master Smith, it would be bad enough. What occasioned the laughter was far worse. Captain Merriweather fell *in* the chamber pot. That is to say, he stood up to give a toast and his crutches slipped and his arm went into the chamber pot, which then tipped over, spilling its contents over the table. And, I might add, over the clothing of everyone present." His aggrieved glance fell on his breeches, which, Sybilla now noted, were quite damp and smelled strongly of spirits.

"Merry wasn't hurt when he fell, I hope," Sybilla said anxiously.

"Hurt! Not at all! He had the servants refill the chamber pot with champagne and proposed another toast. It was then that I decided to leave. Not even to spare the feelings of my noble host would I consent to participate any longer in such debauchery!"

The laughter died out of Sybilla's eyes. "What a dreadful thing to say. Joshua is *not* debauched. He's merely enjoying himself in the company of good friends, who, like him, fought for their country. And who, unlike him, thank God, were badly wounded in the service of their country. You shouldn't begrudge them their reunion."

"I'll thank you not to presume to tell me what to think, young man. I trust I know how a gentleman behaves."

"Then why don't you act like one? A true gentleman is kind and helpful and doesn't judge his friends."

Lady Verity gasped. "Will Smith! How dare you speak to Mr. Cranborn in that fashion? He's one of the greatest gentlemen I know."

Her temper getting the better of her, Sybilla snapped, "Oh, why? Because he writes silly verses that don't scan?"

Stiffening with outrage, Verity rose. "Mr. Cranborn, I think we should go." Trailed by her mousy companion, Mrs. Laleham, and Augustus, she walked toward the door, nearly colliding with Joshua and Merry and Lieutenant Preston, who were just entering the drawing room.

"You're leaving, Verity?" Joshua said in surprise. His smile was slightly owlish, and there was a faint slur in his voice. Like Augustus, he smelled of spilt champagne.

"Indeed, I am. Your little friend, Will Smith, has insulted Mr. Cranborn. You could hardly expect me to stay under the circumstances."

Joshua shook his head, as if to clear his mind from the fumes of champagne. His eyes bored into Sybilla. "Is it true, Sy—Will? Did you insult Mr. Cranborn?"

Sybilla said, dropping her eyes, "Yes. I suppose so. I told him to act like a gentleman. I also said his verse didn't scan." Her temper flared again. "He deserved it. He accused you and Merry and Lieutenant Preston of debauchery, simply because you were drinking champagne toasts out of King Joseph's chamber pot!"

Joshua and the two ex-cavalrymen dissolved into helpless laughter. Merry was in such a state that he had to be supported on his crutches. Lieutenant Preston helped him to a chair.

Her beautiful face rigid with anger, Verity stalked past Joshua. He caught her arm as she reached the door. Still shaking with laughter, he said, "I'm sorry. I didn't mean to make light of Will's behavior. But I'm sure he didn't mean to be rude. I know he'll be willing to apologize to Mr. Cranborn. Can't we let bygones be bygones?"

Verity's eyes flashed. "I might have known you'd condone that boy's disgraceful conduct. It's all of a piece. Since he came to town, you've pampered him and lavished attention on him at my expense. When I think of how many engagements you've broken because you were rattling about with that boy in tow! And what is he, after all, to merit such attention? His father was a nobody, a ne'er-do-well black sheep connection of an illustrious family. But no, the way you're treating him, anyone would think he was your own child, not the son of some undistinguished officer of your regiment!"

All trace of his usual warmth and gaiety vanished from Joshua's face. His gray eyes were icy cold. "Since you feel that way, it would be useless to ask you to stay. Let me call your carriage."

Chapter 8

SYBILLA LOOKED up from her breakfast, her face clouded with apprehension, as Joshua entered the dining room the next morning. Without speaking, he went to the sideboard, ignoring the array of covered dishes, and poured himself a cup of coffee.

"You're not hungry, Joshua?" asked Sybilla as he sat down.

He gazed with loathing at the mound of bacon and ham and eggs on her plate. "I never want to eat again," he growled. He didn't look well. His eyes were bloodshot, and his skin was grayish beneath the bronze of his tan. The aftermath of too much champagne, Sybilla suspected. After Verity had stormed out of the house last night and the flustered and embarrassed Prestons had left, Joshua and Captain Merriweather had retired to the dining room. There, more likely than not, they'd cracked several more bottles.

"Joshua, I'm sorry I ruined your dinner party," Sybilla began, feeling a need to relieve herself of the guilt that had caused her to toss sleeplessly for most of the night. "I shouldn't have said what I said to Mr. Cranborn."

"Was what you said true?"

"Well . . ." A blue flame appeared in Sybilla's eyes. "He had no right to accuse you of debauchery!" she

106

exclaimed. "And he *does* write terrible verse!" She bit her lip. "That doesn't excuse me. I should apologize to Mr. Cranborn, and yes, to Lady Verity. I ruined her evening, too."

Joshua put down his coffee cup. A line between his brows told Sybilla he had a raging headache. "It will be quite unnecessary for you to apologize to anyone. You're the injured party. Verity should apologize to *you*."

"But, Joshua—"

He cut her off. "You're my guest, my honored guest, and I don't allow my guests to be insulted in my own house, by my fiancée or anyone else." He rose and walked toward the door, saying, "I'm going to my library to read my newspapers in peace and quiet. This afternoon, if you still want to attend the fair at Peckham, I'll be at your disposal."

Feeling utterly dejected, Sybilla watched him go. Verity had been so angry last night. Joshua had been angry, too, and with rather more justification, in Sybilla's opinion. True, he should have been on hand to welcome his fiancée to his home. Then, too, perhaps he ought to have guessed that Verity's sweetness of manner had masked a resentment at the amount of time he was spending with his protégé, "Will." Certainly he hadn't improved matters by virtually ignoring Verity at the dinner table to rehash old battles with his cronies. As for keeping her waiting in the drawing room while he got foxed drinking champagne toasts out of a silver chamber pot . . . Despite her concern, Sybilla's mouth widened in a grin.

No, really, it was no laughing matter, she reminded herself sternly. On thinking it over, she had to acknowledge that prim and proper Lady Verity had been sorely tried. But then—another small voice took over in Sybilla's mind— shouldn't Verity have been a little more understanding? Why hadn't she been able to overlook Joshua's lapses when she'd witnessed his delight in renewing the camaraderie of his military days?

Pushing aside her plate, its contents only half-eaten, Sybilla left the dining room. Casting a wistful look at the library door as she passed—she hoped Joshua's headache would soon be better—she wandered aimlessly through the house. She ended in the stables, where a visit to Midnight temporarily took her mind away from her problems. She'd been riding the black stallion every day this week in her morning rides with Joshua in Hyde Park. With each ride the bond between her and the horse had deepened. Oh, how she'd miss Midnight when her visit with Joshua was over!

With a final loving pat on the horse's velvety muzzle, Sybilla returned to the house. In the morning room she sat down with a book open in her lap, nursing her gloomy thoughts anew. Was Lady Verity's tiff with Joshua a mere lovers' quarrel, or was she angry enough to cry off from her betrothal? If that should happen, I'd be responsible, Sybilla reflected, once more overcome with guilt.

Mrs. Roper bustled into the morning room, pausing with an unconvincing start of surprise when she saw Sybilla. "Not going out this morning?"

"No. We're going to a country fair this afternoon."

The housekeeper wandered about the room, straightening a cushion here, an ornament there. At length, abandoning her pretense of domestic zeal, she said, "Lady Verity left quite early last night, I hear."

Sybilla met Mrs. Roper's curious eyes and said crossly, "Everything would have been quite all right if Captain Merriweather hadn't brought that silver chamber pot with him."

Clearly the housekeeper was familiar with most of the details of last night's disaster and only wanted the opportunity to discuss them. "There! Remember what I told you? That Francis Merriweather, he's bear-leading His Lordship into trouble again. Drinking out of a chamber pot! It's indecent—" She broke off as a footman peered into the morning room. "What is it, Briggs?"

"Captain Merriweather fer Master Smith, ma'am. That's to say, the captain wanted ter see 'is Lordship, only 'is Lordship, 'e'd already told me 'e didn't wish ter see nobody this morning. So then the captain, 'e said could 'e talk ter Master Smith."

"Show Captain Merriweather in," said Sybilla quickly. Mrs. Roper left, her spine rigid with disapproval.

Merry hobbled into the morning room, dropping into a chair with a sigh of relief. "Getting to be an old man," he complained. "Didn't used to feel this bad the morning after I was castaway the night before." The captain looked, if anything, worse than Joshua. The bright blue eyes were squeezed almost shut against a potentially hurtful ray of sunshine, and his skin color resembled the underside of a fish. Even the crisp carroty curls looked limp. "Could you draw those draperies, young Will?" he said, grimacing. "Thank you, that's better." Cautiously Merry opened his eyes wider. "Now, then, why won't Linton see me?"

"It's nothing to do with you, Captain. I don't think he wants to see anyone."

"Well, is he angry with me? The thing is, I don't recall much of what happened at the dinner party after I spilled the champagne. Except I seem to remember Lady Verity being cross as crabs about something or other, and I did just wonder—"

"She *was* cross. She left the party in a tremendous taking."

"Did she, by Jove. Why was that? I say, did it have something to do with—"

"With King Joseph's chamber pot? Yes, I'm afraid it did. But mostly it was my fault. I said unkind things to Mr. Cranborn, and Lady Verity took his part. And then, later, Joshua took *my* part, which he shouldn't have done, and that sent Lady Verity up into the boughs . . ."

"And she stormed out," finished Merry. "It's coming back to me. Lord, what a shocking coil!"

"Yes," Sybilla agreed miserably. "I'm so afraid Lady Verity might break her engagement, and it would all be my doing. I've offered to apologize to her. But Joshua won't let me. . . ."

"Always stubborn, Linton. Very loyal to his friends, too. Well, now, as I see it—" Merry sat up straight and immediately gasped with pain. "Oh, my cursed head. Let this be a lesson to you, young Will. Don't drink. Or at any rate, don't dip too deep. Well, then, as I was about to say, there's nothing for it but to go behind Linton's back and *both* of us apologize to Lady Verity. Can't have Linton wearing the willow, though it's not what I'd care for myself. Being leg-shackled, I mean. So off we go, lad."

Half an hour later, sitting in the drawing room of Lord Dunsford's house in Cavendish Square, Sybilla murmured to Captain Merriweather, "What if she won't see us?"

"Take that fence when we come to it—"

He broke off as Verity entered the room. She was pale but composed. There was very little warmth in her manner. "You wanted to see me?"

Merry proceeded to use his charm and his considerable talents as a raconteur to coax Verity out of her megrims. He related a rousingly exciting tale about the capture of King Joseph's chamber pot by officers of his regiment. He played on her heartstrings by describing the devotion of military men to comrades who had shared their dangers. "And if I could go on my knees to beg your pardon for my behavior last night, Lady Verity, I assure you I would," he finished. "Only, as you can see, that's quite impossible, what with my having left a leg in Spain. Young Will now, *he* could do it."

Verity's frigid features melted into a smile. "That won't be necessary. Perhaps I was somewhat hasty myself last night. I didn't quite perceive that the silver—the silver object was a regimental trophy. You say it will be enshrined in the regimental mess, brought out to mark the greatest of patriotic occasions? So the—it—might almost be called a badge of honor. I fear I don't hold with drinking from—but we shan't quarrel about that, shall we? And of course I do understand that gentlemen occasionally imbibe a little too freely in all male company."

Verity's smile became a little less warm when she looked at Sybilla, saying, "Certainly I agree with Captain Merriweather that you're to be commended for feeling great loyalty to Joshua. He's been most kind and generous to you. Still, one can hardly condone your rudeness to Mr. Cranborn under any circumstances."

"My mother would be the first to agree with you," said Sybilla contritely. "She'd be shocked to learn I'd been discourteous to one of Joshua's guests. I assure you it won't happen again. Pray convey my apologies to Mr. Cranborn.

I'm not likely to see him again. In a few days I'll be going home."

"Really? So soon? But, of course, you'll be returning to school." In the twinkling of an eye Verity appeared to recover her good humor. She reached over to pat Sybilla's shoulder. "Well, we shall miss you, Will. You must be sure to study hard at school and make Joshua proud of you."

The visit ended in complete cordiality. "Will's" transgressions, and the captain's, were as if they had never been. As Merry and Sybilla rose to go, Verity said with a sweet smile, "Tell Joshua for me, Will, that I look forward to seeing him tonight at Lady Cartwright's rout."

As they drove out of Cavendish Square, Merry said with relief, "I was afraid Lady Verity might cut up stiff with us, but now I fancy we'll be all right and tight. A month or so from now we'll be proposing toasts at Linton's wedding."

"*You* will, Captain."

"Lord, I'd forgotten. You told Lady Verity you were leaving London soon to go back to school. Well, now, mind you don't study too hard. Books never did anyone any harm, I collect, but they don't do much good, either." As he left Sybilla off in Bedford Square, the captain said cheerfully, "I can smell the orange blossom already. We've done a good morning's work."

Sybilla wasn't so sure. Verity wasn't angry anymore, but how did Joshua feel? Sybilla walked into the house and tapped on the library door. "It's me, Joshua."

"Come in."

When she entered the library, she found Joshua seated in an armchair, his nose in a newspaper. Several discarded newspapers were strewn on the floor around his chair.

"Are you still planning to go to the Peckham Fair, Joshua?"

He lowered his newspaper, gazing at her with raised eyebrows. "Certainly. Why would I change my mind?" His color had improved, and his gray eyes looked clearer. His smile was unforced. There was an underlying brittle quality in his voice, however, that told Sybilla he wasn't his usual lighthearted self. "Actually," he went on, "a nice vulgar fair will be a welcome distraction. The newspapers are depressing. I don't think the siege of San Sebastian is going very well."

"Naturally. You aren't there to advise them," murmured Sybilla wickedly.

"That will be quite enough out of you, minx." Rising, he went to the bell cord. "I'll send word to the stables that we want the curricle."

Sybilla blurted, "Joshua, I have a message for you from Lady Verity."

Swinging around abruptly, he skewered her with gray eyes that had turned icy. "You've seen Verity today?"

Sybilla gulped. She was looking at a different Joshua. She could easily visualize this man leading his dragoons in a wild cavalry charge, the light of battle in his eyes. "Captain Merriweather and I went to Cavendish Square to apologize to Lady Verity."

"You did that against my express wishes?" The gray eyes were even icier.

"Yes, I did," retorted Sybilla, roused to indignation. "And it was the right thing to do, too. Both Captain Merriweather and I were afraid our behavior would cause Lady Verity to cry off from your betrothal. So we explained everything to her, and she's not angry anymore. In fact . . ." Sybilla doubled up, suddenly convulsed with laughter. "In fact," she gasped, "Lady Verity's now calling the chamber pot a trophy of war. A badge of honor!"

An odd mixture of expressions battled for supremacy in Joshua's face. Anger. Annoyance. Stiff-necked pride. Hilarity. Grabbing at the nearest chair, he sat down, holding his sides and laughing until his eyes were streaming. At length, after he caught his breath, he said, "What a brass-faced female you are. At least life is never dull when you're around!"

Sybilla said anxiously, "You're not in bad skin with Lady Verity anymore?"

Joshua's familiar cheerful grin was back. "No, confound your impudence. Verity was simply no match for you and Merry. The two of you would try the patience of a saint. So what's the message my affianced sent along with you?"

"She said she looked forward to seeing you at Lady Cartwright's rout this evening."

"Oh, God. If I believed in reincarnation, I'd wonder what I was being punished for in this existence. Well, Sybilla, before I must needs go to the slaughter, we'll enjoy ourselves at the fair."

The village of Peckham was a short five-mile drive from the center of London, south across Westminster Bridge. The town was situated in an area of carefully tended market gardens and lush pastures, where cattle drovers rested their herds before bringing them to the markets of London. The main activity of the annual fair was centered around the Kentish Drovers Public House in the High Street.

Wandering along the crowded street with Joshua, going from booth to booth, Sybilla was soon lost in enchantment. Nothing in Yorkshire compared to the delights of the Peckham Fair. There was something for every taste, although, it occurred to Sybilla, the fastidious Lady Verity would probably find it all impossibly vulgar!

Joshua and Sybilla explored the wares offered by the booths selling toys and gimcracks, china, confectionaries and ribbons. They marveled at the skills of the jugglers and the rope dancers and a man named Fighting Frank, who put on a demonstration of foil play, backsword, cudgeling, and other pugilistic arts. They laughed at the puppet show and stood open-mouthed in front of the conjuror's booth when he caused rich red apples to appear on what, minutes before, had been a barren and desiccated tree.

In only one aspect did the Peckham Fair disappoint Sybilla. She walked away from an exhibition of "curious monsters" after only a halfhearted glance. Joshua caught her arm as she marched off toward the upper end of the High Street. "What is it, Sybilla?"

"I don't like looking at a 'Pig-faced Lady,' or a four-legged child," she said in a trembling voice. "They're not monsters. They're poor, suffering people. They shouldn't be put on display to be ogled and laughed at."

Joshua's fingers tightened on her arm in a warm, comforting clasp. "You're an uncommon girl," he said huskily. He cleared his throat. "Of course you're right. These people aren't monsters. But you can't change their situation. Look, at the very least they're earning a few pennies to put food in their mouths." He gave her a little shake. "Speaking of food, are you hungry? I'm starved. You ate a gargantuan breakfast this morning, as usual, while I couldn't force myself to eat a morsel."

In a quick reversal of mood, Sybilla retorted, "Don't blame me for your empty stomach. Nobody forced you to get shot in the neck last night."

"You've got the tongue of an adder," Joshua complained. "I pity your poor husband, if you're ever fortunate enough to catch one."

A little later, standing with Joshua in front of a confectioner's booth, Sybilla finished off a lemon ice after consuming an apple tart, a currant bun, some seed cakes, and several glasses of orgeat. Licking her fingers, she remarked, "I really think the ices are better at Gunther's, don't you?" She looked up in faint surprise when Joshua didn't answer. He was staring at something off in the middle distance.

"Sybilla, look over there to your right," he said in a low voice. "See that man in the brown coat and breeches?"

The man in question was stocky, grizzled, middle-aged and modestly dressed. A hat with a low, flat-topped crown sat squarely on his head. The eyes in the weather-beaten face were keen and alert, as Sybilla discovered when she met his gaze. He quickly looked away again. "What about him?" she asked.

Joshua turned his body slightly so that he could continue to keep the strange man under observation without appearing to do so. "The fellow's been following us. Every place we've gone in the past half hour, he's been right behind us."

Sybilla sneaked another look. The man was still there. "Do you think he's a thief? I've heard that cutpurses and pickpockets swarm around these fairs. And you have the look of a well-breeched swell, Joshua."

"You'd think he'd be a little less obvious if he were out to rob me." Joshua frowned. "Besides, Mrs. Roper mentioned something to me yesterday. She said a man of this fellow's description had been loitering outside the railings in the square for the past several days. Of course, it's not unusual for vagrants to congregate in the better residential squares. But this man is different. He doesn't beg or try to sell anything. Just stands about, watching, or lingers at the kitchen door or the entrance to the stables, trying to talk to any of the servants who come out."

"What could he want?"

"I haven't a notion, but I'm damned well going to find out." Joshua wheeled, striding purposefully toward the stranger, who turned and melted into the crowd. Joshua dashed after him, scattering startled fairgoers. Five minutes later he returned, slightly out of breath. "Chased him all the way to the end of the street. Then he disappeared into an alley, and I lost track of him. I don't like this at all. Fellow's up to no good, I can feel it."

Sybilla didn't answer. She was too deep in her thoughts. A frisson of unreasoning fear had shot through her when she heard Mrs. Roper's tale of the man loitering in the vicinity of Linton House. It couldn't have anything to do with her, she told herself. No one could possibly know she was staying at Joshua's house. In any event, there was no reason for anyone to try to discover her whereabouts. Was there? She recalled the low-voiced conversation she'd overheard at the castle one night, which had sent her fleeing from Yorkshire in fear of her life. During these past two weeks in London, however, as she'd gone over and over those few cryptic remarks, turning them inside and out, she'd begun to wonder if she could have been mistaken. Perhaps she'd acted like a child, seeing trolls and ogres behind every shadow.

"What?"

Joshua repeated himself patiently. "I said, do you want anything more to eat? Perish the thought you might feel hunger pangs before it's time to sit down to dinner."

"No, I've had enough. Joshua, it's getting late, and you have an engagement this evening. Let's go home."

Joshua nodded. "To tell the truth, I don't fancy being in a crowd like this knowing that prying fellow in the brown suit is on the loose. Not in your company, anyway. Left to myself . . ." His eyes kindled. "I'd love to get into a mill with that fellow. It'd be bellows to mend with him in about two seconds!"

On the drive back to Bedford Square, through the orchards and flower gardens of Camberwell and on to Walworth and Elephant and Castle, both Joshua and Sybilla were unusually silent. At length Joshua said, "I'm sorry that Peeping Tom of a fellow ruined our excursion, Sy—Will."

Sybilla resisted the impulse to glance back at the tiger. Joshua was growing careless in his use of her Christian name. She wondered if her masquerade was any longer a secret to the shrewd Cockney eyes of the tiger. Not that it mattered. The boy cared for nothing except Joshua's horses and Joshua, in that order. She was sure he wouldn't talk. And soon the problem wouldn't exist. Soon she'd no longer be there.

"The excursion wasn't ruined at all, Joshua. I can't remember when I've enjoyed myself so much. The Peckham Fair will be a wonderful memory of my last day in London."

"Your last day? What do you mean?" Joshua's tone was sharp.

"Well . . . my next to the last day, then. It's two weeks today that I came to London. We haven't received any word from Henrietta Place, so I presume that neither Aunt Lucretia nor her housekeeper has returned to the house. And you did say you were going to put me on a stagecoach for home if I hadn't heard anything from my godmother in two weeks."

"Oh. I hadn't realized how the time was slipping by. . . . It's possible, you know, that the caretaker lost the message I left with him, telling the housekeeper to contact me. We'll go to your godmother's house to check for ourselves."

Standing in front of Number 21, Henrietta Place, knocking repeatedly on the door without an answer, Sybilla had a curious sense that history was repeating itself. As she lifted the knocker to pound on the door again, she reflected that it was probably unjust to blame the caretaker for failing to answer her knock. All of Aunt Lucretia's friends must know she was away from home. To give him his due, the caretaker wouldn't be expecting anyone to call.

Finally the door opened a crack, and the beady eyes under the thatch of untidy hair that she remembered from her previous visit peered out at her. After a long look the man clucked with disapproval, "Oh, ye're 'ere again. Ye're wastin' yer time, young 'un. 'Er Ladyship, she ain't 'ere, nor yet the 'ousekeeper, Miz Endicott. And I ain't got no idea *when* the pair o' 'em will be back, neither."

Sybilla slumped in dejection. Joshua spoke over her head. "See here, my man, have you still got that slip of paper with my name and address on it that I left with you to give to the housekeeper?"

"Wot d'ye take me fer, Guv? 'Course I do. An' as soon as Miz Endicott comes back, she'll 'ave it."

Joshua reached through the crack in the door to drop several coins on the caretaker's palm. "See that you do. Let's go, Sy—Will."

Seated once more in the curricle, Sybilla said, with an attempt at raillery that she didn't feel, "Well, am I going home by common stagecoach? Or will I be traveling in style with the Mail?"

Joshua didn't reply for a moment. Then he said, a frown clouding his handsome face, "I don't know. Let me think about it." He continued deep in glowering silence until they reached Bedford Square. As they climbed down from the curricle, he said abruptly, "Come to the library. We need to talk."

Leaning against the edge of his desk, his arms folded across his chest, Joshua stared at Sybilla as she stood near the door of the library, waiting for him to speak. She had the curious sensation he was looking at her as if he'd never seen her before, or as if he were seeing her anew. At length he said, "Tell me the truth. Do you want to return to your home tomorrow?"

She felt an electric quiver of excitement rising in her. "No, I don't. The longer I stay away from—from my home, the more time my uncle will have to reflect on the wisdom of forcing me to marry my cousin."

A flicker of amusement showed in Joshua's face. "Conniving wench. If you stay away long enough, you think your uncle will be so relieved to see you that he won't insist that you marry his son."

"Something like that." Sybilla eyed Joshua with dawning hope.

Throwing up his hands, he exclaimed, "The devil take the hindmost! I know I shouldn't be contributing to your poor uncle's distress, I know I ought to restore you to his loving arms immediately, but what difference can a few days make? Sybilla, if you'd like to stay another week in Linton House, you're welcome to do so. Perhaps in another few days your godmother will have returned from Ireland. And besides"—he shot her an unwilling grin—"I rather enjoy having you around."

Chapter 9

"I THINK little Joe recognized us, Joshua," Sybilla observed, watching Lem Wyatt's son play happily with a paper windmill on the floor of his father's bedchamber in the farm at Epsom. She and Joshua had brought the toy when they arrived earlier from London to visit the ex-dragoon.

"No doubt about it, Master Smith, little Joe reckernized ye an' the major," said Lem Wyatt, beaming. "Little Joe, 'e's small, like, but e' knows when 'e's well off, so ter speak. 'E knows who took 'im fer a ride in a grand carriage wi' two beautiful 'orses and brought 'im ter live in a fine 'ouse wi' 'is dad."

Sybilla reflected that little Joe didn't look like the same child she and Joshua had rescued from the squalid slum where he'd been living with his mother and her paramour. He was clean now and not as thin, and he was dressed in respectable clothes. He was wearing loose trousers buttoned to a short jacket, a style Mrs. Simmons, the farmer's wife, had called a "skeleton suit," and which, she'd informed Sybilla, was the height of fashion for little boys.

"He looks very well, Lem, I'm happy to see," said Sybilla. "I asked Lord Linton to bring me out here today because I wanted to know how the two of you were getting on before I left London."

"Ye're going away, sir? Sorry I am ter 'ear that. Depend on it, little Joe and me, we'll think o' ye often, an' bless yer kindness."

"I'll keep Master Will informed about you, Wyatt, when he's back home in Durham," said Joshua, rising. "You're coming along well, Mrs. Simmons tells us."

"Oh, indeed I am, Major—Yer Lordship. My broken leg's mending apace, an' Miz Simmons, she brought me ter a doctor in Epsom, and 'e says I kin soon be fitted wi' a wooden leg. I'll be earnin' my keep wi' Farmer Simmons quicker'n a cat kin wash be'ind 'is ears."

"Splendid. Well, if you need anything, tell Mrs. Simmons. She'll relay the message to me." Nodding to the ex-dragoon, Joshua left the bedchamber with Sybilla. Downstairs, Mrs. Simmons waylaid them with a bountiful tea. She bridled with pleasure when Sybilla complimented her on little Joe's new clothes.

"'Twasn't no trouble, Master Will. Fact is, I like doin' fer a child again. My own son, 'e don't show no signs of givin' me a grandchild!"

Sybilla remarked to Joshua with a laugh, after they had gorged themselves on cream buns and scones and had made their escape from the cozy farm kitchen, "I'd lay you a tidy sum, if I had it, that you couldn't remove little Joe from Mrs. Simmons's care with a barge pole."

"Yes, she does seem to have a soft spot in her heart for children," Joshua agreed. "She had only the one child of her own, you know. When I was a lad, she was used to dissolve in tears when it was time for me to return home after a visit with my godfather. And that was after I'd made her life miserable with my pranks. Once I let the bull out of the pasture. Another time I pulled all the feathers out of her tom turkey's tail."

Circling the stables, they walked to the little brook behind the orchard, each of them carrying a fishing rod that Mrs. Simmons had unearthed from a dusty storage shed. Standing on the bank, Sybilla flicked her wrist, making a cast upstream. "I hope the Old Gaffer is still here," she said with a grin, watching the fly float down toward her on the surface of the water. "I have every intention of catching him today."

Joshua eyed her performance critically. After a moment he said in mock chagrin, "Is there no useful art your papa didn't teach you? You're a bang-up fiddler, a bruising rider, an expert shot, and now I discover you're a 'compleat angler,' too."

Sybilla laughed. "He certainly didn't teach me such ladylike and useful accomplishments as playing the pianoforte or sewing a fine seam or painting on glass. Mama and my governess would get so cross when they couldn't find me to take my lessons. I was always out on the estate somewhere with Papa."

Making another cast, she continued to chatter happily as she added to the motion of the fly by working it with short pulls from the rod-top. "I'm so glad we came out here today, Joshua. I'd have hated to leave London tomorrow without knowing how Lem Wyatt and little Joe were getting on."

"As I told Lem, I'll be happy to send you news of them in Durham. Which reminds me, don't forget to write down your uncle's direction before you leave so I'll know where to send my letter."

"Oh. Yes, of course. I'll do that." Though the sun was still shining brightly, it seemed to Sybilla that the day had turned somber in an instant. She'd awakened this morning with a firm resolve to enjoy her last day in London and not to think about what might happen afterward. Now Joshua's remark had made it impossible for her to ignore reality. After today she'd never hear another word about Lem and little Joe. After tomorrow she'd never see Joshua again.

A sudden pull on her line distracted her. Her mouth set in concentration, she gradually tightened the rod until she had fixed the hook. Slowly she reeled in the trout. "Joshua," she breathed in excitement. "He must go nine, ten pounds. Have I caught the Old Gaffer?"

Joshua gazed at the trout with a measuring eye. "I'm not personally acquainted with the Old Gaffer, worse luck," he said in a tone of mingled amusement and envy, "but I'm dashed if I don't think this might be the elusive old fellow.

You're downy as a hammer, Sybilla. When I think of all the times I tried to catch that dratted trout with no success whatever!" He shrugged philosophically. "Mrs. Simmons will bless you. He'll make a fine supper for her."

Sybilla took another long look at the trout as it lay flopping on the grass. With a sudden quick movement she removed the hook and gently released the fish back into the stream.

"Sybilla, what the devil—?"

"I wanted the fun of catching the Old Gaffer. I don't want him eaten. I hope he lives out his life without ever being caught again."

Joshua gave a shout of laughter. "Oh, Sybilla! What am I going to do with you?" He put his arm around her shoulders in an impulsive hug. She looked up at him, and their eyes locked together for a long moment. Then, drawing his breath sharply, Joshua dropped his arm, saying, "Well, if the Old Gaffer isn't to provide Mrs. Simmons's supper, we'd best catch her a few substitutes. Lay you a shilling I'm a better fisherman than you."

"Done!"

An hour later, as she and Joshua drove along the farm lane leading to the London road, Sybilla extended her hand. "Here's your shilling. You caught more trout than I did."

"Keep your blunt," Joshua said, grimacing. "I've no reason to be proud of myself. I caught exactly two fish. Hardly enough to crow about."

Grinning, Sybilla put the shilling back in her pocket. As they neared Tooting, a thought occurred to her. "Could I do a little shopping before we go home?"

Giving her a curious glance, Joshua said, "Certainly. What is it you want to buy?"

"Well, it's Mrs. Roper. She's been so kind to me. I'd like to buy her a little gift to show her my appreciation."

Joshua smiled. "That will please her, but you must remember that if she's been kind to you, it's because she likes you. We'll go shopping for a gift in Oxford Street. If you can't find what you want there, you won't find it anywhere in London."

Left to herself, Sybilla thought, as she and Joshua left the curricle to stroll up one side of Oxford Street and down the other, she could have spent a full day peering into the enticing windows of myriad shops. Joshua had been right. The shops here sold every conceivable item a customer could want. Lamps, fans, parasols, and silverware. Shoes, toys, jewelry, and linens. Her eyes lingered on a delicate fan of painted gauze. Mrs. Roper would probably never have the occasion to use such a thing, but Sybilla suspected the housekeeper would display it proudly to all her friends.

In the end Sybilla settled on an inexpensive bottle of lavender water at a perfumer's shop. Small as the purchase was, it depleted her tiny reserves. The only money she had was the handful of sovereigns she'd won from Joshua in their shooting match at Manton's Gallery.

"Don't be a ninnyhammer," Joshua had expostulated when she refused to buy the fan on the grounds it was too expensive. "I have plenty of blunt with me. If you think Mrs. Roper would like the fan, let me buy it for you."

Sybilla had shaken her head. Joshua had already done so much for her. Her conscience writhed at the thought of accepting anything more from him. Especially since she was planning to deceive him again tomorrow by remaining in London after he put her on the stagecoach.

She found her scruples weakening, however, when she stopped to look at a gown in the window of Madame LaTouche's dress shop. "Oh . . . how beautiful," she murmured, staring entranced at a dress of delicate white lace over a satin slip of deep blue. The tiny puff sleeves were of blue satin slashed with white lace, and the hem of the skirt was adorned with a drapery of white lace entwined with pearls and full-blown white roses.

"I think I'd die happy if I could wear a gown like that just once in my life," she said wistfully.

"That blue matches the color of your eyes," observed Joshua. "Cornflower blue. I've never met anyone with eyes like yours." He seized her arm and pulled her toward the door of the shop.

"Joshua, what on earth—?"

"I'm going to buy that gown for you."

Sybilla came to an abrupt stop, bracing herself against the

pressure of Joshua's hand. "What a bacon-brained notion to take into your cockloft. What would I do with a ball gown?"

"Wear it to a ball, what else? We'll go to the masked ball at the Argyll Rooms tonight."

Sybilla looked hard at Joshua. He was smiling, but it wasn't a joking kind of smile. "You're serious, aren't you? Oh, how I wish . . ." She shook her head. "It wouldn't fadge, and well you know it."

"I don't know it. Look, you've been wearing nothing but boys' clothes for weeks now. I'm sure you must be sick to death of coats and pantaloons and Hessians. Why shouldn't you become a girl again for one night, your last in London, and attend a ball, all decked out in full feather?"

The temptation was almost too much for Sybilla. She stole another look at the gown and hardened her resolve. "I can think of a number of reasons. That gown probably wouldn't fit me. If it did, how could I appear suddenly in your house in a ball gown when all your servants think I'm a boy? What's more, you don't even like to dance. You've said so often enough! But all that's beside the point. What matters is that you've promised to escort Lady Verity to the theater tonight."

Pulling Sybilla closer to the storefront, out of the way of the busy stream of shoppers, Joshua said, "I hate argumentative females. Let's dispose of your silly objections one by one. If the gown doesn't fit, we'll find another. We won't let my servants see you in the dress. I never said I don't like to dance. I just don't like crowded balls where I'm deprived of the opportunity to dance with the lady of my choice. As for Verity and the theater"—a wary note crept into his voice— "I'll send word I'm indisposed. She's seen so many plays, it surely won't be any great deprivation to miss this one. I have it. I'll suggest she ask Augustus Cranborn to escort her. He likes plays. After all, he writes them!"

"No. It wouldn't be right."

"My dear pea goose, will you answer me one question? Would you *like* to attend a ball tonight?"

"Well, of course, but—"

"That's all I wanted to know." Before the startled Sybilla quite realized what was happening, Joshua had turned her around, grasped her firmly by both shoulders, and marched her into Madame LaTouche's shop.

The proprietress, a rather overblown lady with artfully colored Titian curls, approached Joshua with a broad smile. The smile became somewhat uncertain when she focused on the slight boyish figure beside him. Sybilla suspected that Madame frequently did business with prosperous-looking young bucks like Joshua, who came into her shop to buy fripperies for their ladybirds. Few of her customers, however, would make their appearance with a callow stripling in tow. "How may I help you, sir?" she asked Joshua, her eyes sliding over Sybilla.

"I—" Joshua paused. A blank expression settled over his face.

Sybilla stifled a giggle, and the last bothersome shreds of her conscience ceased to trouble her. Poor Joshua! Lies were tricky and dangerous, she'd long since decided. Especially in the case of an imposture like hers, one had to be constantly alert to avoid stepping out of character. Joshua hadn't thought ahead to invent an excuse for his purchase of the white lace ball gown.

Well, she and Joshua had already told so many bouncers, singly and together, during these past few weeks that a few more wouldn't matter. She smiled at the proprietress. "My brother and I would like to buy a birthday gift for our sister."

"Ah." The faintly puzzled look vanished. "To be sure. Your sister is a young lady making her come-out, perhaps?"

"That's it," said Joshua with a grateful look at Sybilla.

"Then might I suggest a shawl? Or a reticule? A pelerine?"

"Well, as a matter of fact, ma'am," said Joshua, "we'd like to buy that dress in your window."

"The white lace with the blue satin petticoat? Oh, dear me, no, sir, begging your pardon. I created that gown for Lady Anne Crofton."

"What are you charging her?"

"Sir?"

"I'll double your fee. Triple it. Name your price. I want that gown."

Her conscience springing to life, Sybilla poked her elbow into Joshua's ribs. "Don't be an idiot," she muttered.

Madame's face was an interesting study in cupidity. "Lady Anne is one of my best customers," she protested halfheartedly. "Triple my price, did you say? But what am I thinking of? How tall is your sister? Is she slender, plump? Really, sir, I can't sell a gown to a customer, sight unseen. I must consider my reputation."

"Fetch the gown from the window," said Joshua curtly. Sybilla could hear the faint echoes of a thousand cavalry commands. She wouldn't have been surprised if Joshua had lifted his arm and yelled, "Charge!"

Obeying the voice of authority, Madame LaTouche removed the gown from the display window and brought it to Joshua. "But, sir, the fit—your sister wouldn't wish to wear a gown that didn't fit properly."

"Hold it up against Will. He and our sister are of a size. Take after our mother's family, you know."

Sybilla sent Joshua a speaking glance of admiration. He choked, trying to suppress a cackle of laughter.

"Well . . ." Madame measured the gown against Sybilla's slender frame. "*If* you were a young lady, I suppose this dress might suit you."

"We'll take it," said Joshua briskly. "How much?"

Madame named a sum that made Sybilla blench. Joshua took out his purse, counting out a wad of banknotes that caused Madame's eyes to glisten. Gazing at the purse, she said, "I've made a toque of white satin, with pearls and ostrich feathers, to match the costume."

"We'll take that, too," said Joshua.

As he and Sybilla were walking out the door of the shop, Madame called after them, "Indeed, I thank you, I'm sure, and I hope your sister will enjoy wearing the gown."

"Oh, I'll see to that!" Joshua exclaimed over his shoulder. Turning to Sybilla, his eyes dancing, he said, "You'll help, too, won't you, Will?" Before she could answer, his eye fastened on something behind her in the street. Abruptly he thrust the parcels containing gown and toque into her hands and raced away from her. Gazing after him, Sybilla watched him pursue a vaguely familiar figure who dived into a waiting hackney cab and was driven away before Joshua could catch up to the vehicle.

Ignoring the curious stares of passersby who had observed his wild chase, Joshua walked back to Sybilla. She studied his grim expression. "Was it—?"

He nodded. "The same man who was following us at the Peckham Fair." He hesitated. "I don't want you to be alarmed," he said in a low voice, "but I fancy I've seen the fellow several times in the past week." He hit his fist against his palm. "Damnation. I wish I knew the fellow's lay."

Sybilla felt chilled. Could Joshua have a secret enemy? What an absurd thought. Joshua, with his sunny good nature, his vast tolerance for other people's foolishness, had probably never made a serious enemy in his life. Instinctively she knew that this mysterious surveillance must be in some way connected with herself. But why? How? What purpose could it serve?

"If this fellow keeps following us, I'll go to the Runners," Joshua muttered as he took the reins from his tiger and climbed into the curricle. "They'll find out, soon enough, what he's up to."

Sybilla opened her mouth to speak and shut it again. The thought of going to the Bow Street Runners appalled her, but she certainly couldn't make her feelings known to Joshua.

Mrs. Roper received the gift of lavender water with a gratified smile, though she felt obliged to make a ritual protest. "Miss, you shouldn't have."

"I wish it were more. You've been so kind to me."

The housekeeper brushed a sudden tear from the corner of her eye. "It's been a pleasure having you here. The house will seem very empty when you're gone, that it will." She cleared her throat. "But that's neither here nor there. I don't wish to throw a damper, but I must tell you I cannot approve of His Lordship's scheme to take you to a masked ball. It's not an affair at which I'd choose to see a respectable young female. I don't rightly know what His Lordship can be thinking of."

"Oh, I know masked balls aren't quite the thing, and I'd feel so responsible if Joshua were to catch cold at it. . . ." Sybilla's voice grew wistful. "But, Mrs. Roper, I'm leaving tomorrow. Tonight may be the only opportunity I'll ever have to dance at a London ball."

Propriety versus romanticism waged a war in Mrs. Roper's soul, and the tender emotion won. "Bless you. What harm can it do, after all? Turn around, do. Let me fasten these little buttons at the back of your gown."

Sybilla gazed at her image in the cheval glass and gasped in surprise. The blue satin slip and tiny puffed sleeves of the gown exactly matched her eyes, making them glow with a blue radiance. More, the bodice was so low-cut and so clinging that it emphasized her femininity in a way that both shocked and delighted her. Feathery ringlets of hair on either temple escaped from beneath the roguish white satin toque. Taking another long look at herself, she murmured, "I look rather nice, don't I?"

"You're a beautiful girl. Have you never noticed that before? I'm sure His Lo—" Mrs. Roper broke off, clamping her lips tightly together. Her face suddenly looked troubled.

A knock sounded at the door. Mrs. Roper admitted Joshua, looking superbly handsome in his evening dress of black coat and breeches, silk stockings and pumps. He had a long garment of some sort draped over his arm, which he threw down on a chair as he advanced into the room. He paused, gazing at Sybilla in frank admiration. "By Jove, if you're not prime and bang up to the mark!" he exclaimed. "I *knew* that gown would become you." He walked over to her, handing her a small box covered with worn velvet. "It just occurred to me that you needed some jewelry to complete your costume. These belonged to my mother. If she were still here, I know she'd be delighted to have you wear them tonight."

Wonderingly, Sybilla opened the box. "These" comprised a necklace of sapphires and diamonds with matching bracelet and earrings. Beside her, Mrs. Roper sighed with reminiscent pleasure. "Oh, Master Joshua. I haven't seen this parure in donkey's years. I'd forgotten how lovely it was. Well I remember seeing your mother wear it when she went to parties at grand places like Carlton House. In those sapphires Her Ladyship looked like a princess."

Shutting the box, Sybilla handed it back to Joshua. "Thank you for your kind thought, but I can't possibly wear these. They're a family heirloom. If anything should happen to them while I was wearing them—"

"Nothing's going to happen to them," said Joshua calmly, opening the box. "I'll be with you, remember? I certainly have no intention of allowing thugs or footpads to lay a hand on my mother's sapphires! Turn around." As Sybilla faced the cheval glass, he draped the necklace around her neck and fastened the clasp. "There. *You* look like a princess. Now put on the bracelet and earrings."

Once she'd donned the full parure, Sybilla's qualms fell an easy victim to the seductive azure gleam of the Linton sapphires. She took one long look at herself in the cheval glass, and the battle was lost. Never in all her life had she looked so magnificent. What possible harm could there be in wearing the lovely things for one evening only?

"I have another little gift for you," he said, grinning.

"Oh, no, I can't accept anything more—" Sybilla broke into a chuckle as Joshua handed her a black velvet mask. Placing it over her eyes, she peered into the cheval glass. She looked mysterious, alluring, *older*. Nothing like provincial Sybilla Trent from the moors of Yorkshire.

Mrs. Roper sniffed. "I collect you've forgotten something quite important, Master Joshua. How do you propose to whisk Miss Sybilla out of the house without being seen by the servants? Quite a commotion it would cause, I daresay, if she suddenly appeared as a young lady."

"Dash it, woman, I didn't serve in the military all those years without paying attention to logistics," said Joshua loftily. He picked up the garment he'd thrown across a chair when he entered the room and draped it around Sybilla's shoulders. It was a voluminous hooded cape, worn and weather-stained, that trailed on the floor around Sybilla's feet. A nostalgic note crept into his voice as he said, "This cloak is an old friend. It saved me from perishing from wind and rain and cold in the Peninsula. It's a bit long, of course. You'll have to be careful you don't trip yourself up, Sybilla. But the cloak will certainly conceal every bit of your finery from curious eyes."

The hackney coach, a sad-looking castoff from some nobleman's carriage house, was waiting on the corner of Charlotte Street near the eastern end of Bedford Square. As soon as Joshua had helped her into the coach and closed the door, Sybilla succumbed to the laughter that had been threatening to engulf her for several minutes. When she was able to speak at last, she wiped her eyes, saying, "I think you're wasted in civilian life. What a masterly campaign you've waged to enable me to go to a ball. First, this cloak I'm wearing. It does cover me from head to toe, but, your servants might have thought it odd that I was wearing such a garment on a lovely July evening, so you had Mrs. Roper execute a feint. She distracted the attention of the footman in the front hall so that you and I could slip out the door without being seen. Then this hackney. I never in the world would have thought of that."

"Yes, I fancy that was a stroke of genius," said Joshua with a cheerful grin. "It's true, we might have gone to this ball in style in my own town carriage, but my coachman, after all, is one of my servants, too. Why run the risk of his recognizing you when we could outflank him by using a hired carriage?"

Sobering, Sybilla reached over to press his hand. "There can't be anybody like you in the whole world."

"Oh, the devil. I just want you to enjoy your last night in London."

He sounded embarrassed, and there was a kind of electrical tension in the air that made Sybilla vaguely uneasy. Gazing about her at the shabby interior of the coach, which had a distinct smell of mildewed hay, she forced a smile, saying, "You've gone beyond the call of duty by riding in this vehicle. Have you *ever* ridden in a hackney before?"

"Certainly. I was an impecunious lieutenant once, remember?" They both laughed, and they were comfortable with each other again.

The Argyll Rooms were situated on the northeast corner of Little Argyll Street. After he and Sybilla had descended from the hackney, Joshua had her remove his old campaign cloak, which he then tossed into a corner of the carriage. He slipped on his own mask and turned to the driver. Handing the man several pound notes, he said, "Wait for us, and I'll see you don't lose anything by it."

For country-bred Sybilla the brilliantly lit ballroom of the Argyll Rooms, with its fashionable decor and its impressive classical wall motifs, was a dazzling sight. The room seemed pleasantly full. A country dance was in progress as they entered. Gradually, as she looked around at the dancers and the spectators, she became aware that it was a mixed crowd. Everyone was masked, and many of the ladies and gentlemen were dressed, as she and Joshua were, in expensive, fashionable clothes. Judging by their clothing and deportment and scraps of overheard conversation, however, many of the people were from the lower ranks of society.

"Yes, you'll find all kinds at these masked balls," Joshua commented when, wide-eyed, Sybilla pointed out to him a lady in a bright red satin gown. The bodice of the gown was practically nonexistent, and the lady's partner was fondling her in a most ungenteel way. "The Argyll Rooms can be respectable, you know. The Philharmonic Society gives concerts here. Unfortunately, this is also the scene of the annual Cyprians' Ball." He added with a tinge of misgiving, "Probably I shouldn't have brought you here. Ladies of quality don't go to masked balls."

"But I'm not a lady of quality," she said saucily. "I'm a waif from the hinterlands, and I don't want to waste a minute of the fun. Shall we join that Scotch reel?"

For Sybilla the evening at the Argyll Rooms went by in an enchanted blur. If Joshua really disliked dancing, he gave no sign of it. He partnered her in every reel and country dance with the greatest of enthusiasm. Only once did they encounter any unpleasantness in the mixed crowd, when Joshua went off to fetch her a glass of arrack punch.

He came back to find her fending off the advances of a stout and inebriated young gentleman in an unfortunate cravat.

Joshua seemed to grow a foot taller on the instant. Impaling the young man with an icy gray gaze, he inquired, "How old are you, my man?"

"Er—I'm twenty-five."

"If you're interested in reaching the age of twenty-six, I'd advise you to apologize to the young lady."

"I'm sure as 'ow I never meant no 'arm, miss," said the man, keeping an uneasy eye on Joshua, who dismissed him with a nod. The man darted into the crowd and disappeared.

Turning to Sybilla, Joshua said, "I'm sorry. I didn't use good judgment bringing you here." But Sybilla wasn't listening. She was facing the orchestra dais, tapping one foot to the lively rhythm of a waltz. "My dear Miss Smith," he said with a slow grin, "I presume you know that respectable young females don't dance the waltz in public. You could blast your reputation if you accepted an invitation to waltz at Almack's."

She shot him a provocative glance from behind her mask. "But we don't happen to be at Almack's."

"Sybilla, you rogue, where did you learn to dance the waltz?"

"Oh, I was visiting a friend whose brother had just come back from a diplomatic posting in Vienna. He taught both of us the waltz. He warned us, though, that we must never, never attempt to do so in public. Joshua, do *you* know how to waltz?"

Chuckling, Joshua placed his arm lightly around Sybilla's waist. "By an odd coincidence, I'm an expert waltzer. Portuguese ladies are far less prudish than the hostesses at Almack's."

Afterward Sybilla couldn't really remember dancing with Joshua. It was more like floating, mesmerized, in a magic web of melody and movement and intense awareness of his masculine strength and grace. Time and again their eyes locked and his arm tightened around her waist, and still they didn't miss a beat. At the end of the evening, as they were leaving the Argyll Rooms, she said in a tone of discovery,

"The orchestra never played another reel or country dance after that first waltz."

"So they didn't."

At the quiver of amusement in his voice she exclaimed, "Joshua! Was that your doing?"

"Guilty as charged," he admitted cheerfully. "The orchestra leader couldn't resist a bribe."

Faithful to his trust, the hackney cab driver was waiting for them around the corner in Argyll Street. The driver's face wore an expression of perfect bliss a little later, when he drove away after leaving them off in Charlotte Street, near the entrance to Bedford Square.

Gazing after the departing hackney, Sybilla exclaimed, "You gave him twenty pounds! That's a small fortune to a man like that. I'm sure he'll never forget you."

"He deserved it. I'll never forget this evening."

Sybilla looked up at him. They had both taken off their masks in the carriage, and in the soft light of the full moon she could see his face clearly. It looked young and wistful and yearning. "Joshua, this has been the most wonderful night of my life. I can never thank you enough—"

Putting his hands on her shoulders, he said huskily, "You could kiss me. I can't think of a nicer thanks."

Slowly, inexorably, his arms drew her closer. She seemed to have no will of her own. She lifted her face, slipping her arms around his neck, and their lips met, gently clinging at first, growing hungry and more urgent. "God, Sybilla, you're so lovely," Joshua murmured against her mouth.

The sound of wheels broke the slumbering silence of the street and rescued Sybilla from the sweet drowning abyss into which she was falling. She looked over Joshua's shoulder to see a town carriage rolling past them down Charlotte Street.

Chapter 10

"My DEAR, you must take it."

"What?" Sybilla looked up from the small portmanteau into which she'd been packing the boys' wardrobe she'd accumulated during her stay at Linton House. She'd been standing in front of the portmanteau for several minutes, she now realized, without adding a single item to its contents or hearing a word Mrs. Roper was saying.

"I said, you must take your lovely gown," said the housekeeper. "How could you bear to leave it behind?"

"Oh—I don't think I'll have much need for it where I'm going."

"But—you'll be attending parties, surely, when you go home?" Mrs. Roper paused, looking stricken. "Is it your father? Are you afraid he'll keep you shut up like a prisoner if you refuse the match with that dreadful old man? You'd have no use for pretty clothes in that case, of course."

For a moment Sybilla's mind was blank. She'd almost forgotten she was supposed to have an unfeeling father who was forcing her into a loathsome marriage. A by now familiar wave of guilt swept over her. She'd lied to Mrs. Roper, who'd repaid her with kindness and consideration, and she was still lying to Joshua. And perhaps it was sheer illogic, but she knew she'd feel even guiltier if she took with her that exquisite dress. No, she'd leave that behind, as a form of self-punishment.

"Please don't worry about me, Mrs. Roper. I'm sure Papa will be so relieved to see me that he won't insist on marrying me off. Not to that old gentleman, anyway. But the dress—well, you see, we don't lead a very grand life in Durham. The dress really wouldn't be suitable."

Turning away from Mrs. Roper's puzzled gaze, she walked to the window, staring out over the square, blinking against the dry scratchiness behind her eyes. She hadn't slept well last night. For hours she'd tossed restlessly, remembering how it felt to be cradled in Joshua's arms, reliving the touch of his lips.

The kiss shouldn't have happened, she thought miserably. Joshua was happily engaged. He had no romantic interest in her. She must have done something to entice him, to lead him on. Gentlemen didn't need much enticing, or so she'd heard. Engaged or no, probably Joshua would have kissed any pretty girl in the moonlight after a night of dancing and arrack punch. It didn't mean anything. Joshua, too, had apparently realized immediately that the kiss had been a mistake. He'd looked guilty and confused when she broke away from his embrace.

"Is there anything else I can do for you, miss?"

"Oh, no, thank you. You've done so much for me already. Thank you for laundering all my linen and for the loan of the valise." Sybilla put her arms around the housekeeper and hugged her. "Thank you for everything."

"Oh, come now, there's no need to thank me. I was only doing what I'm paid to do," protested Mrs. Roper, but a pleased smile softened her severe, bony features. "I declare, the house won't be the same without you clattering in and out with Master Joshua, at all hours of the day and night."

Sybilla concentrated on fastening the straps of the portmanteau. "It will be better for Joshua when I'm gone. He'll have more time for his own friends then. I've been taking up far too much of his time for weeks now."

"Indeed, and I'm not so sure of that," retorted the housekeeper. "His Lordship will doubtless be spending more time with that Francis Merriweather, and I can't see *that* as an improvement. One-legged though he is, Captain Merriweather will find some mischief to inveigle Master Joshua into!"

Sybilla turned away to hide a smile. Mrs. Roper would never forgive or forget the redheaded cavalryman's transgression with King Joseph's silver chamber pot.

When the housekeeper left, Sybilla wandered down the stairs and out to the stables. After she'd said goodbye to Midnight, the horse Joshua had bought for her at Tattersall's, she'd be ready to leave Linton House. She was packed. Nothing remained to be done.

"That Midnight, e'll miss ye, Master Smith," remarked one of the grooms to her as she stood outside the loose box, stroking the horse's mane. "O' course, ye'll be seein' 'im again soon. 'Is Lordship, 'e says 'e'll be sendin' Midnight to yer home up north."

"Yes, His Lordship is very kind," Sybilla agreed. But as she walked into the house from the stables, the aching void in her heart seemed to grow wider. She'd never see Midnight again. Joshua wouldn't be able to send the horse to an imaginary address in Durham. Suddenly the thought of Joshua's anger and disappointment when he discovered how thoroughly she'd deceived him was too much to bear. She'd be far away by then. She wouldn't have to see it.

As she came into the hall, Joshua was entering the library, a bundle of newspapers under his arm. "Come in," he called. Seating himself in his favorite armchair, he motioned to the newspapers, saying, "The news from the Peninsula isn't very good this morning. The Second Division's had hard fighting at the Maya Pass. Hill's been forced to retire. Oh, well, I'm sure Wellington has the siege of San Sebastian in hand."

Perched on the edge of the desk, Sybilla said, smiling, "I know you'd feel easier in your mind about the campaign if you were there."

"Oh, certainly, if I were at San Sebastian, I could change the course of battles—and empires, too. I'm indispensable," Joshua retorted. His grin was unforced as he made fun of himself. Earlier, at breakfast, he'd seemed subdued, as if he, too, hadn't slept well. And he'd avoided looking at her directly. "Are you all packed?"

"Yes, all ready to go."

Putting his newspaper down, Joshua said, "See here, we've hours before it's time to take you to the General Post Office to catch the Edinburgh Mail north. Would you like to do something, go somewhere, this afternoon?"

"No, you've done quite enough for me," Sybilla was saying when a commotion erupted on the other side of the closed library door.

"What the deuce is that?" said Joshua irritably. "A fine household establishment I've got if a man can't have peace and quiet in his own library." He rose, walking toward the bellpull. The door burst open. A footman tried desperately to bar a furious Augustus Cranborn from entering the room.

Motioning to the footman to leave, Joshua stared down his nose at Augustus. "Come in, Cranborn. What can I do for you? I collect this must be an emergency, or you'd have had yourself properly announced."

Flicking a glance at Sybilla and then ignoring her, as if she were a piece of furniture, Augustus snapped, "Yes, you can do something, Lord Linton. You can read this." He thrust a note into Joshua's hand. The poet wasn't himself. His normally placid face was twisted into a scowl of rage, and he'd obviously dressed in haste. His neckcloth wasn't up to his usual standards of perfection.

Tearing open the note, Joshua scanned it quickly. His mouth hardened as he read. Looking up, he said, "Thank you, Cranborn. Is there anything else?"

Augustus's eyes flashed. "Is that all you have to say?"

"That's all I have to say to you. My correspondence, like the rest of my affairs, is none of your concern."

"None of my concern?" Augustus flared. "None of my concern, when you've betrayed the trust of an angelic creature who is so far above you that you're not fit to touch the hem of her garment? Lady Verity and I saw you last night, Linton. There you were in all your brass-faced impudence, fondling your lightskirt in public, practically in front of your own house! Fouling your own nest, as I told Lady Verity!"

Sybilla gasped. Neither of the men paid any attention to her. Clearly Augustus had failed to recognize her as the despised fancy-piece he'd seen in Joshua's arms the night before. Apprehensively she stared at Joshua. She'd seen him angry on several occasions. Never had she seen him as he was at this moment. His face was a mask of granite, and he spoke in a tone so cold that it would have frozen the marrow in Augustus's bones if the poet hadn't himself been so angry.

"May I ask," Joshua inquired with an icy courtesy, "how it was that you and Verity came to be in the vicinity of Bedford Square last evening?"

"It was quite by chance, I assure you," Augustus said shortly. "Lady Verity, needless to say, had no intention of spying on you. She'd asked me to escort her to the theater when you begged off by reason of being indisposed. *Indisposed*! Then, kind to a fault, as always, she was driving me to my rooms in Gower Street after the performance, since I don't keep a carriage of my own. You can imagine her shock, her *grief*, when she saw you embracing that prime article in the middle of the street. So exquisite are her sensibilities, however, that she would not allow me to leap out of the carriage and confront you. Instead, she asked me to bring you her note this morning."

"I see." The chill in Joshua's voice was several degrees colder. "My betrothed acquainted you, I take it, with the contents of her note?"

Augustus glared at him. "She did. She's broken off her engagement to you, and I must tell you I'm happy to learn she's seen the light at last. You're not fit to marry a pure soul like Lady Verity."

Joshua bowed. "Thank you for favoring me with your opinion. If you have nothing further to say, I'll bid you good day."

"Ah, no, you don't get rid of me that easily. I do have one more thing to say to you." Augustus removed one of his York Tan gloves—with some difficulty, for they were inordinately tight-fitting—and slapped it across Joshua's face. "Name your second, my lord."

After a moment of disbelieving shock, Joshua doubled up with laughter. "Oh, for God's sake, stop talking such fustian," he choked. "I'm not going to fight you. Have you ever so much as cocked a pistol or unsheathed a foil? Think of Lady Verity's reputation, for one thing. Think of mine! What would the ton think of me if I allowed a cloth-head like you to call me out?"

Augustus lost all control of himself. He rushed at Joshua, arms and fists flailing. Calmly warding off the ineffectual blows, Joshua finally wearied of the unequal contest. Cocking his fist, he disposed of Augustus with one short, sharp blow to the chin. He stood looking down at the unconscious poet for a moment, brushing back a lock of tawny hair that had fallen over his forehead. The disheveled hair was the only evidence that he had been in a fight. His breathing was quite normal. He pulled the bell cord. When a footman appeared, Joshua pointed to Augustus. "Mr. Cranborn is leaving. Pray help him to his carriage."

The wide-eyed servant stared wordlessly at the unconscious figure on the floor. Then, darting out of the room, he returned shortly with a second footman. Carefully they lifted Augustus and carried him out of the room. Only when the library door had closed behind them did Sybilla break her silence.

"Joshua, did Lady Verity really cry off from your engagement?"

"She did." Joshua's voice, like his face, was impassive, but Sybilla could sense the tightly coiled tension beneath his calm.

"It's my fault, all my fault," Sybilla burst out. "I shouldn't have come to stay in your house, I certainly shouldn't have allowed you to take me to that ball. Let me go to Lady Verity. I'll explain that you were treating me to one last outing in London. I'll tell her that the kiss didn't mean what she thought it meant, that I was simply expressing my gratitude to you for your many kindnesses."

Joshua made a slight, involuntary movement. His lips compressed, he said shortly, "You'd also be exposing your masquerade and risking the loss of your reputation. I won't let you do it."

Aghast, Sybilla exclaimed, "And I won't let *you* sacrifice your future happiness because of me! You *must* explain to Lady Verity what really happened and ask her to forgive you."

"I haven't done anything wrong, nor have you," said Joshua with a level look.

"But surely you must see that Lady Verity was justified in thinking the worst of us. What would *you* have thought if you'd come upon her embracing a strange man in the street?"

"Before I passed judgment, I'd have gone to her and asked for an explanation."

So that was it, thought Sybilla. Poor Joshua, he was devastated by what he considered Verity's lack of trust, and he was too stiff-necked to make the first move toward a reconciliation. Well, perhaps time would mend the breach, she mused, grasping at straws so that she'd feel less responsible for causing Joshua's broken engagement.

He broke into her thoughts by saying, "Well, this development changes our plans." He reached again for the bell. "Since I'm no longer engaged, there's nothing to keep me in London. I'll drive you all the way to Durham. I never did like the notion of your taking the Mail."

"No!"

"Oh, stop making a goose-cap of yourself," he said impatiently. "You can't look forward to spending two and a half days in a coach, stopping only for meals and to change the horses."

"Joshua, please think carefully," Sybilla pleaded. "If you go off like this, without making any attempt to contact Lady Verity, she'll think you don't care a fig for your broken engagement. It will be much harder to make it up with her."

Even as she spoke, Sybilla felt like a hypocrite. She wanted Joshua to reconcile with Verity, yes, but her principal reason for refusing his well-meant offer was entirely selfish. If he insisted on driving her to Durham, it would be virtually impossible for her to sneak away from him and lose herself in London as she'd planned. She put up her chin. "I thank you, but I don't wish you to drive me to Durham. I'd as lief go by the Mail."

Her remarks had no effect on Joshua's highhandedness. He simply ignored her. When a footman arrived to answer the bell, he said, "Tell the stables I want my traveling chaise at the door in a quarter of an hour. Four horses. One of the grooms will ride postilion and bring back the horses from the first stage." As the footman turned to leave, Joshua asked, "Mr. Cranborn has left?"

"Oh, yes, m'lord. 'E was jist wakin' up when Ben an' me puts 'im in the hackney. Looked a bit confused, like."

Nodding a dismissal to the footman, Joshua said to Sybilla, "The chaise will be more comfortable than the curricle for a long trip. Give me a few minutes to pack some clothes, and I'll be with you."

Actually, it was only a few minutes after the quarter hour when Joshua climbed into the chaise beside Sybilla. A groom let up the steps and closed the door, another groom released the wheelers' heads, and they were off.

"I had to fight a rear guard action with my valet before I could get away," Joshua observed with a smile that didn't quite reach his eyes. "He seemed to think I couldn't exist for six days without him. I wonder how he thought I survived the Peninsula, making do with only the services of a batman?"

Sybilla didn't return his smile. She felt bewildered and not a little resentful. Totally ignoring her protests, Joshua had whisked her through a hasty leave-taking with Mrs. Roper and bustled her out of the house and into the carriage before she quite realized what was happening. Reality was only now setting in. Joshua was about to drive her to an imaginary destination in Durham, and catastrophe loomed. Sybilla sat back against the squabs in a corner of the chaise and cudgeled her brains. She had to find a way to elude Joshua, and do it as soon as possible.

It proved even more difficult than she'd anticipated, as they took the Great North Road through Highgate and Finchley into Middlesex and on into Herts and the pleasant low hills of Huntingtonshire. On another occasion Sybilla would have enjoyed the luxury of traveling in Joshua's well-sprung chaise with the Linton crest on its doors, which commanded instant attention wherever they went. At all the posting houses, ostlers rushed to change their horses without a moment's delay. When they stopped for meals, bowing landlords ushered Joshua and his companion into their best private parlors. But during that long first day of the journey, Sybilla never found an opportunity to slip away.

At ten o'clock they stopped for the night at Stamford in Northhamptonshire, ten hours and ninety miles from London, on the edge of the fen country. In the dining parlor of the inn Joshua was cheerful and talkative—as he'd been all day, except on the subject of his broken engagement, which he refused to discuss. "You're not eating," he accused Sybilla as he carved another slice from an excellent capon. "It's not like you. You're the heartiest trencherman I've ever met."

"I'm not very hungry. It's been such a long day, and I'm tired. Would you mind if I went up to bed?"

She thought he looked a little disappointed to be deprived of her company, but he waved her off, saying, "Capital idea. You'll need your rest. We make an early start tomorrow. I'm going to sample some of our landlord's excellent port."

Joshua had greatly impressed the landlord by ordering a separate bedchamber prepared for his young friend, Master Smith. Stepping into her snug, well-appointed room, Sybilla put out her candle, but, except to take off her boots, she didn't undress. It was almost midnight. Sitting at the window, looking down into the inn yard, she waited impatiently to hear Joshua's footsteps in the corridor outside.

He came at last. She heard him enter the bedchamber next to hers, and she listened to the small sounds a man makes when preparing for bed. The splash of water in a washbowl. The thud of boots dropped on the floor. The gentle creaking of bedsprings. For another quarter of an hour she sat motionless. Then, carrying her boots in one hand, her portmanteau in the other, she tiptoed across the room. The door squeaked protestingly as she opened it.

She and Joshua had laughed together over the sound earlier when the inn servant had shown them to their rooms. "Sounds like a cat whose tail had been stepped on," Joshua had commented.

At the door Sybilla paused for a moment, listening intently. Nothing stirred in the quiet of the inn. Reassured, she began walking toward the staircase, her stockinged feet silent on the boards of the flooring.

"Going somewhere, Sybilla?" came a quiet voice behind her.

She whirled about. Joshua stood in the doorway of his bedchamber, holding a lighted candle. He, too, was completely dressed except for his boots.

"How did you—?"

"I was waiting for you to leave," Joshua replied coolly. "I knew I'd hear your squeaking door." He motioned toward his bedchamber. "Come in. We can't talk out here." He followed her into the room and closed the door. Setting down the candle on a low table next to his bed, he crossed his arms over his chest and gave her a long, measuring gaze. "Now, then, you exasperating female, I'd like to know why you absconded from your bedchamber in the small hours of the morning and what you proposed to do when you left the inn."

Recovered from the initial shock of being waylaid by Joshua, Sybilla stared back at him truculently. "What do you mean, you were waiting for me to leave?"

"What a gudgeon you must think me. You simply weren't yourself today. You scarcely spoke. You showed no interest in the passing scenery. You pecked at your food. Add to all that your obvious reluctance to accompany me, and it was quite easy to deduce that you were planning to run away."

"Well, why didn't you say something, then, instead of playing your cat and mouse game with me?" Sybilla demanded, glaring at him. "You sat downstairs, swilling down port, knowing full well I was up here waiting for you to go to bed."

Joshua threw up his hands. "*Touché.* I'm sorry, that wasn't very sporting of me. It was just—I thought we were better friends than that. I didn't like to think you'd sneak away from me without saying goodbye. And I daresay I resented your belief that you could bubble me so easily. Why *were* you running away?"

"You know why. Or you should. I don't want to return to Durham, to be forced into a marriage with my cousin Barnaby."

"Oh, the devil. Have you been fretting about that in secret? Why didn't you come to me about it?"

"Because I'm not your responsibility. Look, Joshua, I can fend for myself. Just let me go and forget about me."

"The way you were fending for yourself when I found you, unconscious on the pavement?" Joshua's face had turned grim. "No, my girl, I won't allow you to go off by yourself into the stews of London. Neither will I allow you to leave your family in ignorance of your welfare any longer. Good God, they may be thinking you're dead, or lost forever. No, I'm taking you home to Durham. If you wish me to do so, I'll speak to your uncle. Perhaps I can persuade him to change his mind about this marriage, if he's still set on it. He may not be, you know."

"No."

Joshua's eyes narrowed. He said suddenly, "I want your word of honor that you won't try to escape from me before we reach Durham."

Oozing defiance in every pore, Sybilla stared back at him without speaking.

"It's either that or share a room with me for the rest of tonight and again tomorrow night. I don't say I'll like sleeping in a chair braced in front of the door, but then I learned to do without comforts in the Peninsular campaigns."

Sybilla looked at Joshua's implacable face and admitted defeat. For the time being. Carefully phrasing her reply, she said, "I wouldn't dream of putting you to so much hardship. Very well. I promise not to run away from you before we reach Durham."

"Good." Joshua's expression softened, and he bent to brush a light kiss against her cheek. "I promise you won't regret it. Get to bed now. We have a long day tomorrow. I hope to get as far as York. Better than a hundred miles. Fourteen hours or so."

The next day was largely a repetition of the first. The hours and the miles flew by as Lincolnshire merged into the flat fertile lowlands of Nottinghamshire. In late afternoon they passed through Doncaster in the West Riding of Yorkshire, and Sybilla's heart began to feel at home—and almost immediately to feel a sense of loss. For, though she was close now to the beloved dales of the North Riding, she wouldn't be seeing them on this journey, nor on any other in the near future.

Reaching York after nine that evening, they settled into an inn on the Stonegate, not far from the Cathedral. After supper in one of the private parlors, Joshua said abruptly, "Are you sleepy? Shall we stroll in the garden?"

The warm summer night was redolent with the spicy scent of the heliotrope and the mingled fragrances of mignonette and rosemary and lavender. Walking with Joshua in the little garden, Sybilla drew a quick breath as she caught sight of the Minster, exquisitely outlined against the sky in the brilliant moonlight.

Breaking stride, Joshua put his hand on her shoulder and turned her until she was facing him on the path. "You hardly spoke to me again today. I hate to see you so unhappy. I hate to be the ogre forcing you to do something you don't want to do. The chances are, you know, that your uncle will be so relieved to see you that he'll give in to you about this marriage. Whether he does or not, though, it's infinitely better to face your problems than to run away from them."

The tenderness in Joshua's voice caused a lump to form in Sybilla's throat. She was putting him to so much trouble. She'd cost him so much already. In spite of all that, the temptation to throw herself into his strong capable arms, admit her identity and the problems that confronted her and ask for his help, was almost irresistible. She forced herself to say sharply, "Why don't you practice what you preach? You're running away from your problems, too. You know you should have stayed in London and patched up your quarrel with Lady Verity. You love each other, and yet both of you are letting stubborn pride keep you apart."

Joshua stepped back from her. His voice was aloof as he said, "My concerns aren't your affair."

"Precisely. Nor mine yours. Shall we retire? We have another long day tomorrow."

Sybilla experienced another near sleepless night. At breakfast Joshua was unusually silent. Perhaps he hadn't slept well, either. He remained uncommunicative as they left York shortly before eight o'clock that morning for the last lap of their journey north.

At Northallerton they stopped for lunch. Sybilla was in an agony of apprehension to get away from the place. This market town in the North Riding was too close to her native dales for comfort. She hadn't often visited here. Her face wouldn't be familiar to any of the inhabitants, but there was certainly a slim chance that she might encounter an acquaintance from the vicinity of her home at Castle Wycombe.

It was probably because she was so alert to the possibility of meeting someone who might recognize her that she noticed the man in the brown suit. As she and Joshua came out of the inn after lunch and walked to their carriage, she glanced around her. A flash of movement caught the corner of her eye. She turned to spy a stocky man in a serviceable suit with a hat pulled squarely over his eyes. He climbed hurriedly into a hired post chaise and was driven away.

Clutching at Joshua's arm, she muttered, "That man who was following us in London—he just drove away in a post chaise."

Flashing her a startled look, Joshua ran to the gate of the innyard. He came back a moment later, shaking his head. "It couldn't have been our man. That chaise was going south, in the direction of Thormanby."

Sybilla relaxed, grateful that in addition to all her other troubles, she needn't concern herself with a mysterious pursuer. Gradually, however, as the chaise traveled northward, her nerves began to tighten again. They had now entered the undulating plains of the county of Durham. In midafternoon they passed through Darlington. Three hours later they crossed an ancient bridge over the River Wear, lined with quaint houses. A short drive uphill brought them to a triangular marketplace. Off to their left, on a peninsula formed by a great loop of the river, a towering cathedral and an impressive castle rose from the wooded banks of the Wear.

"Well, Sybilla, as I don't need to tell you, this is Durham," said Joshua quietly. "You're home. Where shall I tell the postilions to go?"

Sybilla huddled against the side of the carriage, staring out unseeingly at the old church that dominated the square. It wouldn't be possible now to find an opportunity to evade Joshua's vigilance and slip away from him. She'd promised not to attempt to escape before they reached Durham. Unfortunately, she hadn't been familiar with the distances in this part of the country. She'd assumed that, as usual, they would arrive in the city so late that Joshua would elect to take a room for the night and drive her to her fictitious home in the morning. Before morning came she would have been gone.

"Well, Sybilla? Do you and your uncle live in the city or outside it?"

She drew a deep, hopeless breath. "Neither. I've been lying to you. I don't live in Durham. This is the first time I've ever set foot in the place."

Chapter 11

JOSHUA'S FACE slowly turned to stone. "So you don't live in Durham. Do you live anywhere near here?"

Sybilla shook her head. Her throat was too constricted for her to speak.

"Are you going to tell me where your home is?"

Again she shook her head.

Joshua's hand clenched. For a split second Sybilla wondered if sunny-tempered, tolerant Joshua was going to hit her. Inhaling a sharp breath, he opened the door of the chaise and called out to the postilion, "We'll stay the night in Durham. We passed a respectable-looking inn just after we crossed the bridge. Go there."

Joshua didn't address another word to Sybilla as they drove to the Crown and Sceptre, nor could she muster up the courage to talk to him after a long searching look at his unreadable face. He remained silent during their supper in a private dining room of the inn. As he ate a hearty meal accompanied by a bottle of claret, however, he gradually began to appear not so much angry as deeply abstracted. Wondering what he was thinking about, Sybilla was able to eat very little. She sat in ever-growing misery, stealing apprehensive glances at Joshua whenever she thought he wasn't looking at her.

After the servants had cleared the table, Joshua ordered a

bottle of port. When it arrived, he poured himself a glass and leaned back in his chair, one hand extended on the table with his fingers around the stem of the wineglass. His cool, considering gaze unnerved Sybilla. It was most un-Joshua-like.

"Did you enjoy pitching me that gammon, Sybilla?"

"I—"

"You bubbled me royally. You sent me off on a wild-goose chase the length of England, and never once in those two hundred and fifty miles did it occur to me that it was a damned hum."

"Joshua, I'm so sorry—"

"Sorry enough to tell me where you live so I can take you home?" At Sybilla's quick shake of her head he said, "I thought not." He sipped at his port, gazing at her over the rim of his glass. "Well, since you won't help me to extricate you from your difficulties, I've come up with my own solution: We'll get married. Unfortunately, since you're a minor and I can't obtain the consent of your parent or guardian, we can't get married in England. There's nothing for it but another long day's journey. Tomorrow we go to Scotland."

Sitting bolt upright in her chair, Sybilla made an instinctive protest. "No! I won't let you do it. You know very well you haven't the slightest desire to marry me."

"Actually, I haven't the faintest desire to marry anyone," he replied acidly. "My recent experience with females has left me with a jaundiced opinion of the fair sex! Since you won't allow me to restore you to your family, however, marriage is the only answer. As Lady Linton, you'll be safe and well cared for until you come to your senses. I'm not suggesting a permanent arrangement, naturally. I doubt either of us would survive it! After the marriage has served its purpose, you can divorce me or apply for an annulment, whichever you choose."

Temptation wound its enticing coils around Sybilla's heart. If she married Joshua, she'd have breathing space. She'd have time to plan her next move. She'd have time, possibly, to discover whether the menace that had sent her fleeing from Yorkshire was real or imagined. And she could

continue to enjoy Joshua's warm and vital companionship
for a little longer. Was she being monstrously selfish even
to consider such a marriage? As he'd said, it wouldn't be a
permanent arrangement. She'd be disrupting his life for
only a short period of time. . . .

Revulsion quickly set in. What kind of a poor, weak
creature was she to think seriously of taking further advantage of Joshua's generosity? Rising, she said, "No. It's
out of the question. What's more, I can't accept any more
help from you. Tomorrow morning we part company. I'm
taking the first stagecoach south to London. You can't stop
me."

In one fluid motion he got up from his chair, planted
himself squarely in front of her, and seized her arm. His
gray eyes were cool and confident. "Can't I? You underrate
me, my girl. Try to get away from me, and I'll follow you
to the ends of the kingdom."

He'd do it, too, Sybilla thought. She was sure of that.
She was learning that beneath his lazy charm Lord Linton
had a will of iron. "Why are you being so stubborn? Think
of Lady Verity—"

"Because I'd never have another moment's peace of
mind, knowing you were adrift somewhere in the city," he
interrupted. "And I *am* thinking of Verity. She's jilted me,
which means that in another few weeks I'll be in Dun
Territory. If I'm not married by my thirtieth birthday, I lose
my Uncle Lucius's fortune. I'm calling in your vowels,
Sybilla. If I've ever done anything for you, you can return
the favor by marrying me and keeping me out of the River
Tick."

Afterward, Sybilla could never quite decide whether it
was Joshua's persuasiveness or her own unruly desires that
made her accept his proposal. "Well . . . I wouldn't care
to see you under the hatches."

"Now you're being sensible." Joshua put his arm around
her and squeezed her shoulders briefly. "By this time
tomorrow night you'll be Lady Linton."

Sybilla sat by the window of her bedchamber, watching
pedestrians and carriages come and go across the ancient

bridge over the River Wear. The sun was streaming into the room, but her hands felt cold and clammy. At intervals during the night and into the morning hours, she'd become increasingly dubious about her promise to marry Joshua. In the short run, yes, the marriage would benefit both of them. She would have a safe refuge until she could put some order into her life, and he would achieve financial security. But what about Joshua's love for Lady Verity, which she was convinced was only dormant beneath his hurt and resentment? He'd realize eventually he'd made a mistake, but would Verity ever forgive or understand? Would she care to marry a divorced man? Would it, indeed, be as simple and easy as Joshua had indicated to obtain a divorce or annulment?

Her head had begun to ache fiercely by the time Joshua knocked at her bedchamber door. He came into the room laden with parcels and looking distinctly harassed. It had dawned on him and Sybilla over breakfast that it would be exceedingly awkward to ask a clergyman or anyone else to marry them while she was dressed in boys' clothing. It would be nearly as awkward for Sybilla, disguised as a boy, to walk into a modiste's shop and order a lady's wardrobe. So, unwillingly, Joshua had agreed to do the shopping.

"There," he growled, as he tossed the parcels on the bed. "I hope they fit. If they don't, pray keep your opinions to yourself. Or go complain to Madame Romaine. *I* will never again set foot in a dress shop as long as I live!"

Forgetting her own problems momentarily, Sybilla looked at Joshua's scowling face and began to laugh. "Was it so very bad? What happened?"

He glared at her. "Well, first off that damned Frenchwoman assumed I was buying clothes for my ladybird. Probably she thought I'd just plucked someone out of the gutter because I told Madame I needed *everything*. Dresses, a hat, a pelisse, shoes. As it turned out, she had a number of dresses made up. Some hadn't yet been delivered to the customers who'd ordered them, others had been returned. None of them would have fit you. They were all made for dwarfs or for very stout ladies. So then I observed that

Madame was about your size and I offered to buy *her* clothes. And there they are. I wish you joy of them."

Still laughing as Joshua left the room, Sybilla turned her attention to Madame Romaine's castoffs. The two dresses of figured muslin fit tolerably well, although they were somewhat too short and a little loose at the waist. But the pelisse of pale green kerseymere, lined with white sarcenet, and the matching French bonnet, trimmed with a nosegay of flowers and an ostrich plume, were very wearable. The soft kid slippers were slightly large but fit well enough when she wadded a bit of paper in either toe. Madame Romaine had also included in her packet several pieces of underwear—petticoats, drawers, and a set of linen stays with front buttoning.

She quickly put on the undergarments and one of the muslin dresses, and checked her appearance in the mirror. Yes, the dress would pass muster. She brushed her hair, reflecting how convenient it was that her short, curly coiffure appeared so suitable with either male or female garments.

Half an hour later, having put on the kerseymere pelisse and the French bonnet, Sybilla opened her door slightly and peered cautiously into the corridor. Seeing none of the inn servants—who might have thought it odd to see a fashionable young lady emerging from a stripling's room—she scurried out of the bedchamber with her portmanteau and down the stairs to the front door and the waiting chaise. With the change of postilions, she thought, no one would be the wiser that Joshua had arrived at the inn with a male companion and had departed with a young lady.

After the postilion had guided the chaise out of the inn yard and headed it north for the border, Joshua gave Sybilla an appraising look. "Very nice," he said. "I think I like you better as a girl."

"You have good taste," Sybilla replied with a grin. "One would think you had lots of practice buying ladies' clothes."

"Saucy chit. I never could abide a brazen female. I've half a mind not to marry you after all."

The resumption of their familiar give-and-take bantering should have made Sybilla feel more at ease, but it had the opposite effect. Suddenly renewed waves of guilt and uncertainty swept over her. "We shouldn't be doing this," she said in a rush. "Please. Let's go back to London. Perhaps my godmother has returned from Ireland—I can go live with her, and you won't have to worry about me any longer. Perhaps there's a message waiting for you from Lady Verity, telling you she's changed her mind. Perhaps—"

"Perhaps you'd like me to put a gag over your mouth so I won't have to listen to your falderal," Joshua cut in rudely. She laughed in spite of herself, and Joshua brushed his finger lightly against her cheek, saying, "That's better. My dear pea goose, we've begun our advance, and there's no turning back in this campaign. You've pledged me your troth, and I'm not about to let you cry off."

He quickly changed the subject, pointing out the sights of the countryside, including the remains of a medieval priory to the north of the town. His cheerful chatter gradually caused Sybilla to relax. Soon they were back to their old impudent sparring. Her improved spirits lasted until they reached Morpeth, north of New Castle, where they stopped for a late lunch.

If the food at the King's Arms hadn't been so abominable, they might not have encountered the man in the brown suit again. Stringy roast beef and tasteless vegetables, however, drove them from their table in the private dining parlor only minutes after they sat down to eat. The man in the brown suit, undoubtedly confident he had time to spare before his prey reappeared, was still sitting in the coffee room over a pint and a cold platter.

Glancing idly into the coffee room as she and Joshua passed, Sybilla stiffened and stopped in her tracks.

"What is it?" Joshua asked. He followed her gaze, erupting into sudden movement at the very moment that the man in the brown suit looked up from his beer. At the sight of Joshua coming toward him, the man pushed back his chair and rose so hastily that the chair crashed over on its back to the floor.

Ignoring the startled glances of the other occupants of the coffee room, Joshua strode over to the man in the brown suit, grasping him by his cravat. "I'll give you five seconds to start explaining why you've been following me!" Joshua exclaimed between clenched teeth. "After that you may find it difficult to breathe."

" 'Ere, now, take yer dabblers off'n me," protested the man. He looked around him, appealing to his fellow diners. "Ye ain't goin' ter let this young gentry mort do 'arm ter a peaceable bob-cull like meself, are ye?" His voice broke off as Joshua's fingers tightened the knot of his cravat.

"Your five seconds are up," said Joshua. "Nod your head if you've decided to answer my questions."

Clutching at his throat, the man gazed about him desperately, finding no support from the other occupants of the room, who carefully turned their eyes away from him. Sybilla thought their reluctance to come to the man's aid was quite understandable. Joshua looked positively awesome in his wrath. Beginning to turn a dull blue, his victim gave a frantic nod. Joshua loosened his grip. "Well? Start talking."

"Not 'ere, m'lord," the man gasped. "I'll speak ter ye in private."

Transferring his hold from the man's cravat to his arm, Joshua said curtly, "Very well. Come with me and the lady."

In the parlor, where the remains of his and Sybilla's miserable lunch still lay on the dining table, Joshua closed the door behind them and stood with his back to it. "I collect this is private enough, my man. Now you'll tell me why you've been following me. First off, what's your name?"

"Well, then, it's Sebastian Scunthorpe," came the reluctant answer. "And I ain't done nuffing wrong, nor yet illegal."

Joshua raised an eyebrow. "Nothing wrong? Nothing illegal? When you've been skulking after me these past two weeks—" He paused, gazing at the man with narrowed eyes. "You're a Robin Redbreast," he said suddenly. "You're not wearing that famous red waistcoat, but I'd venture a more than modest bet that you're a Bow Street Runner."

Scunthorpe appeared torn between pride and chagrin. "Ye've a keen pair o' winkers, m'lord," he said after a moment. "Yes, I be a Runner. Took off my weskit, I did, or ye might 'ave rumbled my lay long since."

Joshua stared at Scunthorpe appraisingly. At last he said, "I collect you're not pursuing us in your capacity as thief-taker. What *is* Bow Street's interest in me?"

Hesitating, opening and closing his mouth several times, Scunthorpe said finally, "I was 'ired by a private party ter follow ye, m'lord. More'n that I can't say."

Joshua took a menacing step toward him. "I can make you talk, you know."

It seemed to Sybilla that the Runner grew visibly in stature and dignity. "Nay, m'lord," he said quietly. "Oh, I 'ear ye're a proper man wi' yer fives, an' I 'ave no doubts ye could mill me down, but ye'll not make me breach the confidence o' my client."

Sybilla held her breath. She would have staked her life and everything she owned that Joshua was no brutal bully. On the other hand, she had never seen him so angry. His eyes were blazing with fury. Gradually he regained control of himself. He opened the door. "Get out. And keep out of my way." He paused, glancing from Sybilla to the Runner. "Scunthorpe, if the thought has passed your mind that there's any connection between this lady and the lad who's been staying at my house, you'll keep your suspicions strictly to yourself, or you'll wish you'd never been born!"

The Runner touched a finger to his hat. "Beggin' yer pardon, m'lord, I b'lieve I knows when ter keep my mouth buttoned. Good day, sir, ma'am."

Staring after the man with drawn brows, Joshua muttered, "There's no rhyme or reason to this. It's—it's insane. Why the deuce would anyone order a Robin Redbreast to follow me?" Squaring his shoulders under the many-caped greatcoat, he took her arm, saying, "Well, there's no help for it now. First things first. We'll have to hurry if we expect to get across the border tonight."

As she walked with Joshua out of the inn, Sybilla felt her

heart pounding so hard that she wondered why he couldn't hear its agitated beat. After learning the Runner's identity, she'd immediately jumped to the conclusion that he was after *her*. But how was that possible? No one could have discovered she was living in Joshua's house, disguised as a boy. In all of London only Mrs. Roper and Joshua knew her identity and whereabouts. But if she wasn't the object of the Runner's pursuit, it must be Joshua. And try as she would, she could think of no reason why anyone would want to follow him.

As they entered the courtyard of the inn, the Bow Street Runner was standing in plain view beside his hired chaise. He was probably feeling relieved, Sybilla reflected, that he no longer had to hide his presence. As soon as Joshua handed her into the carriage, Scunthorpe, too, stepped into his chaise, which then kept pace with them throughout the day.

For Sybilla the long journey into Scotland dragged on interminably. Plagued by uneasiness over the Runner's pursuit and a strong sense of guilt that she was taking advantage of Joshua, she remained largely silent, lost in her thoughts, speaking only when spoken to. Joshua didn't appear to notice. All his attention was focused on the Bow Street Runner. His inability to prevent Scunthorpe from following them kept him in a state of simmering resentment. At each posting stop the sight of the stolid, impassive-faced Runner sent Joshua into a fresh paroxysm of rage, even though Scunthorpe said or did nothing overt. He merely watched their every move.

"I promise you this, Sybilla," Joshua said at one point, "the first chance I get when we return to London, I'm going to pay a visit to the chief magistrate at Bow Street. I'll find out soon enough who's behind this persecution."

It was ten o'clock that night when they reached the River Tweed, marking the border between England and Scotland. On the north side of the river, spanned here by a graceful five-arched bridge, lay the town of Coldstream, almost as famous a Mecca for eloping lovers as Gretna Green to the west. It had begun drizzling earlier in the evening. Now the drizzle had turned into a downpour.

The keeper of the bridge emerged reluctantly from the tollhouse, his cloak streaming with rain in the uncertain light of his upraised lantern. "The nicht, 'tis not fit fer man nor beastie," he grumbled loudly to the postilion, as if to reproach the man for disturbing him in such inclement weather.

Joshua opened the door of the chaise and beckoned to the tollkeeper. Peering inside the carriage, the man's sour expression changed into a knowing grin. "Ye needna' tell me why ye're here, sir. Ye wish tae marry the lassie. Weel, then, step intae the tollhouse. Half a guinea—and anything else ye care tae gi'e me—and a minute o' yer time, and the deed's done."

Joshua shot him an irritated look. "I don't propose to be married on a bridge in the middle of a thunderstorm. What's the name of a good inn?"

The tollkeeper's face grew sullen as the vision of a fat fee and tip vanished. "That'll be the White Hart i' the High Street," he muttered. His expression brightened when Joshua threw him a coin.

The pelting rain had turned into a deluge by the time the chaise drew up in front of the White Hart, a comfortable-looking establishment whose windows streamed with a welcoming light. During her brief dash to the door of the inn, the rain penetrated Sybilla's light pelisse and turned her bonnet into a sodden mess. She felt a throb of sympathy for the shivering postilion, who had endured hours of battering from wind and rain.

Not misled by the state of Sybilla's bonnet, the smiling landlord immediately recognized the arriving pair as members of the Quality and begged to know how he could assist them.

"You can start by throwing that fellow out of your establishment," declared Joshua. He pointed to the bedraggled figure of Sebastian Scunthorpe, who had just come into the foyer, dripping pools of water from hat and greatcoat.

"But, sir ye canna ask me tae turn away a customer, and on sich a nicht, forbye," protested the landlord.

"You won't lose anything by it. I'll engage all your vacant rooms. Make your choice between us, landlord. I won't stay the night in the same hostelry with the fellow."

Scunthorpe gazed at Joshua reproachfully. "M'lord, I wouldn't 'ave thought ye'd be so 'ard-'earted, I wouldn't, indeed. I've already sent my driver and carriage ter the stables. Ye wouldn't force me out on foot inter sich weather, would ye? It's rainin' cats an' dogs out there. It's begun ter *hail*! Lightnin' could strike!"

"I fancy you'll survive the experience. You've a very thick skin." Joshua raised an eyebrow at the proprietor of the inn. "Well?"

Scunthorpe's mention of Joshua's title had worked its magic. The innkeeper bowed low, saying, "Happy tae obleege, sir—my lord." He turned to the Runner. "I'm verra sorry, sir, but I canna help ye. Ye maun see how 'tis."

"Stow yer whids, mate," sniffed Scunthorpe. "I ain't dicked in the nob. I know there's no contest between me an' a swell like Lord Linton." He opened the door and plodded back into the storm. Sybilla actually felt a pang of pity for him.

"Noo, then, my lord, please tae come wi' me. I'll take ye tae yer bedchamber," began the landlord.

"Hold on a moment," said Joshua. "The lady and I wish to be married immediately."

The landlord beamed. "Ach, nothing could be simpler. If ye'll juist step intae the parlor there—"

"I wish to be married by a clergyman," Joshua interrupted him.

"But, sir, 'tis quite unnecessary. In Scotland, do ye ken, ye need only declare yer intent tae wed in front o' witnesses, and I should be happy tae be yer witness—"

"Thank you, I prefer that a clergyman officiate. Pray fetch the nearest parson."

"But, my lord, it's sae late, and there's the weather—" The innkeeper ceased his protests when he saw the five-pound note in Joshua's fingers. "I'll send fer the Reverend Cameron. I dinna ken if he'll come at this hour o' the nicht . . ."

Waiting with Joshua in a private parlor of the inn, her nerves still tight with tension, Sybilla asked, "Why did you insist on a clergyman? The ceremony with the landlord would have been perfectly legal."

Joshua was taking off his caped greatcoat, which had received a thorough drenching. Giving it a hearty shake that sent droplets of water flying, he glanced up, saying with a frown, "Because I don't want a hint of anything havey-cavey about this marriage. I should think that would be self-evident." His expression softened. He walked over to her, reaching out to remove her bonnet. "You look soaked through. Take off that pelisse. Even your dress is damp," he added, running his fingers along her sleeves. His touch was like a mild charge of electricity. Suddenly every nerve end in her body felt exposed. What she was feeling, he seemed to feel, too. He took a hasty step away from her. "You'll have to change clothes as soon as possible, or you'll catch your death," he said, summoning up a rather strained smile. "You owe something to your brand-new husband, you know. You wouldn't want to leave me a sorrowing widower after four-and-twenty hours of marriage, would you?"

His nonsensical remark dissolved the hard knot in Sybilla's stomach. She was able to talk quite naturally to Joshua until, ten minutes later, a severe-looking figure in deepest clerical black arrived in the private parlor. His clothes were drenched, and he wore a decidedly sour expression. Sybilla suspected that only a summons by a person he believed to be a peer of the realm would have pried the clergyman from his comfortable bed on such a miserable night.

He quickly confirmed her impression. Gazing at Joshua down the length of his nose, the clergyman said in a hostile voice, "It's verra late. One trusts this unseemly haste is truly necessary, my lord—?"

"Linton. Viscount Linton," Joshua replied, drawing himself up with a glacial dignity. Very Lord-of-the-Manorish, Sybilla thought. She marveled anew at the ease with which he could shrug off his usual amiability to confront impudence. "I beg to inform you, sir, that there is nothing either hasty or unseemly about my marriage plans."

The clergyman gulped. "Indeed, my lord. Shall we begin?"

During the brief ceremony, Sybilla tried to overcome her feelings of unreality. At intervals during her tomboyish girlhood, she'd dreamed of a romantic wedding, imagining herself at the altar with a handsome bridegroom who would make her happy forever after. And here she was, marrying a handsome and charming and lovable man whose prime ambition was to rid himself of his new wife at the earliest possible opportunity.

The Reverend Cameron departed, his dour expression failing to conceal his pleasure in the several banknotes that Joshua had slipped into his hand. The hovering landlord came up to extend his congratulations. "Weel, noo, my lord, my lady, I've roused Cook. Wha' do ye say tae a nice wedding supper?"

"Capital. I could eat my weight in hyenas," said Joshua. He paused to finger the damp sleeve of his tailcoat. "Lady Linton and I have been standing about in our wet clothes quite long enough," he told the landlord. "Send the meal up to our bedchamber when it's ready. Come along, Sybilla."

As a servant girl led her and Joshua up the stairs, the palms of Sybilla's hands began to feel clammy. "Our" bedchamber? Surely she hadn't heard right? She had. She gazed around the large, pleasant room with its high tester bed and a cheerful fire blazing in the fireplace. As soon as the servant had left, she turned to Joshua, trying to hide her panic. "You did ask for two bedchambers? I believe the landlord has a number of vacant rooms—"

"Now, please don't be missish, Sybilla," Joshua begged. "We're newly married. What would the landlord think if I asked for two bedchambers? He'd think it was a rum go, that's what he'd think. You'll take the bed, and I'll sleep in that chair over there, and we'll be all right and tight."

He tugged off his limp cravat and shrugged out of his damp coat and waistcoat, which he hung in the wardrobe. "That's better," he said, shaking out the sleeves of his shirt and extending his hands to the fire. Over his shoulder he said, "Get out of those wet clothes, Sybilla." She caught the hint of laughter in his voice. "Don't worry. I intend to be a perfect gentleman. I'll keep my back turned."

Her fingers were trembling with nervousness as she knelt to open the small portmanteau that a servant had brought up earlier. "Oh, no!" she exclaimed. Either she hadn't fastened the case properly, or the catch was defective, it didn't matter which, and the driving rain had seeped in to soak the contents of the portmanteau.

"What is it?" Joshua asked without turning his head.

Sighing, she explained what had happened while she lifted out a dress and several articles of underclothing and festooned them on the furniture. "They'll dry in a few hours," she said, coming to warm herself at the fireplace. "And the maidservant said she'd hang my bonnet and pelisse beside the kitchen fire tonight. They should be dry by morning."

"What are you going to wear in the meantime?" Joshua said sharply. "You're shivering so hard your teeth are chattering." He dived into his own portmanteau. "Here." He handed her one of his shirts and a silk dressing gown.

"I can't—"

"You can and you will. I don't want a dead body on my hands."

Sybilla didn't argue. This was Major Waring of the 4th Dragoons speaking, not the charming and amiable Lord Linton. While Joshua turned his back, she quickly peeled off her damp gown and undergarments and pulled the linen shirt over her head. It came to her knees and was much too large in every respect. She folded back the sleeves and slipped her arms into the dressing gown, which trailed on the floor. Pulling the garment around her, she tied the sash, and, holding up the skirts to avoid tripping, she joined him at the fireplace. "I must look a regular guy," she murmured.

Joshua turned to face her, putting a finger beneath her chin. His lips curved in a tender little smile. "Why, you're blushing. There's no need for you to feel embarrassed. You're much more modestly clothed than you were in that fetching blue gown you wore to the ball at the Argyll Rooms."

Almost absently his fingers brushed her cheek, glided lingeringly along her throat, and buried themselves in her hair. "God, but you were beautiful that night," he muttered. "You're so beautiful now. Your skin is like the softest velvet, your hair is like silk. And your eyes—I've never seen such eyes. I'm drowning in them. . . ."

His hands cupped her face and he slowly bent his head, claiming her mouth in a kiss that sent a cascading flood of sensual awareness coursing through her body. An inner voice breathed a faint warning and fell silent as she returned Joshua's kiss with eager lips. He shuddered, pulling her close to him, moving his mouth rapaciously from side to side until he had forced her lips apart so that his tongue could taste the honeyed delights within.

Then his fingers were fumbling at the sash of her dressing gown. In one fluid movement he pushed the garment off her shoulders. It fell in a silken pool to the floor. He pulled her against his body in a sudden fierce embrace and sought her mouth again, and now, through the double thickness of fine linen, she could feel the pounding irregular beat of his heart.

Tearing his lips away from hers, he rested his head against her hair, still holding her closely with one arm while his other hand slipped inside the opening of her shirt to caress the sensitive skin beneath. Drawing a ragged breath, he whispered into her hair, "I want you, Sybilla. We *are* married . . ."

Sybilla's inner voice came to life again, jolting her with a shrill warning. If she allowed herself to slip into the sweet dangerous abyss of Joshua's sensuality, there would be no going back. She pushed against him violently, catching him by surprise. He stumbled back, saving himself from falling by grabbing at a chair. A knock sounded at the door. A voice called, "We've brought yer supper, my lord."

Joshua's eyes cleared. Straightening his shirt and running a hand through his disheveled hair, he muttered, "Oh, my God, Sybilla, I'm sorry . . . Here." He picked up the dressing gown and draped it around her shoulders. "Go stand over there behind the bed until they leave."

Two servants, carefully keeping their eyes to themselves,

carried in a table laden with covered dishes and several bottles. They left immediately, looking gratified by the size of Joshua's tip.

Sybilla emerged from her hiding place behind the bed, tying the sash of the dressing gown so tightly she could scarcely breathe. "Something smells good," she said, removing the cover from one of the dishes to inspect a haunch of venison. She sat down, unfolding her napkin, and avoiding looking at Joshua. What was he thinking of her? She felt cheap and weak and out of control. And what was there to say, after they'd narrowly avoided doing something they would regret for the rest of their lives?

Sitting down opposite her, Joshua observed, "The land-lord seems to have done very well by us. Here's what appears to be a very fine stewed carp." He sounded quite normal, but Sybilla, stealing a quick glance at him, noticed the lines of strain around his mouth.

Suddenly he reached across the table to clasp her hand. "Sybilla, will you forgive me? I swear it will never happen again."

She looked up at him, realizing with a flood of gratitude that his eyes reflected only their old easy friendship. "There's nothing to forgive," she said, smiling. "We were both—we were both carried away. It's been *such* a day."

"It was, wasn't it?" Joshua looked immensely relieved. "Lord, I'm hungry. Let me help you to some of this capon."

Rather to her amazement, Sybilla was soon eating with her usual hearty appetite. The landlord had provided a bottle of a very decent burgundy. She drank several glasses. Joshua, growing increasingly mellow as he polished off more than his fair share of the burgundy and started on a bottle of claret, began making plans for the future.

"As soon as we return to London, Sybilla, I'll go see my solicitor to inform him about our marriage. That will take care of Uncle Lucius and his blasted will. Then I'll send a notice to the *Times* and the *Morning Chronicle*." He paused. "No, better not. A shocking coil that would be, to announce I was married to one Sybilla Smith, only to have it transpire that my bride's name was Cholmondely, or some such thing." He cocked his head hopefully. "Unless you're willing to tell me your real name?"

Sybilla shook her head. Her nerves tightened, though Joshua didn't appear especially upset with her. "Before you do anything else, you *must* go to Lady Verity," she said quietly. "Think how she'll feel if she first hears about our marriage from someone else."

"Oh." Joshua's face closed up. "Yes, I'll do that." Abruptly he changed the subject. "I suppose that infernal Redbreast will be loitering at the door of the inn first thing tomorrow morning. Probably he'll dog us all the way to London." He scowled. "Well, as I told you, it won't take me long, once we get back, to find out who's employing him."

"Joshua, please leave it alone—" The words had slipped out involuntarily. Sybilla broke off, biting her lip.

Joshua gazed at her, his eyes narrowing. "You know why the Runner is following us, don't you?"

Sybilla looked away. "I—no."

He stared at her in a heart-pounding silence, raking her face with eyes that seemed to search her soul. At length he said flatly, "You're lying." Rising, he came around the table and jerked her upright, grasping her shoulders. "You've lied to me from the very beginning. Have you ever spoken a word of truth to me? Do you really have an uncle who's trying to force you into an unwelcome marriage with your cousin? I doubt it. You could be a runaway wife, or an absconding servant, or—or a murderess, for all I know."

His fingers tightened on her shoulders. "You've made a shambles of my life, Sybilla. The woman I loved and was going to marry has thrown me over. I could be the center of an ugly scandal the moment the public learns you've been living in my house for three weeks disguised as a boy. I'm married to a woman I don't know and can't trust. Are you going to tell me the truth now? Who are you? Where do you come from? Why are you so afraid of the Runner?"

Sybilla gazed up into the blazing gray of Joshua's eyes and longed to place her burdens on his strong and capable shoulders, but she couldn't force the words past her lips.

Joshua released her. Walking over to the fireplace, he turned his back to her, staring down at the flames. "Go to bed," he said in a tired voice. "You've won. We'll play out this farce according to your rules. But I can't face any more of it tonight."

Chapter 12

SYBILLA STRUGGLED to fasten the last two sets of copper hooks and eyes at the back of her frock. Finally succeeding, she glanced down at her figured muslin gown and sighed. It badly needed pressing. She needed a maid, she reflected, to help her into her gowns and to keep her clothing in order.

Then the enormity of her predicament swept over her again, and she sat down with her head in her hands. The hiring of an abigail was the least of her worries. She must have been queer in her attic—and so must Joshua have been—to think that a temporary marriage to him would solve her problems.

Neither of them had thought far enough ahead to the situation in which they would find themselves when they returned to London. Why hadn't they considered the possibility that a man of Joshua's rank and social importance couldn't suddenly produce a wife without a shred of background and expect to have her accepted by the ton? Sybilla Smith, a nobody from nowhere, had snared the season's prime catch in the Marriage Mart. Almost inevitably her appearance on the scene would cause a storm of gossip and conjecture, and then, sooner or later, her disguise was bound to be penetrated. She'd have disrupted Joshua's life for nothing.

She sat back in her chair, letting her eyes roam around the

pretty blue and pink bedchamber that Joshua's mother had occupied before her. Her new husband had escorted her to the room late last night when they arrived in Bedford Square from Scotland and had left her alone in it, bidding her a curt good night.

"Good morning" and "good night," and a few bare monosyllables in between had, in fact, been the sum total of Joshua's conversation during their entire three-day journey from Coldstream. Grim and tense, obviously making a tremendous effort to hold his temper in check, he'd sat in silence on his side of the chaise while they traveled from Scotland to London. He'd looked so forbidding, so unlike her carefree, irrepressible companion of the past few weeks, that Sybilla hadn't dared to attempt to cross the invisible wall that separated them.

Even the continuing pursuit by the Bow Street Runner, Sebastian Scunthorpe, had failed to shake Joshua out of his angry self-absorption. As he'd predicted, Scunthorpe was waiting for them outside the inn at Coldstream on the morning after the wedding. The imperturbable Runner had lifted his hat and wished them "werry happy." But Joshua had ignored this bit of impudence, and during the journey south he'd simply looked through Scunthorpe whenever he encountered him as if the man were invisible.

"Come in," Sybilla called as someone knocked on the door of the bedchamber. She rose, feeling a sudden rush of hope. Perhaps it was Joshua. Perhaps he was over the worst of his anger, and they could now talk calmly about their plans for the immediate future.

"Good morning, my lady," said Mrs. Roper, balancing a tray on one hand while she closed the door with the other. "I'm the housekeeper, Sarah Roper. I thought I'd just bring up your breakfast myself so's I could introduce myself . . ." Her voice trailed off, and the tray wobbled precariously as she met Sybilla's eyes. "Miss Sybilla!" she gasped. She put the tray down on a nearby table and groped her way to a chair, her face reflecting her shock.

For a moment Sybilla forgot her troubles. The temptation to laugh was almost too much for her. Last night on arriving at the house, Joshua had briefly informed the footman who

admitted them that he'd brought home a bride. This
morning the housekeeper, using the breakfast tray as an
excuse, had come up to gratify her lively curiosity about the
new Lady Linton.

Recovering somewhat, Mrs. Roper pelted Sybilla with
questions. "Is it really true? You've married his lordship?
But why—how?"

After Sybilla had given her an unvarnished account of the
elopement, Mrs. Roper seemed more stunned than ever.
"Dear, dear," she murmured. "I can't take it in . . . You
say Lady Verity broke off the engagement? And then, when
you wouldn't tell his lordship where you lived, he decided
to marry you? And now there'll be no trouble about his
Uncle Lucius's fortune?"

Sybilla said wanly, "It's so awful. I should never have let
Joshua persuade me to marry him. I'm convinced that Lady
Verity would have relented eventually if he'd explained to
her why I was living in the house. Now it's too late. I fear
I've ruined his life."

Sybilla had expected the housekeeper to disapprove of
the runaway marriage. Surprisingly, Mrs. Roper shook her
head, saying sharply, "Don't you go ablaming yourself. It
seems to me Her Ladyship acted much too hastily. Gentlemen will be gentlemen, you know, and females must . . .
Well, that's neither here nor there. I understand why His
Lordship couldn't fling you off to fend for yourself. He
always had a soft heart."

"Yes, for stray cats and dogs and waifs off the street,"
said Sybilla bitterly.

"Now, now, Miss—my lady." Mrs. Roper patted Sybilla's shoulder. "What's done is done. The question is, what's
to happen now? Sooner or later, I fear, the servants will
begin to take note of your strong resemblance to Master
Will Smith." Her forehead furrowed in a frown of intense
concentration. "You're Will Smith's cousin," she said
suddenly. "Master Joshua met you when he drove Master
Will to his home, fell head over heels in love with you and
persuaded you into an elopement. There's always been a
strong family resemblance between you and your cousin.

And you'd best start letting your hair grow. The less you look like Will Smith, the better!"

Sybilla burst out laughing. "Oh, Mrs. Roper, what a downy one you are, as shrewd as you can hold together! That Banbury story might just pull the wool over everyone's eyes." Almost immediately the amusement died out of her face. The housekeeper's inspired lie might keep gossip at bay for the time being, but it was no solution to her most basic problems.

Another knock sounded at the door, and Mrs. Roper walked over to admit one of the footmen. He bowed, saying, "My lady, 'is Lordship's compliments, an' 'e'd like ter see ye in the drawing room."

Walking down the stairs, Sybilla felt a vague foreboding. If Joshua wanted to talk to her, why hadn't he come to her bedchamber or asked her to join him in the library? Was he still so angry with her that he refused to speak to her except in a semipublic place, in the formal surroundings of the drawing room?

Her foreboding was justified, but not in the way she'd anticipated. She stopped, frozen, on the threshold of the drawing room, staring at the two men who were confronting Joshua. One of them was tall and elegant, with a handsome, austere face and dark hair going silver at his temples. The other was much younger, tall and slim and gangling, a man who one day would probably look very much like his father.

"Uncle Hubert! Barnaby!" gasped Sybilla.

Three heads turned toward her. Joshua said to the older man in a voice void of expression, "Mr. Trent, I apologize for doubting your word. I collect you really are Sybilla's uncle."

As if released from some form of trance, Barnaby Trent rushed over to her, enveloping her in a crushing hug. "Thank God, oh, thank God, Sybilla darling, we've found you at last, and you're quite safe."

"Barnaby, of course I'm all right." Gently Sybilla disengaged herself and turned to face her uncle, who strode over to her with outstretched arms to clasp her hands. "My dear, I'm as happy to see you as Barnaby, if not quite as effusive!" He added reproachfully, "You gave us such a fright. For a whole month we didn't know if you were alive or dead. Sybilla, why did you run away? You said in the note you left behind that you wanted to see something of the world. Why didn't you come to me? I'd gladly have taken you to London, or anywhere else you wanted to go!"

Tugging her hands away, Sybilla stepped back. "How did you find me, Uncle Hubert?"

Joshua cut in. "Oh, come now, need you ask? Mr. Trent hired the Bow Street Runners." She winced at the contempt in his tone.

Hubert Trent whirled on Joshua with a look of angry dislike. "You have much to answer for, my lord. I'll speak to you later." He turned back to Sybilla, his expression softening. "Yes, I went to the Runners. Not immediately. We didn't know where you'd gone. Then Barnaby remembered you'd been talking of late about visiting London. So I wrote to Bow Street. The only clue I had, of course, was your godmother's address in Henrietta Place. The Runner could discover nothing at first. Lady Madden wasn't at home. Her caretaker didn't know her whereabouts. Finally, after returning several times, the Runner inveigled a clue out of the caretaker. A boy answering to your description had called at the house, leaving a message for the house-keeper, who was also not in residence."

"Don't you mean he bribed the caretaker for information?" inquired Joshua.

Hubert shot him another angry glance. "Call it what you like. Doubtless we offered more than you did! Sybilla, five days ago Bow Street informed me that a young man, believed to be the same lad who had called on Lady Madden in Henrietta Place, was living with a Lord Linton in Bedford Square. A Runner was keeping watch on the pair. We couldn't be sure the young man was you, of course. We could only hope. Barnaby and I started for London the next day, arriving two days ago. Yesterday we called in Bedford Square, only to be told Lord Linton had gone out of town with his young friend, Will Smith. We also paid a call in Henrietta Place."

"Has Aunt Lucretia returned?" Sybilla asked quickly.

"No," replied Hubert with a trace of impatience.

"Her housekeeper told us Lady Madden was visiting an old friend in Ireland," volunteered Barnaby. "Someone named Lady Kilcannon, in—where was it, now?—in a place called Dunmore, in County Clare."

"Oh, the devil, Barnaby, that's not important!" exclaimed his father, still more impatiently. "We no longer need Lady Madden's help to find your cousin. Sybilla, please have a servant pack up your belongings. I don't want you to stay in this house a minute longer than necessary."

Sybilla drew a deep breath. "I'm not coming with you, Uncle Hubert."

"What? You can't mean what you're saying. As an unmarried female of good family, you cannot remain in the home of an unmarried gentleman, unrelated to you, without risking your reputation—"

"One moment, Mr. Trent," interrupted Joshua. "Sybilla may do as she likes, but I believe you're overlooking one important point. I gather you haven't been in contact with Bow Street this morning?"

"I have not."

"Then you don't know that I eloped to Scotland with your niece. Sybilla and I were married three days ago in Coldstream."

Hubert turned a dull red. Barnaby looked desolated. Clearing his throat, Hubert said, "Lord Linton is lying, is he not, Sybilla?"

"No, he's not lying."

Hubert rounded on Joshua, waving an angry fist in his face. "You infernal scoundrel! You've taken advantage of my niece to save your own skin. Oh, I know all about you. You inherited a worthless, impoverished title. To keep yourself out of Dun Territory, you had to marry a girl of fortune, and you found her in Lady Verity Heston, who filled your requirements well enough until you chanced upon one of the wealthiest women in all of England, with a title in her own right. So then you jilted Lady Verity and somehow persuaded my niece to elope with you. How did you succeed in doing that? By rape and violence? If so, you'll answer to me with your life one day. But for now I want Sybilla out of your house."

Joshua shoved Hubert out of his way. "What's this fool talking about, Sybilla? Who are you?"

"I'm not a big enough bleater to swallow that gammon," sneered Hubert. "You'll not make me believe you didn't know Sybilla is Baroness Trent of Castle Wycome in the North Riding, the greatest heiress in all the North Country."

White to the lips, Joshua stared at Sybilla. "Well?"

"Yes," Sybilla faltered. "I'm Baroness Trent, and I do have a huge fortune."

"I see." Except for a quick clenching and unclenching of his hands, Joshua gave no sign of emotion. He looked at her with the face of a stranger.

"Well, whether Lord Linton knew your identity or not, it doesn't matter," said Hubert Trent. "Come, Sybilla. You needn't stay to pack. The servants can send along your belongings later." To Joshua he said, "We'll be at Fenton's Hotel."

"No, Uncle Hubert," said Sybilla steadily. "I wish to stay with my husband."

"Sybilla!" wailed Barnaby. "You can't mean what you're saying. You can't stay with this man."

"No more she will. I wish to hear no more of this nonsense, Sybilla. You're coming with us," declared Hubert, reaching out to seize her arm. As she shrank away, Joshua moved forward to interpose his body between uncle and niece.

"Sybilla doesn't wish to go with you," Joshua said coldly. "I think you and your son should leave."

Hubert Trent took a long look at Joshua's implacable face and tall, powerful form, and stepped back. "Oh, I'll go, but you haven't heard the last of this," he said in a voice trembling with rage. "I don't know what lies or lures you may have used to seduce my niece, but I assure you I'll move heaven and earth to have this infamous marriage annulled and get Sybilla back under the shelter of my roof where she belongs."

Joshua bowed. "You will, of course, do as you think fit." He crossed to the bell and pulled the cord. In a moment a footman appeared at the door. "These gentlemen are leaving," Joshua told the servant. "And I'm not at home to other callers."

Recovering some shreds of dignity, Hubert stalked out of the room behind the footman. Barnaby, after a stricken look at Sybilla, followed suit.

Waiting tensely until she heard the door closing on father and son, Sybilla took an impulsive step toward Joshua, saying, "Thank you for taking my part. I should have known I could depend on you."

She recoiled when Joshua said savagely, "Taking your part? You misunderstand me, my dear. You see, I happen to have a certain amount of family pride. If it wasn't for the fact that you're now a Waring—even if only temporarily—you'd have been out of the door with your uncle. Since you've elected to stay, however, I believe explanations are in order at last—"

He paused, lifting his head to listen to the sound of raised voices coming from the foyer. In a moment the Earl of Dunsford and his daughter entered the drawing room, followed by an unhappy-looking servant, who announced shrilly, "Lord Dunsford and Lady Verity Heston to see you, my lord."

"My dear Linton, your footman told me you weren't receiving today, but I took the liberty of disregarding his efforts to turn us away. I felt sure you would not wish to exclude me and Verity," said the earl, advancing with an affable smile. "As a matter of fact, we called at Linton House yesterday, and the day before that, too. It seems your servants expected you home two days ago, and we didn't wish to delay for a moment our efforts to clear up the unfortunate misunderstanding that has developed between you and Verity."

"Papa," murmured Verity. "We are not alone." Her beautiful face turned a delicate pink from embarrassment.

For the first time the earl seemed to be aware of a fourth presence in the room. He turned a surprised look on Sybilla. Then, his eyes growing intent, he murmured, "Have we met, Miss—?"

Sybilla forced down her panic. "Oh, dear no, Lord Dunsford," she replied with a tinkling little laugh. "I declare, you must have met my young cousin, Will Smith, who was visiting Linton House recently. People are always saying we look almost like twins! I'm Sybilla Trent."

A startled look crossed Joshua's face, and then he said abruptly to the earl, "Actually, Sybilla is Baroness Trent, of Castle Wycombe in Yorkshire. And before this conversation goes any farther, sir—"

Lord Dunsford cut in. "Did you say Castle Wycombe?" he asked, his face alive with the interest he reserved for important subjects like family pedigrees and wealthy estates. He said to Sybilla, "My dear Lady Trent, was your mother by any chance the daughter of old 'King' Moreton, who owned half the coal fields in Lancashire?"

Taken aback, Sybilla said, "Why, yes, my grandfather was John Moreton."

The earl beamed. "I thought so. I have a memory for such things. Well, now, I'm happy to make your acquaintance. Will you be visiting long in London?"

"I—"

Joshua cut in. "As I was saying, sir, before this conversation goes any farther, you should know that Sybilla and I were married in Scotland three days ago."

Verity gasped. "Married?" She turned pale.

"Married?" the earl repeated, sounding stunned.

Prim, calm, controlled Verity burst into tears. "Oh, Joshua, how could you? You should have known I didn't mean it when I broke our engagement. In fact, it was only hours after I sent you the note that Papa pointed out to me how easily I could have misunderstood what—what I saw you doing. So then of course he brought me to Linton House immediately to make amends, but it was too late. You'd left town with that boy, Will Smith. And now—and now everyone in London will be saying you threw me over for a fabulously wealthy coal heiress from Yorkshire. Oh, Joshua, Joshua!" Sobbing uncontrollably, she threw herself into his arms.

He'd turned very nearly as pale as Verity, Sybilla noted with a pang, and he looked hideously uncomfortable. While Verity's tears dampened the fine broadcloth of his coat, Joshua patted his ex-fiancée's shoulder, saying huskily,

"Oh, for God's sake, Verity, I never meant to hurt you. But I thought you'd jilted me, so then when—" He bit off his words.

Even now, when I've turned his life upside down, he can't bring himself to betray me, thought Sybilla.

Verity lifted her head. Despite her tear-stained cheeks, she still looked far more beautiful than any ordinary woman. "Oh, Joshua," she breathed. "I see how it was. You thought you'd lost me, so you didn't care whom you married." A tremulous smile curved her lips. She straightened her hat, reached into her reticule for a handkerchief to wipe her tears away, and said to her father, "I think we should go, Papa. We wouldn't wish to embarrass Joshua." Her smile held an edge of triumph as she said to Sybilla, "I wish you happy, Lady Linton."

The earl bowed stiffly. "Pray accept my felicitations also, Lady Linton, Lord Linton." He extended his arm to his daughter. "You're quite right, my dear. It's time to go."

After Verity and Lord Dunsford had left the drawing room, and the footman had closed the outer door of the house behind them, Joshua broke the silence into which he'd retreated. "Come with me to the library, Sybilla. I want to talk to you where no one can interrupt us."

As soon as the library door shut behind them, Sybilla said, "I'm so sorry. Oh, how I wish I'd never involved you in my affairs. If I had it to do over . . ."

Sitting down behind his desk, Joshua leaned forward, his hands clenched in front of him. "If you had it to do over, you'd act exactly the same," he snapped. "You're a selfish, willful child, bent on having your own way, and hang the consequences. Tell me this: Did you have any real reason to run away from your home?"

"Yes, I did. I told you, Uncle Hubert was determined to make a match between me and Barnaby."

"Fustian. Your uncle seems a decent man, perfectly respectable. Naturally, he'd prefer that you marry his son, but he couldn't—and I'm sure he wouldn't—have forced you to the altar. You simply wanted a fling in London. Well, I can understand that, I daresay, though you shouldn't have left your uncle and your cousin to stew about your safety. But why, after your little escapade was finished, why didn't you let me take you home? Why didn't you confide in me, as I begged you to do, over and over? Now we're all in the basket—you, me, Verity, your uncle, your cousin Barnaby—and I don't know how we're going to get out of it."

Clasping her hands tightly together to control their trembling, Sybilla said, "I know it's very bad, but surely there's a way out eventually? When we got married, you said it was only for a little while. We'd get a divorce or an annulment in a few months. Why don't you divorce me immediately? Then you'll be free to marry Lady Verity—"

Joshua glared at her. "Damnation, woman, don't you see I'm not free to do *anything*? I didn't know when I proposed that insane marriage scheme that you were one of the wealthiest women in England with a title in your own right. There's no way we could obtain a quiet divorce or annulment immediately, considering your position and fortune and that confounded romantic runaway elopement to Scotland. We'd be the center of the most colossal scandal to rock London in a generation. I'd be the laughingstock of the ton for being such a gull. Do you seriously think Verity would marry me after all that? No, I'm chained to you for the foreseeable future. In a year's time, or several years from now, we can start divorce proceedings. Until then, my dear, you're Lady Linton, and I expect you to live up to your new position with such grace as you can muster."

He rose, pulling the bell. To the footman who appeared, he said, "Tell the stables I want my curricle."

Waiting until the servant had left, Sybilla asked, "Where are you going, Joshua? I'd like to talk—"

"There isn't anything more to say," he replied, seating himself at the desk again to scribble a few lines. "As soon as I've sent this notice of our marriage to the newspapers, I'm going to White's, where I won't have to see you or talk to you for the rest of the day."

When Joshua arrived at White's Club, it was not yet three o'clock, and the card room was still very thin of company. He sat down at a table, ordered a bottle of wine, and, picking up a deck of cards, desultorily played Patience until several of his acquaintances arrived to make up a table of whist. He was still there, hours later, when Captain Merriweather swung himself on his crutches into the card room.

Pausing at Joshua's table, the captain said with a grin, "Hallo, Linton, my lad. Where've you been for the past week?"

Joshua looked up with an owlish expression. He replied in a slurred voice, "For your information, Merry, I've been up in Scotland, getting married."

The other whist players at the table gaped, putting down their cards. After an astonished pause the captain said, "Congratulations, old fellow. Married in Scotland, were you? Don't know why I thought you were marrying Lady Verity next month in St. George's, Hanover Square."

Joshua poured himself another glass of wine. "You've got the wrong bride. I married Sybilla Trent—*Baroness* Trent. She owns half the coal mines in Lancashire."

His bright blue eyes narrowing at the hint of venom in his friend's tone, the captain glanced at the pile of counters beside Joshua's elbow. "Played enough whist? You look like a winner. Come have a bite of supper with me."

"*Looks* like a winner! Hah!" said one of the whist players bitterly. "Linton's had a run of luck I wouldn't have believed if I hadn't seen it myself. He's already won half my town house."

"Oh, I daresay he'll be delighted to give you the opportunity to recoup your losses at some other time," said the captain with an easy grin. "Now, if you'll excuse us, I'd like to put some food into him before he falls on his face." He put his hand on Joshua's shoulders. "Come along. I'm starving."

"Oh, for God's sake, Merry, I'm not castaway, just a little bit on the go," protested Joshua, but after asking his partner to cash in his counters, he yielded to Merriweather's persuasions and accompanied his friend out of the card room. "You said you wanted to have supper," he said, mildly surprised, when the captain proceeded past the door of the dining room.

"We'll have a bite later. First I want a word with you."
Merry opened the door of the library and peered into the
room. "Good. There's nobody here. We'll not be interrupted."

A moment later the captain lowered himself awkwardly
into a chair in the library and dropped his crutches to the
floor. "Still can't use the confounded things properly," he
said with a withering glance at the crutches. His face
beneath the mop of carroty curls was unwontedly serious as
he said, "Sit down, old chap. Now, then, tell me how it is
you've married a lady I never heard of, and why, instead of
being in the company of your brand-new bride, you're
spending the evening getting foxed at White's."

At Joshua's instinctive glare of resentment at the invasion
of his privacy, Merry said quietly, "On your high ropes, are
you? I thought we were friends, *Major Waring*. And friends
can help, or at least listen."

Joshua relaxed, heaving a deep sigh. "Lord, Merry, you
wouldn't believe the muff I've made of things."

"Try me."

During Joshua's somewhat incoherent account, the captain kept shaking his head in wonderment. At one point he
gasped, "That nice lad, Will Smith, is really Baroness
Trent? My God!" When Joshua finished his story, Merry sat
in silence for a few moments. Finally he said, "Well,
you've landed yourself under the hatches, right enough, but
you know, it could be worse. For one thing, between your
Uncle Lucius's legacy and your wife's fortune, you'll be
rich as Croesus."

Joshua stiffened.

"All right, all right," said Merry hastily. "Money's not
everything. It can be dashed important at times, though, let
me tell you! What I really wanted to say is this: It may not
be such a bad thing, being married to Will. I mean Sybilla.
I liked the lad—er, girl. A very good sort, I thought. Loyal
and kind. Look how hard she tried to mend your rift with
Lady Verity, that time I fell into King Joseph's chamber pot.
Fine sense of humor, too. And now I think of it, she's
probably quite pretty when she's dressed like a young lady."

Joshua exploded. "She's a scheming, lying minx who

doesn't care two pins for anyone but her own selfish self!"
He lunged out of his chair. "I need a drink."

"You're better than half-sprung already. Don't be an ass.
You can't stay at White's forever, trying to drink their
cellars dry. Sooner or later you'll have to go home to your
wife. Why not go with me now?"

Sybilla glanced at the ormolu clock on the mantel.
Almost midnight. She'd been sitting in her bedchamber, not
bothering to undress and prepare for bed, since an early
dinner, eaten in solitary state in the great dining room
downstairs. Joshua hadn't returned. During the long hours
that had elapsed since he left the house earlier in the day,
she'd done nothing but think about her disastrous marriage
and the problems it had caused. After those hours of thought
she was no closer to a solution of the problems than she'd
been in the beginning.

On the face of it the situation was simple enough. Joshua
was in love with Verity. He'd marry her if he could. But
until he obtained a divorce or annulment, he couldn't make
her his wife. And divorce or annulment wasn't possible at
this time, because Joshua was quite right, the circumstances
of his marriage and Sybilla's position as one of the greatest
heiresses in England would combine to create the juiciest
scandal in years. Verity would never be able to face it.
Possibly she wouldn't have the patience, either, to wait for
Joshua to become free, after he'd finally shed the galling
yoke of his marriage to Sybilla.

At the sound of voices outside in the silent corridor,
Sybilla stirred. They were male voices, and they seemed to
be arguing. Going to the door, she opened it slightly and
looked out. Joshua and Francis Merriweather stood in the
corridor, facing each other.

"Damnation, Merry, it's no use your saying I need a
doctor, because I won't have a sawbones!" Joshua exclaimed. "You'd think I was dying! I've lost a little blood,
that's all." He put a hand to his shoulder and winced. There
were dark stains on the front of his coat.

"Joshua!" Sybilla screamed. She ran out into the hall.
Giving her a glance of cold contempt, Joshua walked slowly

down the corridor to his bedchamber, opened the door, and went in.

"Merry, what is it? How did Joshua get hurt? How serious is it?" Sybilla stopped, biting her lip. She'd given herself away. She wasn't supposed to know Francis Merriweather.

"It's all right, Will. I mean Sybilla," said the captain. He put his arm around her in a brief hug. The affectionate gesture nearly caused him to lose his balance. "Damn these crutches," he said without heat. "Don't you worry. Joshua's told me all about you. Be sure I won't tell anyone you and Will are the same person. Now I think we'd better see to that stubborn ass of a husband of yours. I don't know how badly he's wounded."

Inside his bedchamber they found Joshua sitting in an armchair in his shirtsleeves. His ashen-faced valet, who had apparently already removed Joshua's coat and waistcoat, was attempting to pull the bloodstained shirt over his master's head.

"Sybilla, go take the shirt off," said Merry. "That valet, silly gudgeon, is about to faint."

Pushing the valet out of the way, Sybilla ignored Joshua's look of angry protest and pulled the shirt over his head. She drew a deep, quivering breath when she saw the deep cut in his right shoulder, which was still bleeding, but not profusely.

Leaning down as far as he could without falling, the captain peered at Joshua with the knowledgeable eye of one who had seen many a battlefield wound. "Well, it's worse than a flesh wound, but I don't think it's really serious," he commented.

"That's what I told you—"

Sybilla interrupted Joshua to insist, "I think we should send for a doctor."

"No doctor," he growled. "Dalrymple"—he gestured to his valet—"go fetch some hot water and some linen for bandages." With a pointed look at Sybilla and the captain, he said, "I don't need either of you. Dalrymple will do very well by me. And if you don't mind, I'd like to get a bit of rest."

Merry shrugged. "We'll leave you, then. Sybilla?"

"But I still think—" She looked at Joshua's unyielding expression and ceased arguing.

Following the captain out of the bedchamber, she said urgently, "What happened, Merry? That was a stab wound, wasn't it? Was Joshua attacked?"

Merry knit his brow. "Well, he was, but I'm hanged if I can make heads or tails of it. We were coming out of White's, on our way to my curricle—I'd sent Joshua's curricle home with his tiger—when a fellow rushed up to Joshua out of nowhere, slashed away at him with a wicked-looking knife, and ran off. There was no attempt at robbery, no move to attack me. On the face of it the ruffian was out to kill or injure Linton, but why, in heaven's name? I could have sworn Joshua didn't have an enemy in the world. Dashed if I don't think the thug simply mistook him for somebody else."

"Yes, I'm sure that was the case," said Sybilla between lips that had suddenly grown stiff. "I'm glad you were there, Merry."

"Wasn't the first time I've seen action with Linton," the captain replied with a grin. He hesitated. "I hope you won't feel I'm intruding, but he told me you and he were experiencing difficulties. My dear, I'm sure it'll all come right in the end. I think you'll be very good for old Joshua."

"Thank you. I hope so." Sybilla managed to keep a smile on her face until the captain had hobbled off down the stairs. Then she walked slowly to her bedchamber, feeling crushed under an intolerable burden. Someone had tried to murder Joshua, and it was all her fault.

Chapter 13

HURRIEDLY CLOSING the portmanteau, Sybilla shot a worried glance at the clock over the mantel. Past five-thirty. She'd overslept, on this of all mornings. Perhaps, with luck, she'd be able to avoid meeting any of the servants who might be astir. Carrying the portmanteau, and pausing to pick up the note she'd written the night before, she left the bedchamber. She walked along the silent hallway to Joshua's room, where she tucked the note underneath his door. Then, proceeding cautiously, she started down the stairs. At the first landing she stopped to peer over the railings. There was no one in the foyer. Quickly she descended the remaining steps, pushed back the chain, and went out the door of Linton House.

Bedford Square was deserted in the early morning light. Sybilla knew that tradesmen and domestic servants would soon be abroad, however. Half-running, half-walking, she slipped past the gates of the square and rounded the corner into an adjoining street. Only then did she feel safe from observation.

Walking briskly, she made her way toward the Tottenham Court Road. The random thought crossed her mind that it felt odd to be wearing pantaloons again. During the past few days she'd grown accustomed to dresses and a bonnet and pelisse. As a runaway, though, she knew she'd appear far less noticeable disguised as a respectably dressed stripling.

The idea of fleeing from Linton House had occurred to her almost at the same time she realized that Joshua's life was in danger. It had taken her a little longer to decide on a destination.

Emerging from Tottenham Court Road into Oxford Street, she stood irresolutely for a moment. Which way should she turn? She was going to Ireland. At some point during the night she'd remembered her cousin Barnaby's remark that her godmother, Aunt Lucretia, was visiting a Lady Kilcannon at Dunmore in County Clare.

Making up her mind, she turned left. At one of the coaching inns in Holborn she'd surely be able to obtain a seat in a coach going to Bristol. An accommodation coach, not the Mail. It had cost her almost five guineas, including tips and meals, to travel by the Mail in an inside seat from Yorkshire to London. She couldn't afford to take the Mail to Bristol. In her pocket she had only the few pounds she'd won from Joshua—how long ago it seemed!—in their shooting match at Manton's Gallery. An outside seat on an accommodation coach would be within her means, and if she pinched her pennies, buying little or no food, she probably had enough money to get to Ireland.

Though it was so early, the wheeled traffic on Oxford Street, mostly produce carts, was beginning to grow heavier. Deep in concentration, she didn't notice the hackney cab that rolled past her. She did hear the familiar voice calling her name, however. She looked up to see a lanky figure scramble out of the hackney cab and start running back toward her.

"Sybilla, I wasn't sure . . . It *is* you!" exclaimed Barnaby as he came up to her. "What on earth are you doing on the street at this hour, alone and dressed like a boy?"

Sybilla bit her lip. For a fleeting moment she'd thought that Joshua had come after her. But he'd have no reason to do that, not after reading the note she'd left. "What are *you* doing here at this hour?" she countered.

"I was coming to see you, of course. Sybilla, I'm worried. My father isn't himself. He's talking wildly, saying he's going to swear out a warrant accusing Lord

Linton of kidnapping you. Think of the scandal that would cause! So I decided to come see you before Father woke up—he was dipping pretty deep last night, so it'll be some time before he's out of bed—and try to persuade you to come home with us."

Sybilla shook her head.

"You can't continue living with a complete stranger," Barnaby protested. "I don't know how that man, that Lord Linton, managed to persuade you to elope with him. Perhaps he *did* kidnap you. But you needn't stay married to him. Father will help you obtain an annulment. . . ." He swallowed hard. "Look, if you ran away because Father and I were pressuring you to marry me, I withdraw my proposal. Just come back to Castle Wycombe. I swear I won't say a word about marriage to you unless you bring it up first."

Sybilla shook her head again. "I won't go back to Yorkshire, but I'll not be staying with Lord Linton, either. In fact, I'm sure he'll soon divorce me." Suddenly she realized it was fortunate that Barnaby had intercepted her. He could be her messenger. "Go back to Uncle Hubert and tell him Joshua and I are divorcing. And don't worry about me." She turned on her heel and began walking along Oxford Street in the direction of Holborn.

With several long strides he caught up with her, grabbing her arm. "Where are you going?"

She tried to shake off his hand. "I can't tell you."

"You mean you won't. Sybilla, I'll not allow you to go off to some unknown place by yourself." His mouth hardened. "You can kick or scream or bite, whatever you choose, but I'm putting you into that hackney cab and you're going back to the hotel with me."

Her blood ran cold. Barnaby was young and coltish and rather inept in most things he attempted, but he was stronger than she was. If he tried to force her into the cab, it wasn't likely that any passerby would interfere. He could always claim she was his runaway younger brother.

"Listen to me, Barnaby," she said with a desperate intensity. "I'll tell you why I can't go back to Castle Wycombe. . . ."

* * *

Sybilla awoke with a start, momentarily bemused to find herself in an easy chair in front of a dying fire. After a long day's fishing with Barnaby, she'd come to the library after dinner to begin reading Mr. "Monk" Lewis's novel, *The Bravo of Venice*, which had arrived that day in the carrier's cart from Harrowgate. Terrifying as the book promised to be, she'd apparently fallen asleep over the first chapter.

At the sound of Uncle Hubert's voice behind her, she yawned and started to get up from her chair. Then the sense of what he was saying penetrated into her drowsy mind. She shrank back into the chair, scarcely daring to breathe.

"If she won't consent to the marriage, I'll be forced to desperate measures. I may need your help," said Uncle Hubert.

"Well, sir, I've always been yer man, I can't say bettern' that." The second voice belonged to Sam Raynell, the steward of Castle Wycombe. Two years ago, when Uncle Hubert had arrived at the castle to assume his guardianship of the estate after the death of Sybilla's father, he'd pensioned off Jack Watts, who'd served as steward for over thirty years. In Watts's place, Hubert had brought in Raynell, an outlander from Northumberland.

"I'll hold you to that, Raynell," said Hubert. "I'm prepared to do anything that's necessary to stay out of debtors' prison. That last trip to Harrowgate finished me. I lost a hundred thousand pounds at the tables. If Sybilla won't marry my son, I'm ruined. You know, even better than I, that I can't wring a single extra penny out of the estate, thanks to my damned brother's will. I can't touch Sybilla's principal, only her income."

"Yes, I believe ye once told me the late Baron Trent put his entire personal property—including his wife's inheritance—into a trust."

"Exactly. Sybilla receives only the income from the trust, until she turns twenty-one. In the event she marries, her income from the trust will be at her sole disposal. If her husband predeceases her, her income, and then the trust itself, remains in her hands. If she dies without issue, the trust devolves on her next of kin, not on her husband, if any. In the ordinary way of things, of course, a husband assumes full control of his wife's personal property, which passes to *his* family, not to hers, when he dies. My brother set up this trust because he was determined that Sybilla's fortune was not going to fall into the hands of a conniving husband *or* his family."

"That's all very well and good, Mr. Trent, but if ye can't touch the principal . . ."

Hubert laughed. "If Sybilla marries Barnaby, my creditors will stop hounding me. They'll expect my son's wealthy wife to tow me out of the River Tick when she comes into her legacy. Certainly her trustees won't make any difficulties about that. *I'm* one of her trustees!"

"Well, now, sir. I don't think ye need worry," said Raynell, sounding more confident. "It's plain as the nose on yer face that Her Ladyship is fond of Master Barnaby. Ye'll be posting the banns before long, I have no doubt."

"Let's hope you're right." Hubert's tone hardened. "One way or another, though, her fortune comes to me, or I go under."

Sybilla heard a desk drawer being opened and shut. "Confound it, Raynell, I wanted to ask you about that lease, but I seem to have mislaid it," Hubert remarked in vexation. "It must be in the estate office. Well, it can wait until morning."

Sybilla remained frozen in her chair until she could no longer hear the receding voices of her uncle and the steward as they went off down the corridor. Then she raced to her bedchamber, where, for long agonizing moments, she mulled over the meaning of the conversation she'd overheard in the library.

On the face of it, Uncle Hubert was planning to kill her if she didn't marry Barnaby, in order to keep her fortune in the family, thereby saving himself from debtors' prison. Despite what she'd heard, her heart rebelled against believing in such villainy. Uncle Hubert had always been loving and kind to her. Surely he could never bring himself to kill her. Near the breaking point about his financial worries, he must have spoken out of desperation, not really meaning what he was saying.

No. She might be misjudging Uncle Hubert horribly, but her sturdy common sense told her she couldn't take chances with her life by staying at Castle Wycombe until she'd discovered her uncle's real intentions. She walked to the wardrobe, taking out a portmanteau, and began throwing clothes into it. Midway through her packing, she paused. It would be much easier to travel as a boy. Picking up a candle, she stole down the corridor to Barnaby's bedchamber. She cautiously opened his door, shielding her candle, and listened for a few moments to her cousin's rhythmic snoring. Barnaby was a *very* heavy sleeper. He didn't stir while she rummaged through his belongings for some of his older garments that he'd outgrown. . . .

"My God, Sybilla, you can't believe my father would want to kill you," gasped Barnaby. Pedestrians were passing them on the pavement, and the stream of carriages, carts, and wagons was steadily increasing on Oxford Street, but Sybilla and Barnaby were so deeply absorbed that they were scarcely aware of the presence of other people.

"I didn't want to think so. In these weeks I've been away, I'd begun to believe my imagination might have played tricks on me. Maybe I'd misinterpreted what Uncle Hubert had said. But last night, Barnaby, I realized your father was a murderer. He tried to kill my husband."

Turning pale, Barnaby said, "He couldn't have done. He was never out of my sight last night."

Briefly she explained about the attack on Joshua in front of White's. "The man made no attempt to rob Joshua or his friend, Captain Merriweather. It was a purposeless attack, unless he meant to kill Joshua. I think Uncle Hubert hired him to do so."

"But why in heaven's name would my father do such a thing?"

Sybilla looked at him in pained surprise. It seemed so obvious to her, but Barnaby had never been especially quick-witted. "To make me a widow, of course. If I stay married to Joshua, I'd probably have a child, and that would be the end of Uncle Hubert's expectations. With Joshua

dead, my trust fund would remain in the family, and Uncle
Hubert could renew his scheme to marry me off to you."

"Oh, God." From his pinched features and the desolation
in his voice, it was clear that Barnaby was convinced at last.
"What's to be done, then?" he asked after a long pause.

"I hope Joshua will start divorce proceedings immediately. That way he'll be safe. If he's not married to me, your
father will have no reason to harm him."

Barnaby winced. Then curiosity made him forget his
misery temporarily. "Does Lord Linton want a divorce? But
then, why did you two get married?"

She ignored the last question. "Joshua wants a divorce
eventually," she said steadily. "He'd like to postpone it for
a year or more, to avoid scandal, however, and I can't allow
that. If Uncle Hubert made another attempt on him during
that time, I'd have Joshua's death on my conscience. So I'm
forcing the issue. I'm going away. I've left him a note,
telling him I refuse to live with him any longer, and for him
to divorce me for desertion, or on any other grounds he sees
fit. The fact that I've left him will itself be a scandal, so
he'll have nothing to lose by instituting proceedings immediately."

"I see." He gave her a long look. "I think you're in love
with the man, my dear," he said, sounding wistful.

She flinched. "Goodbye, Barnaby."

"Wait." He caught her arm. "I meant what I said. I won't
let you go off alone. I'm coming with you."

A great weight slipped off Sybilla's shoulders. She and
Barnaby had always been so close. She loved him dearly, as
a brother if not as a husband. Why shouldn't she accept the
comfort of his company on the long journey to Ireland?
She'd been dreading the trip, uncertain as she was of her
reception from Aunt Lucretia, and worrying if her meager
funds would last until she arrived.

She hesitated. "Uncle Hubert will be very angry with you
when he finds out you've helped me escape from London.
And I expect he will find out."

"Yes, he will," Barnaby replied shortly. "I intend to tell
him. Father and I are finished. You must see that. I couldn't

possibly live under the same roof with him, now that I know what he's capable of."

"But what will you do?"

"I'll manage. I have a small income my Uncle Dick—my mother's brother—left me. I may buy a pair of colors. I always wanted to join a cavalry regiment."

Barnaby's grown up, Sybilla thought. Aloud, she said, smiling, "Thank you. I accept. I hope you have some money. *I* can't afford to pay your shot!"

For the first time that morning Barnaby's face lit up with genuine amusement. "Pots of it," he said, laughing. "Enough to go to the Indies. Or as near as makes no difference! Where are we bound?"

"Ireland. I'm going to stay with my godmother."

"Of course. Why didn't I think of that? The very best place for you. Well, let's get started."

They walked over to the hackney cab. The driver had been waiting patiently for his passenger to finish his conversation. Barnaby told the driver, "Take us to the nearest place where we can buy a ticket on a coach going to Ireland."

"Well, sir, I reckon that'd be the White Horse in Fetter Lane, Holborn. Leastways, that's wheer I seen the coaches leavin' fer Bath an' the West."

It was only a little past seven o'clock when Sybilla and Barnaby arrived at the White Horse Inn. They learned they'd have a considerable wait before their coach started on its western run at nine o'clock. After a spot of breakfast in the coffee room they whiled away the time watching the endless, bustling activity in the coachyard. Ostlers, stableboys, store-keepers, chambermaids, and porters vied to serve the stream of passengers descending from the night coaches or heading for seats on the outgoing day coaches.

"Someone told me that Chaplin—he owes this inn and the Swan with Two Necks, also—has more than two thousand employees," Barnaby observed. "I can well believe it."

Finally they took their seats inside the shiny red and black coach. The guard climbed up on his perch, shouting, "All right," the stableboys let go the leaders, the coachman cracked his whip, and they were off.

Sybilla heaved a sigh of relief as the coach rumbled out of the inn yard. Outside passengers had taken every available seat atop the coach, but she and Barnaby, at least at this stage of the journey, were the only occupants of the interior. Though this privacy gave them the opportunity to talk without being overheard, both of them were oddly silent.

Sybilla could guess what Barnaby was thinking of. Despite his brave words, he must have some regrets about the coming breach with his father. He must be wondering, too, if he'd be able to make his own way in the world.

She shivered. She had the same problem. Until she was twenty-one she had no income. For the next two years Uncle Hubert would control the purse strings, and she had no intention, ever, of living at Castle Wycombe until she could force Hubert out. If Aunt Lucretia wouldn't allow her to stay . . . There was Joshua, of course. But no, she'd never accept a penny from him. Not that he was likely to offer her anything, not after that note she'd left behind for him to read. She'd burned all her boats with her brief, cold announcement that she wanted out of their ill-considered marriage and that she hoped she'd never see him again. She was sure she never would.

Even though the coach was going at a fast clip, the miles seemed to drag as they traveled through Middlesex to Berkshire and on into Wiltshire, making stops at Maidenhead, Newbury, Reading, Hungerford, and numerous points in between. Deep in her thoughts, Sybilla paid little attention to the towns or their names, being conscious mostly of a growing weariness as the day wore on. Two more inside passengers had climbed aboard at Maidenhead, making the coach more crowded, and further inhibiting any desire Sybilla and Barnaby might have had to discuss their situation.

At seven in the evening, after the coach had traveled through the outskirts of Savernake Forest, several long blasts of the guard's horn announced that they were nearing another town.

"Marlborough," said one of their fellow passengers. "The guard told me we'll have thirty minutes here for dinner."

Sybilla flexed her legs, which had fallen asleep. They'd been on the road for ten hours already, and it would be another five before they arrived in Bristol. She wasn't hungry, but she welcomed the opportunity to walk around and stretch her cramped limbs.

The coach rolled into the pretty market town, which consisted mainly of one broad street lined with lovely old houses, and came to a stop in the yard of the Angel Inn. Sybilla was the first passenger out when the guard opened the door and let down the steps. She found herself facing an immovable obstacle.

"Good evening, my dear," said Joshua. "I've been waiting for you for half an hour. Didn't you see my curricle passing your coach? The guard blew his horn at me."

"Sir, you're blocking the door. I should like to get down," came a querulous voice from inside the coach.

"Your pardon, sir," Joshua called. He grasped Sybilla by the arm and pulled her away from the coach. "It's time to talk, my dear wife," he murmured.

"One moment, my lord," said Barnaby, scrambling down the steps and running up to them. "Sybilla is with me."

Joshua took out his quizzing glass, an accessory he used so infrequently that Sybilla had forgotten he owned one. He looked through it at Barnaby. "Ah—Trent. So you're here, too. It didn't take long for Sybilla to find someone to replace me, did it? For the present, however, she's still my wife, and I claim my conjugal privileges."

At Sybilla's quick, involuntary jerk, Joshua tightened his grip. "Don't be alarmed. I'm speaking only of a conversational privilege. At least for the time being. Come along."

Feeling strangely numb, Sybilla allowed him to march her into the inn, where, after a brief conference with the landlord, he procured a private parlor. Putting an arm across the door when Barnaby attempted to follow Sybilla into the parlor, Joshua said curtly, "I want a private word with my wife."

Barnaby clenched his fists.

"Don't try it," Joshua warned.

"It's all right, Barnaby," Sybilla said quickly. "Wait for me in the corridor. This won't take long."

Joshua shut the door, and in that moment Sybilla noticed how pale he was, and she remembered that he'd grasped her arm with his left hand. "Joshua—your wound. Did you see a doctor?"

"No. It's the merest scratch."

"I think you're in pain."

He said indifferently, "So? It will pass. You can't drive seventy-five miles with a dickey shoulder and not expect a little discomfort. I'd have caught up to you several stops down the line if my shoulder and arm had been up to snuff."

Suddenly reminded she was a runaway, Sybilla asked, "How did you know where I'd gone? And why did you come after me?"

"I may not be up to every rig and row in town, but I'm no nodcock," said Joshua with a mocking smile. "If you wouldn't return to your uncle, and refused to stay with me, where else would you go but to your godmother's house in Ireland? There's nothing wrong with my ears, Sybilla. I heard your cousin tell you that Lady Madden was visiting in County Clare. So after I read your note this morning, suspecting you might have run off disguised as a boy again, I asked Mrs. Roper to check your bedchamber. Sure enough, your boys' clothes were missing. After that it was simply a matter of inquiring at a number of coaching inns until I arrived at the White Horse and discovered that a lad of fifteen or so, in the company of a young man, had purchased a seat on the nine o'clock coach to Bristol. Ergo, my runaway wife, and, very probably, her cousin Barnaby."

Sybilla bit her lip in chagrin. She'd thought herself so clever, and it had been child's play for Joshua to track her down.

"As to why I came after you," he continued, "you already know the answer. I told you yesterday that I won't permit you to embroil me in a nasty scandal. Neither will I let you make me the laughingstock of London, a man whose wife ran away from him after less than a week of marriage!

You'll come back with me to London now, you'll remain my wife for a year or two years, or however long I find it necessary, and then you can have your divorce."

"I won't go with you. You can't make me."

"You mistake the matter," said Joshua coldly. "If I must, I'll truss you up like a capon and throw you into my curricle." He touched a hand to his pocket. "I happen to have with me our marriage lines. I assure you that no one will lift a finger to prevent me from carting you back to London."

"Barnaby—"

"Forget Barnaby. I can mill him down with my left hand, if need be."

Sybilla's shoulders slumped in despair. Joshua had made up his mind. She could think of only one course that might persuade him to let her go: She could tell him about Uncle Hubert. No. Even if he believed her, which wasn't at all certain, he wouldn't take Hubert seriously. She could hear him saying, "I didn't survive the war in the Peninsula without learning how to take care of myself. Let Hubert Trent do his worst." And while he was laughing at the danger, Hubert would be scurrying around the stewpots of London, searching for yet another assassin.

The door of the parlor slammed open. Uncle Hubert stood on the threshold, looking elegant and distinguished, as he always did. But his eyes were wild. He extended his hand to Sybilla, saying, "You're safe now, my dear. I've come to take you home." Behind him, Barnaby hovered in the doorway, his face reflecting his uncertainty and distress.

"I'll thank you to leave, Trent," said Joshua. "My wife has already indicated she doesn't wish to go with you."

"Ah, no, Lord Linton, you'll not fob me off a second time. I don't know what means you used to coerce my niece into this marriage, but it's obvious she's not a free agent."

"Uncle Hubert—"

Hubert waved his hand. "My dear Sybilla, let me handle this." He turned to Joshua. "If I needed any proof that my niece wasn't acting of her own free will, I discovered it this morning."

"How was that, pray?" said Joshua in a bored tone.

Hubert's eyes looked even wilder. "You may well ask. You see, I called at your house, only to learn that both you and Sybilla were away. Which could have meant, simply, that you refused to see me. So then I persuaded one of your scullery maids to talk. It was quite easy. Five pounds seemed like a fortune to the wench. She told me a rumor was afloat in the household that Lady Linton had disappeared from the house, apparently in the early hours of the morning. She also told me that Lord Linton had ordered his curricle in great haste, telling his servants he would be gone for several days. I may not be awake on every suit, but I'm not an imbecile. It was clear to me that Sybilla was trying to escape from you. As she hadn't come to me, for some reason I'm unable to fathom, she must be attempting to reach her godmother in Ireland. And I was quite right. When I arrived here in Marlborough, my son told me about Sybilla's flight."

Hubert's venomous look at his son caused Barnaby to shrink back and raised the alarm bells in Sybilla's mind. Had Barnaby told his father everything? Did Hubert know she'd overheard his conversation that last night in Castle Wycombe? If so, he might be more dangerous than ever.

"Trent, I've listened to as much as I care to—more, in fact—of your muddled reasoning," said Joshua. "You will now leave, with my assistance if necessary. I might remind you that I'm one of Gentleman Jackson's prize pupils."

"I don't pay any heed to threats." Hubert whipped a pistol from the pocket of his greatcoat, keeping it trained on Joshua.

"Oh, the devil. Give me that thing before you hurt someone, you idiot!" Joshua exclaimed, walking toward Hubert with his hand extended.

"Get back—"

Sybilla heard the rising note of hysteria in Hubert's voice and hurled herself at him, grabbing for the hand that held the pistol. For a split second at the sound of the shot, the four people in the room stood transfixed, as if under a spell. Then Joshua bounded forward to twist the empty pistol from Hubert's hand and turned to Sybilla, his face ashen. "My God, are you hurt?"

"No . . . No . . ." Sybilla was trembling with shock. The shot had barely missed her. She'd felt the heat of its passing on her cheek.

"Why did you do it?" Joshua demanded, his relief turning to anger. "You could easily have been killed. Your uncle was gammoning us. He wouldn't have pulled the trigger."

Suddenly the accumulated strains of the past few days caught up with Sybilla. "I was afraid he was going to shoot you," she blurted. The dam broke. Unable to stop herself, she poured out the story of her flight from Castle Wycombe and the reason for it.

"It's a lie!" exclaimed Hubert fiercely when he could break into Sybilla's narrative. "No, I didn't mean that. Sybilla, darling, you misunderstood what I said that night. Yes, I'm heavily in debt. Yes, I'd like you to marry Barnaby. But you must know I'd never harm a hair on your head. I've loved you since you were a babe." He took a step toward her, arms outstretched.

"You're a liar, Uncle Hubert." Sybilla edged slowly backward, keeping her gaze fixed on her uncle. She gasped in surprise, and then in relief, when Joshua's long arm wrapped itself firmly around her. She looked up at him. "Don't believe a word he says, Joshua. He wouldn't hesitate to kill me. And last night he tried to kill you."

Joshua's eyes widened. "In heaven's name, why?"

"So he could get his hands on my fortune. You see, my father put all my money in a trust. You have no claim to it, nor would your heirs have any claim if you were to die. That's why I ran away to Ireland. If I could convince Uncle Hubert we were about to be divorced, I thought he'd leave you alone."

Joshua's face was a study in mixed emotions, in which a steely anger seemed predominant. He glared at Hubert. "You've tangled with the wrong man, Trent. I'll have you up before the magistrates for this."

"You can't prove anything," said Hubert shrilly. "You haven't the slightest shred of evidence that I tried to kill you or my niece."

Drawing a deep breath, Joshua fought to control his

anger. "I'm not so sure of that, but exposing you would also result in an unpleasant scandal." He walked to the bell rope and pulled it.

"What are you doing?" Hubert asked in alarm.

Joshua didn't reply. From the servant who answered his ring, he ordered paper and pen. When they arrived, he sat down at a table and scribbled a few lines. Rising, he handed what he'd written to Hubert. "Sign that. As long as you refrain from any attempt to injure me or Sybilla, you'll hear no more about it."

Having scanned the sheet of paper, Hubert said in a stupefied voice, "This is a confession in my name. I admit to attempting to shoot you in the presence of witnesses, including my own son." He whirled on Barnaby. "My boy, you wouldn't—"

"Yes, Father, I would," said Barnaby steadily.

Hubert threw the paper down on the table. "I won't sign it."

"Then I go to the magistrates," answered Joshua. "You might end up on the nubbing cheat. At the very least you'll be a pariah for the rest of your life."

Slowly Hubert picked up the pen. Even more slowly he signed his name to his confession.

"Good," said Joshua. He sanded the signature, folded the document, and put it in his pocket. "You can go now." To Barnaby he said, "Will you excuse us? I'd like to finish my conversation with my wife."

Barnaby looked questioningly at Sybilla. She nodded.

When they were alone, Joshua said abruptly, "I've been such a fool. Can you ever forgive me? When I think of what I said to you the night we were married, what I said to you yesterday . . . I accused you of being a selfish child, of lying for the sake of lying, and all the while you were simply trying to save your life and then mine."

Sybilla looked away, biting her lip. "You're being too generous. No matter how much I feared Uncle Hubert, I should never have allowed you to marry me. I've ruined your future with Lady Verity."

"Thank God you did!"

Sybilla gasped in astonishment.

"I don't love Verity," Joshua said in a rush. "I don't think I ever did. I was dazzled by her beauty, that was all. Before I ever met you, I'd begun to wonder if we could ever be happy together. Kissing her was like kissing my sister, if I'd had one." He took a swift stride, gathering Sybilla into his arms. "Not like this," he said huskily, bending his head to kiss her with eager lips. "Sybilla," he murmured against her mouth, "I love you. I don't want a divorce."

Winding her arms around his neck, Sybilla pressed against him, while shooting stars of delight skittered through her blood and her heart pounded wildly against the answering tumult in his breast. "I don't want a divorce, either," she said after he finally released her lips. "It sounds so complicated. We'd need an Act of Parliament!"

With a shout of laughter Joshua held her away from him. "Oh, Sybilla, you wretch, that's why I fell in love with you. You made me laugh." He sobered, and an expression of uncertainty crossed his face. "You haven't said—"

"Darling Joshua, I think I fell in love with you when I opened my eyes to find you bending over me after I collapsed in the street that first morning. I just didn't realize it until a little later."

Joshua's eyes glowed. He slipped his hands inside her coat, running his fingers sinuously over her curves. "Let's stay the night," he murmured, kissing her again.

Sybilla's heart leaped. "Yes. Oh, yes," she whispered.

"Did you bring a nightdress?"

"Yes . . ."

"You won't need it."